P9-CMT-304

Also by Ed McBain

The 87th Precinct Novels

Cop Hater • *The Mugger* • *The Pusher* (1956) *The Con Man* • *Killer's Choice* (1957) *Killer's Payoff* • *Killer's Wedge* • *Lady Killer* (1958) *'Til Death* • *King's Ransom* (1959) *Give the Boys a Great Big Hand* • *The Heckler* • *See Them Die* (1960) *Lady, Lady, I Did It!* (1961) *The Empty Hours* • *Like Love* (1962) *Ten Plus One* (1963) *Ax* (1964) *He Who Hesitates* • *Doll* (1965) *Eighty Million Eyes* (1966) *Fuzz* (1968) *Shotgun* (1969) *Jigsaw* (1970) *Hail, Hail, the Gang's All Here* (1971) *Sadie When She Died* • *Let's Hear It for the Deaf Man* (1972) *Hail to the Chief* (1973) *Bread* (1974) *Blood Relatives* (1975) *So Long as You Both Shall Live* (1976) *Long Time No See* (1977) *Calypso* (1979) *Ghosts* (1980) *Heat* (1981) *Ice* (1983) *Lightning* (1984) *Eight Black Horses* (1985) *Poison* • *Tricks* (1987) *Lullaby* (1989) *Vespers* (1990) *Widows* (1991) *Kiss* (1992) *Mischief* (1993) *And All Through the House* (1994) *Romance* (1995) *Nocturne* (1997) *The Big Bad City* (1999) *The Last Dance* (2000) *Money, Money, Money* (2001) *Fat Ollie's Book* (2003) *The Frumious Bandersnatch* • *Hark!* (2004)

The Matthew Hope Novels

Goldilocks (1978) *Rumpelstiltskin* (1981) *Beauty and the Beast* (1982) *Jack and the Beanstalk* (1984) *Snow White and Rose Red* (1985) *Cinderella* (1986) *Puss in Boots* (1987) *The House That Jack Built* (1988) *Three Blind Mice* (1990) *Mary, Mary* (1993) *There Was a Little Girl* (1994) *Gladly the Cross-Eyed Bear* (1996) *The Last Best Hope* (1998)

Other Novels

The Sentries (1965) *Where There's Smoke* • *Doors* (1975) *Guns* (1976) *Another Part of the City* (1986) *Downtown* (1991) *Driving Lessons* (2000) *Candyland* (2001)

ALICE IN JEOPARDY

A NOVEL

Ed McBain

Simon & Schuster

New York London Toronto Sydney

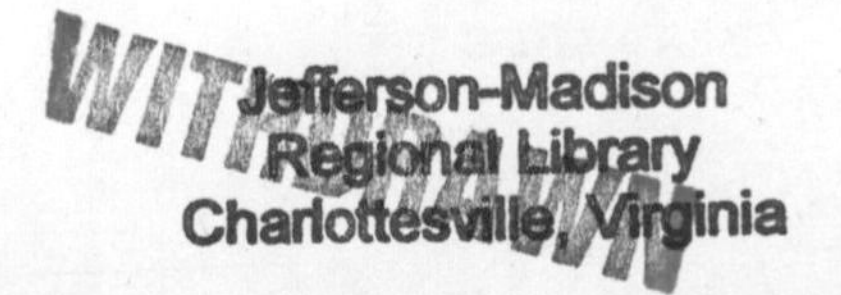

SIMON & SCHUSTER
Rockefeller Center
1230 Avenue of the Americas
New York, NY 10020

This book is a work of fiction. Names, characters, places, and incidents either are products of the author's imagination or are used fictitiously. Any resemblance to actual events or locales or persons, living or dead, is entirely coincidental.

For information about special discounts for bulk purchases,
please contact Simon & Schuster Special Sales:
1-800-456-6798 or business@simonandschuster.com

Book design by Ellen R. Sasahara

Manufactured in the United States of America

1 3 5 7 9 10 8 6 4 2

Library of Congress Cataloging-in-Publication Data

McBain, Ed, 1926–
Alice in jeopardy / Ed McBain.
p. cm.
1. Single mothers—Fiction. 2. Kidnapping—Fiction. 3. Widows—Fiction. I. Title.
PS3515.U585A78 2005
813'.54—dc22
2004052478

ISBN 0-7432-6250-6

I'm sorry, but she's the love of my life, you know.
So this, too, is dedicated to my wife,
Dragica

ALICE IN JEOPARDY

Wednesday
May 12

1

When the same nightmare awakens her, she sits bolt upright in the middle of the bed.

Where am I? she thinks.

And blinks at the bedside clock.

7:15 A.M.

She is instantly wide awake.

"Kids!" she yells. "Jamie! Ashley! Up! We're late! Up, guys!"

She hears grumbling down the hall. Ashley's voice. Jamie hasn't spoken for almost eight months now.

"Guys, are you up?" she shouts.

"Yes, Mom!" Ashley calls.

Ten years old, the elder of the two. Her eyes and her hair brown, like Alice's. Eight-year-old Jamie favors his father. Blond hair and blue eyes. She can never look into those eyes without recalling that terrible day.

She shakes off the nightmare and gets out of bed.

In the shower, she realizes she set the alarm's wakeup time, but neglected to slide the ON-OFF switch to the right. Hurrying to lather, she drops the soap, the heavy bar falling onto the little toe of her left foot. Yelping in pain—it feels as if someone has hit her with a hammer—she yells, "Damn it to hell!" and bends down to recover the slippery bar. Her butt hits the HOT-COLD lever on the tiled wall. The water turns instantly ice cold. She straightens in surprise, drops the soap again, missing her foot this time, and backs away from the icy stream, thinking *None of this would be happening if Eddie were still alive.*

But Eddie is not still alive, she thinks, Eddie is dead—and almost bursts into tears.

She reaches through the slanting curtain of frigid water, and turns off the shower.

The kids are supposed to be at school at eight-fifteen. She is twenty minutes late getting them there. Jamie has forgotten his lucky red cap, so she has to drive all the way back to the house for it, the traffic on U.S. 41 impossible even now in the off-season. By the time she brings the cap to him at school, and then drives to the office on The Ring, it is almost 9:30. Her appointment with Reginald Webster is at ten. She barely has time to check her e-mail, go over the new listings that Aggie has placed on her desk, put on some lipstick, which she didn't have time to do before they left the house, visit the ladies' room one last time, and here he is!

Forty-three years old perhaps, tall and somewhat good-looking in a dissipated way, suntanned from hours spent aboard his thirty-foot Catalina. He is looking for a house on deep sailboat water.

"People call me Webb," he says. "Better than Reggie, don't you think?" Holding her hand. "Anything's better than Reggie. Have you found some good houses for me?"

"I think so," she says, and withdraws her hand. "Would you care for some coffee, or should we just get started?"

"I wouldn't mind a cup, if it's already made," he says.

She buzzes for Aggie and asks her to bring in two cups of coffee. While they are waiting, she shows Webb pictures of the dozen or so houses she's pulled from the internet. He seems interested in two of them on Willard, and another one out on Tall Grass. The two keys are at opposite ends of Cape October. It is going to be a long day.

Aggie comes in carrying a tray with two coffee cups, a creamer, and a sugar bowl on it. As she is placing the creamer and sugar bowl on the desk, she accidentally knocks over Webb's cup, spilling the contents onto his left trouser leg. He jumps up, bellowing in surprise, and then immediately recovers his cool.

"That's okay," he says, and laughs. "I'm about coffeed out, anyway."

She is starting to tell Reginald Webster how Cape October got its name. They have already seen the two houses on Willard Key, and are driving out to Tall Grass.

"Because that's when the first tourists come down," Webb says. "October."

"No, no," she says. "Actually, the name is an odd combination of Seminole and Spanish."

She goes on to explain that when the Spaniards first came to southwest Florida, the Seminole word *tha-kee* for "big" was already in place, and they added the Spanish word *cabo* to it, and came up with the name "Cabo Tha-kee," or "Big Cape." This eventually became slurred and contracted to "Cab'Otha-kee," which was then finally Hispanicized to "Cab'Octubre," which of course was "Cape October" in English.

"Or so the story goes," she says, and turns to him and smiles.

The eastern rim of October Bay is jaggedly defined by U.S. 41, more familiarly known as the Tamiami Trail. Frank Lane, the owner and sole proprietor of Lane Realty, believes that "Tamiami" is redneck for "To Miami." Alice doesn't know if this true or not. But if you follow 41 south, it leads eventually to Alligator Alley, which then crosses the Florida peninsula to the east coast and, of course, Miami. So maybe he's right.

There are four keys off the Cape's mainland. Beyond these so-called barrier islands lies the vast Gulf of Mexico. Sail out due west from the Cape, and eventually you'll make landfall in Corpus Christi, Texas. If you're lucky.

"So how old are you, Alice?" he asks her. "May I call you Alice?"

"Sure," she says.

"So how old are you, Alice?" he asks again.

She doesn't think that's any of his business, but he is a client, and neither does she wish to appear rude.

"Thirty-four," she says.

"Married?"

"Widowed."

"Sorry to hear that."

"Yes," she says.

"Any children?"

"Two, a boy and a girl."

"Tough break."

"Yes," she says again.

"How long ago?" he asks.

"You know," she says, "I'm sorry, but I'd rather not talk about it."

"Okay," he says, and shrugs. "Sorry. I didn't mean to intrude."

"That's okay," she says, and then softens her tone. "It's just that it's still painful."

"Must've been recent then, huh?" he says, and when she doesn't answer, he says, "Sorry."

They ride in silence for several moments.

"Was it an accident?" he asks.

She doesn't answer.

"Sometimes it helps to talk about it," he says. "I figure he had to've been young, right? I mean, you're only thirty-four. So it had to've been either a heart attack or some kind of accident, am I right?"

"He drowned eight months ago," Alice says, and Webb remains silent for the rest of the trip to Tall Grass.

• • •

"The house was built in 1956," she tells him. "Named for Jennifer Bray Healey, who had it designed by Thomas Cooley and his son. They're famous Cape October architects."

"Never heard of them," Webb says.

"They designed a great many of the buildings downtown, I'll take you to see some of them later, if you like. The Healey house is considered a hallmark of the Cape's modern architectural movement."

They are standing in the oval driveway in front of the house. Alice is deliberately postponing that moment when she unlocks the front door and opens it onto the spectacular panoramic view of Little October Bay. It never fails to knock the socks off any prospective buyer.

"The house fell into disrepair after Mrs. Healey died," she says, searching in her bag for the key to the lockbox. "The present owners—Frank and Marcia Allenby—bought it two years ago. They've been renovating it ever since, all in accordance with historic guidelines. The rules are that you can make changes provided you don't alter any 'historically or architecturally significant aspects of the design,' quote unquote."

"Sounds like bureaucratic red tape," Webb says.

"Well, no, not actually. The regulations are there to protect the environment and the property itself. This is a landmark house, you know."

"Mm," he says.

"Ah, here it is," she says, and finds the key to the lockbox, and then opens the box, and removes the key to the front door. "The owners are up north," she says over her shoulder, "they also have a home in North Carolina." She inserts the key into the lock on the front door, twists the key, opens the door, turns to him, and says, "Please come in."

The view is truly breathtaking.

From just inside the front door, one can see through the living room to the sliding glass doors at the rear of the house, and beyond those doors to the wooden platforms that drop gradually from one to the other, down to the dock where a thirty-two-foot Seaward Eagle is moored to the pilings. Out over the bay, a squadron of central casting pelicans swoop low over the calm silent waters.

"Nice," Webb says.

"And you get this same magnificent view from every room in the house," she says.

"Was it a boating accident?" he asks.

"Yes," she says briefly, and leads him through the living room, past the fireplace . . .

"That's fossil stone," she says. "The chimney's been restored, with a new flue and top. The cedar floors are new, too, throughout the entire house."

"Out here on the Bay?" he asks.

"The Gulf," she says, again briefly, and opens one of the sliding doors. "All the windows and doors were replaced during the renovation, this hardware is all new," she says, and steps out onto the first of the platforms.

"The decks were all replaced and enlarged, too," she says. "Highest grade, clean-cut, dense dry wood and stainless steel screws . . ."

. . . and walks him down to the dock itself.

"Note the swimming pool and privacy garden just off the master bedroom," she says.

The Allenbys' power cruiser sits bobbing gently alongside the dock.

"The dock is new, forty feet long. It can hold one large and two small boats, or a second boat up to twenty feet. Dual 50 AMP service to the dock. Full access to the Gulf of Mexico, no bridges on the way."

"When did you start selling real estate?"

"Almost six months ago," she says.

"Lots of widows in the real estate game," he says.

"I hadn't noticed."

"Widows and divorcées. Keeps them busy, I suppose."

She wants to tell him that this is more than busywork, this is her way of starting a new life, her way of coping with the aftermath of her husband's senseless death, when her very existence was shattered . . .

She catches herself, looks out over the water.

"It's so utterly still here," she says.

She allows him to stand on the dock in silence for a while, savoring the solitude and the majestic view.

"Come," she says, "let me show you the rest of the house."

Inside again, she shows him the kitchen with its custom teak countertop and hand-built, hand-painted kitchen cabinets, its Miele and Thermador appliances . . .

"A water softener has been added to the entire house," she says, "and there's a new two-zone air-conditioning system with all new ducts. All the plumbing and plumbing hardware was replaced, too, including a new line to the street. There's a new irrigation system, a new well pump, a new shell driveway. In effect, you'd be getting a brand new house that just *happens* to be a historic landmark as well."

She takes him into the large room on the southern end of the house. From Frank Allenby's spacious desk, the view over the bay is spectacular.

"This is actually a second bedroom," she says, "it has its own private bath. But the Allenbys live here alone, so Frank uses it as an office."

"They say it takes a year," Webb says.

"I beg your pardon?"

"To get over a divorce or a death."

She says nothing.

"I've been divorced for nine months now. You suppose they're right?" he asks.

"I have no idea."

"Are you over it yet?"

"I get by," she says.

Which isn't true. She is struggling. She is struggling mightily.

"The master bedroom is at the other end of the house," she says.

"It's identical to this one. Think of the house as a beautiful butterfly, the living room and dining room as its body, the two bedrooms as its wings."

"How large is the living room?"

"Twenty by thirty. That's a good-sized room."

"And the bedrooms?"

"Each fifteen by twenty. Come, let me show you the other one. Total square footage under air is a bit over three thousand."

She leads him through the house again, past the living room, and into the dining room, and then through to the master bedroom.

"From the bed, you can look right down into the privacy garden and the pool," she says.

"How much are they asking?"

"A million-seven. They've been offered a mill-four but they turned it down. I think they might be willing to let it go for a mill-six, somewhere in there."

"That's a lot of money," he says.

"Not for this location."

"For *any* location," he says. "A million-six comes to more than five hundred dollars a square foot."

"You've got to figure a million for the property alone," she says. "You won't find many other views like this one."

"Well, I'll have to think about it," he says, and her heart sinks.

She gets back to the office at a quarter past noon.

They exchange phone numbers, and Alice promises to have some new houses to show him by tomorrow morning at nine, when they'll go out looking again. She hopes he might call before then with an offer on any of the three houses she's shown him, but she knows this is unlikely.

He'd told her he was looking for something that would cost no more than a million, a million-five, and she'd assured him that getting an eighty percent mortgage would be no problem. That means he would have to come up with $320,000 in cash if he goes for the

Healey house at a million-six. She knows for certain that Frank and Marcia Allenby will never budge below a million-six, never.

Of the seven percent commission on the sale, the agency will keep three and Alice will take home four, which comes to $64,000. She figures that will carry her a good year and more, even if she doesn't make another sale, a likelihood in that she hasn't made a sale thus far, and she's already been working for Lane Realty for almost six months now.

She took the job at the end of November, when she realized she wasn't going to be able to make it on the scant savings she and Eddie had managed to accumulate since their move to Florida. The house she still lives in with the kids is in a good school district, even if it does cost $1,600 a month, which at her present rate of cash flow she will no longer be able to afford come June, unless Mr. Reginald Webster or somebody or anybody *buys* something. Or unless, of course, the insurance money comes through. It was supposed to come through a month and a half ago.

She picks up the phone, dials a number by heart, and waits.

"Briggs, Randolph and Soames," a woman's voice says.

"Mr. Briggs, please," she says.

"May I say who's calling?"

"Alice Glendenning."

"One moment, please."

She waits.

"Hi, Alice," a man's voice says.

"Hello, Andy, how are you?"

"Good, thanks, and you?"

"Fine, Andy. Andy, I hate to keep bothering you about this . . ."

"It's no bother at all," Andy says. "I'm as annoyed as you are."

"Have you heard anything from them?"

"They're still stalling."

"It's been eight months now," she says. "What proof do they *need*?"

"A certificate of death, they say. Which is absurd in this case. The man drowned at sea, his remains were never . . . forgive me, Alice," he says.

"That's all right."

"But the facts . . ."

She knows the facts. Eddie took the sloop out for a moonlight sail. It was a small boat, the waters on the Gulf were very high that night. There was no one aboard when the tanker came across her the next morning, still under sail. Eddie had either fallen overboard or been washed overboard. Those were the facts.

"Garland has no right to withhold payment," Andy says.

"But they are."

"Yes, because there's a lot of money involved here. And because they're in trouble financially, this goddamn administration. With the double indemnity clause, the death benefit comes to two . . . by the way, no one at Garland is claiming that drowning at sea doesn't qualify as an accident."

"Well, they'd be foolish to do that."

"They're foolish to try wriggling out of this in the first place. Other insurance companies *are* paying the same sorts of claims, you know. It's not as if nothing like this has ever happened before, Alice . . ."

"I know."

"Some are taking more time than others, but they *are* honoring their obligations. Quite frankly, Garland's position is contemptible."

"So what do we do, Andy?"

"I'd like to give them till the end of the month. If they don't settle by then, we'll have to bring suit."

"The end of the month," Alice says.

"Yes. I'll call them again on June first. Does that sound okay to you?"

"I suppose."

"Alice?"

"Yes?"

"We'll get the money, I promise you."

"I hope so."

"I promise."

"Okay, Andy, thank you. We'll talk soon."

"I'll let you know the moment I hear anything."

"Thanks, Andy."

"Talk to you later," he says, and hangs up.

She holds the receiver in her hand for a moment, and then puts it back on the cradle, and suddenly she is weeping. She yanks a tissue from the box on her desk, blows her nose, and dries her eyes.

Well, she thinks, the first day of June is less than three weeks away, and I've certainly got enough in the bank to last me till then. But I don't know what to do *after* June first, because by my calculation the account will be getting very low by that time. I suppose I can always get a job waitressing, she thinks, but that would mean having to pay Rosie even more than I'm paying her now. But at least I'll have a steady salary and tips, and I wouldn't have to count on commissions. So far, there has been what one might call a dearth of commissions. So far, the commissions have totaled zero, *nada,* zilch.

She picks up the phone again, dials her home number, and waits. Rosie Garrity picks up on the third ring.

"Glendenning residence," she says.

"Rosie, hi, it's me."

"Hello, Mrs. Glendenning, how are you?"

"Fine, thanks. Everything okay there?"

"Yes, fine. What time is it, anyway?"

"A quarter to one."

"Good. I want to bake a pie before the kids get home."

Rosie comes in at noon every weekday, in time to clean the house and put it in order before the children get home at two-thirty, three o'clock, depending on traffic. By the time Alice gets home at five, Rosie has everything ready to put up for dinner. Rosie works full-time on Saturdays and Sundays, a broker's busiest days.

"Did you see the chicken I left in the fridge?" Alice asks.

"Yes. Will you be wanting the spinach, too?"

"Please. And if you could get some potatoes ready for browning."

"Sounds good. Can you stop for some ice cream on the way home? Go good with the pie."

"What kind of pie?"

"Blueberry."
"Yum. I'll pick some up."
"See you later."
"Bye."
It is almost one o'clock.
She decides to go to lunch.

Grosse Bec is a man-made island that serves as a luxurious stepping-stone between the mainland and Willard Key. If Cape October can claim a Gold Coast shopping area, the so-called Ring on Grosse Bec is it. The rest of the town is all malls. Alice's office is on Mapes Avenue, just off the circle that serves as Grosse Bec's center.

She is just crossing Founders Boulevard, familiarly called Flounders Boulevard by the natives, when she hears a horn blowing, and then the squeal of brakes, and then a woman's voice shouting, "Oh God!" She whirls in time to see the red fender of a car not six inches from her left hip. She tries to spin away again, too late, and then thrusts both hands at the fender in desperation, as if trying to push it off her, away from her. Bracing herself for sudden impact, she feels the bone-jarring shock of metal against flesh, and is suddenly hurtling backward off her feet, landing some three feet away from the car's right front wheel. She feels agonizing pain in her left leg, tries to twist away from the pain, and then does in fact twist away from the car itself, as if it were still a menace.

"Oh God, are you all right?"

The woman is crouched beside her now. Alice looks up into an elegant face, long blonde hair trailing on either side of it, blue eyes almost brimming with tears.

"Are you okay?" the woman asks.

"No," Alice says.

The woman's looming face vanishes. Alice hears a car door opening. Then some clicking and beeping sounds, and then the woman's voice again.

"Hello," she says, "there's been an accident."

She is talking into a cell phone.

"Can you send an ambulance, please?"

The ambulance gets there some five minutes later.

The police still haven't arrived by the time the paramedics load Alice and drive off with her.

The emergency room doctor at October Memorial tells Alice she's broken her left ankle. He tells her he will put her foot in a so-called cuff cast, which will look like an oversized white ski boot. He assures her she will still be able to drive because all she needs for the accelerator and brake pedals is her right foot. He tells her walking will be awkward and cumbersome, but he doesn't think she'll need crutches. He is smiling as he tells her all this. He seems to think she is very lucky.

It takes an hour and twenty minutes for them to clean the wound, and dress it, and put her foot and ankle in the cast. It is almost three o'clock when she limps out of the emergency room. Cumbersome and awkward is right.

The woman who knocked her down is waiting there for her.

"I'm Jennifer Redding," she says, "I can't tell you how sorry I am."

Alice guesses she is a good ten years younger than she herself, twenty-four or -five, in there, a willowy blonde wearing tight white bell-bottom pants with a thirteen-button flap like sailors used to wear, or maybe still did; Alice hasn't dated a sailor since she was nineteen. The pants are riding low on Jennifer's hips, a short pink cotton sweater riding high. In combination, they expose a good four inches of firm flesh and a tight little belly button as well.

"I'm glad you're here," Alice says. "I never got your insurance information."

"Why do you need that?"

"Well, there's been an accident . . ."

"There must be a card in my wallet someplace."

"Didn't the cops ask you for it?"

"What cops?"

"At the scene."

"There weren't any cops."

"Didn't you call the police?"

"No. Was I supposed to?"

Alice suddenly realizes she is talking to a ditz.

"Didn't *anyone* call the cops?"

"What for? The ambulance came, you were already gone."

"I hate to break this to you," Alice says, "but if you drive away from the scene of an accident, it becomes a hit-and-run. If I were you . . ."

"But I wasn't running from anything. I drove straight here to the *hospital.* To see how you were."

"The police may look at that differently. Get on your cell phone again, dial 911, and tell them—"

"Is it broken?" Jennifer asks, looking down at the cast.

"Yes, it's broken."

"I'm sorry."

"You shouldn't have come around that corner so fast. There's a stop sign there. You should have at least slowed down."

"I did. But you walked right into the car."

"I *what*?"

"You seemed to be in some kind of a fog."

"Is that what you're going to tell the cops? That I was in some kind of a fog?"

"I'm not going to tell the cops anything."

"Well, I *am,*" Alice says.

"Why?"

"Because I've had experience with insurance companies, thanks. And there are going to be hospital bills, and I want to go on record about what happened here. Especially if you're going to claim I was in a fog and walked into your car."

"I even blew my horn at you. You just kept walking."

"Jennifer, it was nice of you to come here, really, but I *am* going to report this to the police. You'd be smart to call them first. Otherwise you might find yourself facing criminal charges."

"Oh, don't be silly," Jennifer says. "Have you got a ride home?"

"No, but I'll call my office. My car's—"

"I'd be happy to give you a ride."

Alice looks at her.

"My car's at the office," she says. "On Mapes Avenue. If you can take me there . . ."

"Oh sure," Jennifer says, and grins like a kid with a lollipop.

She doesn't get back to her house on the mainland until almost four that afternoon. She has extracted from Jennifer the promise that she will call the police, but she is eager to call them herself as well. She knows all about claims. She has filed enough insurance claims since Eddie drowned.

North Oleander Street resembles a jungle through which a narrow asphalt road has been laid and left to deteriorate. A sign at the street's opening reads DEAD END, appropriate in that North Oleander runs for two blocks before it becomes an oval that turns the street back upon itself in the opposite direction. Lining these two short blocks are twelve shingled houses with the sort of glass-louvered windows you could find all over Cape October in the good old days before it became a tourist destination for folks from the Middle West and Canada. The houses here are virtually hidden from view by a dense growth of dusty cabbage palm and palmetto, red bougainvillea, purple bougainvillea, white bougainvillea growing in dense profusion, sloppy pepper trees, pink oleander, golden allamanda, trailing lavender lantana, rust-colored shrimp plants, yellow hibiscus, pink hibiscus, red hibiscus, eponymous bottlebrush trees with long red flowers—and here and there, the one true floral splendor of Cape October, the bird-of-paradise with its spectacular orange and bluish-purple crest.

Rosie Garrity greets her at the front door.

Round-faced and stout, in her fifties, wearing a flowered housedress and a white blouse, she glances down at Alice's foot, shakes her head, and says, "What happened to you?"

"I got run over," Alice says.

"Is it broken?"

"The ankle, yes. Where are the kids?"

"I thought maybe you'd picked them up."

"What do you mean?"

"They weren't on the bus."

"Oh dear," Alice says. "Was there a mix-up again?"

She limps into the kitchen, takes the phone from its wall bracket over the pass-through counter, and dials the school's number by heart. Someone in the administrative office picks up on the third ring.

"Pratt Elementary," she says.

Unless a kid is lucky enough to get into Cape October's exclusive public elementary school "for the gifted," officially called Pratt by the school board but snidely referred to as "Brat" by the parents of children who have not passed the stringent entrance exams; or unless a kid is rich enough to afford one of the area's two private preparatory schools—St. Mark's in Cape October itself, and the Headley Academy in nearby Manakawa—then the elementary school educational choices are limited to three schools, and the selection is further limited by that part of the city in which the student happens to live. Jamie has not spoken a word since his father drowned, but he and Ashley are bright as hell, and after the family moved down here both kids passed Pratt's entrance exams with ease.

"Hi," Alice says, "this is Mrs. Glendenning. Did my kids get on the wrong bus again?"

"Oh golly, I hope not. Which bus were they supposed to be on?"

"Harry Nelson's."

"Let me see if I can reach him."

There is a silence on the line. Rosie raises an inquisitive eyebrow. Alice shrugs. She waits. The voice comes back on the line again.

"Mrs. Glendenning?"

"Yes?"

"Harry says they didn't board his bus. He thought you might've picked them up."

"No, I didn't. Can you find out which bus they *did* board?"

"It might take some time to reach all of the other drivers. I got lucky with Harry."

"Last time, they called me from Becky Feldman's house. They got off there when they realized they were on the wrong bus. Would you know which route that might be?"

"I can check. Why don't you call the Feldmans meanwhile? I'll get back to you."

"Thanks," Alice says, and puts the phone back on its hook, and then opens the Cape October directory and looks under the F's for Feldman. She thinks Becky's father's name is Stephen, yes, there it is, Stephen Feldman on Adler Road. She dials the number, and waits while it rings once, twice, three times . . .

"Hello?"

"Susan?"

She can hear children's voices in the background.

"Yes?"

"Hi, this is Alice Glendenning."

"Oh, hi, how are you?"

"I don't suppose my kids are there again, are they?"

"No, they're not," Susan says. "Did you misplace them again?"

"It would seem so. I don't suppose I could talk to Becky, could I?"

"Just a second."

She hears Susan calling her daughter to the phone, hears Becky approaching, hears her picking up the receiver.

"Hello?"

"Hi, Becky, this is Ashley's mom."

"Oh, hi, Mrs. Glendenning."

"Did you happen to see Ashley and Jamie after school today?"

"No, I din't," Becky says.

"Getting on one of the buses maybe?"

"No, I din't."

"Okay, thanks a lot."

"Did you want to talk to my mom again?"

"No, that's okay, thanks, Becky, just tell her bye."

"Okay," Becky says, and hangs up.

Alice replaces the phone on the wall hook. It rings almost instantly. She picks up.

"Hello?"

"Mrs. Glendenning?"

"Yes?"

"This is Phoebe Mears at Pratt?"

"Yes, Phoebe."

"I checked with the loading area guard. Man named Luke Farraday. He knows both your kids, says somebody picked them up after school."

"What do you mean, somebody picked them up?"

"Around two-thirty, yes, ma'am."

"Well . . . who? *Who* picked them up?"

"Woman driving a blue car, Luke said."

"Picked up my *kids*?" Alice says.

"Woman in a blue car, yes, ma'am."

"I don't know anybody with a blue car," Alice says.

"What is it?" Rosie asks.

"Is he still there? The guard. Luke Whoever."

"Farraday. No, ma'am. I reached him at home."

"Well, I . . . can you let me have his number, please?" She listens as Phoebe reads off Farraday's number, writing it onto a pad on the counter. "Thank you," she says. She puts the phone back on its cradle, hesitates for a single uncertain instant . . .

"What is it?" Rosie asks again.

. . . and is reaching for the phone again when it rings, startling her.

She picks up the receiver.

"Hello?" she says.

A woman's voice says, "I have your children. Don't call the police, or they'll die."

There is a click on the line.

Alice puts the receiver back on the cradle. Her hand is trembling. Her face has gone pale.

"What is it?" Rosie asks.

"Someone has the children."

"Oh my God!"

"She told me not to call the police."

"A woman?"

"A woman."

"Call them anyway," Rosie says.

"No, I can't."

"Then what . . . ?"

"I don't know."

The house seems suddenly very still. Alice can hear the clock ticking in the living room. A big grandfather clock that used to belong to Eddie's mother.

"A blue car," she says. "A woman driving a blue car."

"Call the police," Rosie says.

"No. Do you know anyone who has a blue car?"

"No. Call the police."

"I can't do that! She'll kill them!"

"Did she say that?"

"Yes."

"What else?"

"Nothing. Nothing. She just hung up. Oh my God, Rosie, she's got the children!"

"What'd she sound like?"

"I . . . I don't know. A woman. I . . ."

"White? Black?"

"I don't know. How can anyone tell . . . ?"

"*Everyone* can tell. Was she white or black?"

"Black. Maybe. I'm not sure."

"How old?"

"In her thirties maybe."

"Call the police. Tell them a black woman in her thirties has your kids. Do it now, Mrs. Glendenning. A bad situation can only get worse. Trust me on that."

"I can't take that chance, Rosie."

"You can't take any other chance."

The women look at each other.

"Call them," Rosie says.

"No," Alice says.

"Then God have mercy on your soul," Rosie says.

Alone in the house now, Rosie gone in a flutter of dire predictions, Alice first begins blaming herself. I should have bought Ashley the cell phone, she thinks, and remembers her daughter arguing like an attorney for the defense.

"But, Mom, *all* the girls in the fifth grade have cell phones!"

Oh, sure, the same way all the girls in the fifth grade are allowed to wear lipstick and all the girls in the fifth grade are allowed to date, and . . .

"No, Ashley, I'm sorry, we can't afford a cell phone just now."

"But, Mom . . ."

"Not just now, darling, I'm sorry."

Thinking now, I should have bought her the phone, how much would it have cost, anyway? If Ashley had a cell phone, she'd have called me at the office before getting in a car with a strange woman—what on earth *possessed* her? How many times had Alice told them, her and Jamie both, never to accept anything from a stranger, *never,* not candy, not anything, never even to stop and *talk* with a stranger, certainly never to get in a *car* with a stranger, what was *wrong* with them?

No, she thinks, it isn't their fault, it isn't my fault, it's this *woman's* fault, whoever she is, this woman driving a blue car, do I know anyone who drives a blue car? She tries to remember. She's sure she must know *someone* who drives a blue car, but who remembers the color of anyone's car unless it's yellow or pink? A blue car, she thinks, a blue car, come on, who drives a blue car, but she can't think of a single soul, and her frustration leads once again to unreasoning anger. Anger against herself for not having bought the goddamn cell phone, anger at her children for getting into a car with a strange woman, but especially anger at this undoubtedly crazed person, whoever she is, this woman who probably has no children of her own, and who has now stolen from Alice the only precious things in her life, I'll *kill* her, she thinks. If ever I get my hands on her—

The phone rings.

Alice picks up the receiver at once.

"Hello?" she says.

"Mrs. Glendenning?"

The same woman again.

"Yes," Alice says. "Listen, Miss—"

"No, *you* listen," the woman says. "Don't interrupt, just listen. We want a quarter of a million dollars in cash. Hundred-dollar bills. Get the money together by noon tomorrow. We'll call again then. Get the money. Or the kiddies die."

And she hangs up.

Alice puts the receiver back on the wall hook, and stands silently at the kitchen counter for what is perhaps thirty seconds. Then she reaches for the phone again, and immediately calls Charlie Hobbs.

2

She does not think anyone is watching the house.

But she walks swiftly from the kitchen door to the car, and opens the door on the driver's side and gets in behind the wheel, and starts the car, and then backs out of the driveway and into the street and is on her way in less than a minute and a half. Even in off-season traffic, it takes her ten minutes from her house to the Lewiston Point Bridge. From there, it takes her another fifteen minutes to Charlie's house on the northern end of Tall Grass Key.

He is sitting on the front porch of his ramshackle house, waiting for her. Wearing white trousers and a baggy blue shirt, he is smoking a pipe, and he looks like the stereotype of any fisherman you might see on any calendar selling cod liver pills, except that he is not a fisherman, he is a painter of abstract-expressionist canvases, and a damn good one at that. His trousers and shirt are now stained with paint, and there are traces of paint under his fingernails as well, and even in the white beard that clings to his cheeks, his chin, and his upper lip, like leftover lather from a hasty shave. It is ten minutes past seven and still light, the sun hovering above the western horizon as if indecisive about its final descent.

The moment she pulls into his shell driveway, he rises from where he is sitting on the steps. She goes to him, and he holds her close. She is trembling in his arms. Until this moment, she has not realized how frightened she really is. Charlie smells of paint and turpentine and tobacco smoke. He is the only friend she now has in all Cape October, and she loves him to death.

"It's okay," he says. "Everything's gonna be okay."

"I'm so scared," she says.

"It'll be okay. What happened to your foot?"

"I got run over."

"What?"

"Yeah. The ankle's broken."

"Never rains," he says.

She first met Charlie three months ago, when a developer represented by Lane Realty tried to buy the four acres of waterfront land Charlie had been living on since 1970. He'd come down to Cape October after the Vietnam War, having barely escaped death in the massive artillery barrage on Khe Sanh. He was nineteen years old in that March of 1968. He was fifty-six when Alice met him. Frank Lane sent her—new and inexperienced—to negotiate for Charlie's now-precious land. He'd turned her down, of course. But they became fast friends, and Charlie later told her he'd have thrown anyone else off the property sight unseen.

She tells him about the children.

In the gathering dusk, she tells him everything that happened.

Tells him about the school guard, Luke Farraday, seeing the kids getting into a blue car driven by some woman. Tells him she got a call around four o'clock, four-fifteen it must've been, from a woman telling her not to call the police or her children would die. Tells him the same woman called again at six to say they wanted a quarter of a million dollars in cash by tomorrow at noon, hundred-dollar bills . . .

"There's more than just her," she tells him. "She said *we* want the money, *we'll* call again tomorrow. *Should* I call the police, Charlie? I don't know what to do. Rosie said I should call the police. But if I do that . . ."

Inside the house, the telephone rings.

Charlie goes up the steps. Alice follows him.

His studio overlooks the Gulf, where the sun is just beginning to dip low over the water. The huge canvases stacked against the walls resemble sunsets themselves, oranges and reds and yellows streaked in harmonious riot against backgrounds of blues, violets, deeper purples, and blacks. They walk through the studio and into the adjoining kitchen, where Charlie lifts a portable phone from its cradle.

"Hobbs," he says.

"Mr. Hobbs, this is Detective Sloate, Cape October Police Department. Is there a Mrs. Glendenning there with you?"

"Why do you want to know?" Charlie asks.

"We understand she might be in some kind of trouble. If she's there, would you please put her on, sir?"

Charlie covers the mouthpiece.

"It's a police detective," he says.

"What!"

"Wants to talk to you. He knows you're in trouble."

"How . . . ?"

"I think you'd better talk to him, Al."

She takes the phone.

"Hello?" she says.

"Mrs. Glendenning?"

"Yes?"

"This is Detective Wilbur Sloate, Cape October PD. I understand you've got some kind of trouble, ma'am. Would you like to tell me about it?"

"Where . . . ? What makes you think . . . ?"

"We received a phone call from a Mrs. Rose Garrity, says she works for you. Is that right?"

"Yes?"

"She says someone took your children, warned you not to call the police, is that right, too?"

Alice says nothing.

"Mrs. Glendenning?"

This, now, is the moment of decision.

Tell this Detective Wilbur Sloate of the Cape October Police Department that yes, her children were picked up outside Pratt Elementary by some woman driving a blue automobile, year and make as yet unknown, and that she has been told to assemble $250,000 in hundred-dollar bills by noon tomorrow, Thursday, the fifteenth day of May, at which time she will be contacted again. Tell him all this and immediately bring in all the local law enforcement agencies, the Cape October Police, of course—who are already here—and the Sheriff's Department as well, she feels certain, and undoubtedly the FBI . . .

Or—

"I don't know what you're talking about," she says. "My children are here with me this very minute. Anyway, how'd you . . . ?"

"May I speak to one of them, please?"

"How'd you find me here?"

"Mrs. Garrity told us you had a friend named Charles Hobbs, Junior, lived out on Willard. May I please speak to one of the children, ma'am?"

"They're outside playing," Alice says.

"Could you please call one of them to the phone for me, ma'am?"

"I will not have you frightening my children," she says.

"Ma'am," he says, "I'm trying to help you here. If someone has taken your children . . ."

"No one has taken my children. I just told you . . ."

"Mrs. Garrity was there when you received that phone call, ma'am. She told us a black woman—"

"She's mistaken."

"Ma'am, you stay right where you are with Mr. Hobbs, and someone will be there to talk to you."

"I don't *want* anyone to come here," Alice says. "I'm telling you my children are here with me, my children are safe."

"Then let me talk to one of them, ma'am."

"No."

"Ma'am . . ."

"And stop *ma'am*-ing me. I'm not your grandmother!"

"Mrs. Glendenning, I've already called Pratt Elementary and I talked to a Miss Phoebe Mears there who told me you'd spoken to her at a little past four today, asking did your kids get on the wrong bus and all . . ."

"Yes, that was before they came home," Alice says.

"You're saying they finally got home?"

"Yes, they did."

"Then they *weren't* picked up by a woman driving a blue car, is that it? The way Miss Mears says one of the school guards had told her they were?"

Alice says nothing.

"Mrs. Glendenning? Are you there?"

"I'm here."

"Did someone in a blue car bring your kids home to you?"

"No," Alice says. "What happened is they realized they were on the wrong bus, so they asked the driver to let them off at a phone booth. My daughter phoned me at home, and I went to pick them up."

"The driver let them get off the bus?"

"Apparently so."

"And your daughter called home, is that it?"

"Yes."

"She's how old, your daughter?"

"She's ten."

"Knows your home phone number, does she?"

"Of course she does. My office number, too."

"And you went to pick her up?"

"Yes, I did."

"Where was that, ma'am, Mrs. Glendenning?"

"Outside the Eckerd's on Kalin and U.S. 41."

"And she's there with you now, your daughter?"

"Yes. Outside."

"And your son, too."

"Yes, my son, too."

"Then you wouldn't mind showing them to the officer when he

comes knocking on your door in, it should be two, three seconds, will you?"

"Officer? What?" she says, and hears a car pulling into the shell driveway outside.

The uniformed cop standing beside the right front fender of a Tall Grass police cruiser takes off his hat when he sees Alice coming down the steps at the front of Charlie's house. Charlie is walking out just behind her.

"Mrs. Glendenning?"

"Yes?" she says.

"Officer Cudahy," he says. "I'm sorry to be bothering you, ma'am."

"No bother at all," she says. "What is it?"

"We got a call from a Detective Sloate downtown, he says you might be in need of some assistance."

"No, everything's fine, thanks," she says. "But thanks for your concern."

"Mrs. Glendenning," Cudahy says, "I wonder if you'd mind my speaking to your children for a minute."

"My children aren't here," Alice says at once.

Charlie gives her a sharp look.

"It is Detective Sloate's understanding that they're outside playing," Cudahy says.

"He must have misunderstood me."

"It's what he told me on the radio, ma'am."

"Yes, well, he must've heard me wrong."

Cudahy looks at her. Then he turns to Charlie.

"Are you the lady's father, sir?" he asks.

"No, I'm just a friend," Charlie says.

"Would you happen to know the lady's children?"

"I would."

"Are they here, sir?"

"They are not."

"Would you know where they are?"

"I would not."

"Mrs. Glendenning, do *you* know where they are?"

"Yes, I took them to the movies. I'll be picking them up when the show breaks, at nine-fifteen."

Cudahy looks at her.

"That's not what you told Detective Sloate," he says.

"Detective Sloate seems to have misunderstood a great many things," Alice says.

"I'll have to tell him the children aren't here," Cudahy says, and goes back to the car and pulls a mike from the dash. From where Alice stands with Charlie on the front steps of the house, she can hear first some static, and then only some garbled words. She does not know what she can tell the police next. She only knows there is one thing she can *not* tell them. She can not say her children have been kidnapped. If she brings the police into this, Ashley and Jamie will be killed.

Cudahy comes out of the car again.

"Mrs. Glendenning," he says, "Detective Sloate would like to talk to you, please."

"Very well," Alice says. "On the car radio, or does he want me to phone him?"

"In person, ma'am," Cudahy says. "He's asked me to bring you in."

"That's absurd," Charlie says.

"Be that as it may, sir," Cudahy says, and opens the car door for Alice. "Ma'am?"

Downtown Cape October is exactly nine blocks long and three blocks wide.

The tallest buildings here, all of them banks, are twelve stories high. Main Street runs eastward from the Cattle Trail—which is now a three-way intersection with a traffic light, but actually used to be a cow crossing back when the town was first incorporated—to the county courthouse, which, at five stories high, is the tallest building anywhere on Main. The other buildings on Main are one- and two-story cinder-block structures. The banks are on the two streets paralleling Main to the north and south. Alice has learned that when anyone says "downtown Cape October" he isn't talking about a place that also has an uptown. There is no uptown as such. There is merely downtown Cape October and then the rest of Cape October.

The police station here is officially called the Public Safety Building, and these words are lettered in white on the low wall outside. Less conspicuously lettered to the right of the brown metal entrance doors, and partially obscured by pittosporum bushes are the words POLICE DEPARTMENT. The building is constructed of varying shades of tan brick, and its architecturally severe face is broken only by narrow windows resembling rifle slits in an armory wall. This is not unusual for the Cape, where the summer months are torrid and large windows produce only heat and glare.

Cudahy drives Alice around into the parking lot behind the building, and parks the car alongside a white police paddy wagon marked with the words CAPE OCTOBER PD. He leads her to a back door, raps on it, and is admitted by another uniformed officer, who then takes Alice through marbled corridors to the front of the building, and then up to the third-floor reception area, where an orange-colored letter conveyor rises like an oversized periscope from the floor diagonally opposite the elevator doors. There is a desk against the paneled wall facing Alice, and a uniformed officer sits behind it, a woman this time, typing furiously. The clock on the wall above the woman's head reads fourteen minutes to nine. She stops typing the moment Alice gets off the elevator.

"Mrs. Glendenning?" she asks.

"Yes."

"Come with me, please."

Alice feels as if she has been arrested for shoplifting.

Detective Wilbur Sloate is a gangly man in his late thirties, early forties, Alice guesses. He is wearing a rumpled linen suit with a polka-dotted blue tie on a paler blue shirt. His hair is what Alice's mother, rest her soul, would have called dirty blond, a shade darker than Eddie's was. It is parted neatly on the left side of his head. He rises the moment Alice is led into his office.

"Mrs. Glendenning," he says, "please have a seat."

"I want to know why I'm here," Alice says.

"For your own good," Sloate says.

"That's what my father used to say before he whopped me one."

"Look, I can tell you we have reasonable cause to believe a crime was committed, and I can tell you we believe you're withholding evidence of a crime, and I can tell you you're hindering an investigation. I can tell you all of those things, Mrs. Glendenning, and you can tell me to go straight to hell and walk out of here right this minute. But that won't get your kids back if they were kidnapped."

Kidnapped.

The first time anyone has said the word out loud.

Kidnapped.

Alice says nothing.

"I want to help you. I know they told you not to call the police. I know they made death threats. But Mrs. Garrity did the right thing by calling us. I want to help you. Please let me help you."

"How?" she says.

"We can put a tap on your phone, get our people in your house. They won't know we're listening, they won't know we're there, I promise you. They don't have to know we're in this."

"They may *already* know! You brought me here in a goddamn *police* car . . ."

"We were very careful, Mrs. Glendenning . . ."

"Careful? A police car pulled right up in front of Charlie's house! Why didn't you take an ad in the paper?"

"I asked them to show the utmost discretion. Mr. Hobbs's house is in an isolated, heavily wooded part of Willard Key. There were no cars parked on the approach road, no sign of anyone watching the house. Officer Cudahy checked the perimeter carefully before he drove in. And when you arrived here, we brought you in through the back entrance of the facility. I feel certain that the people who kidnapped your children don't know you're here."

Kidnapped.

His using the word again makes it real all at once.

Kidnapped.

Her children have been kidnapped.

Jamie and Ashley have been kidnapped.

She suddenly bursts into tears.

"Here," he says, and yanks a tissue from a box on his desk, and hands it to her.

"Thank you," she says.

"Want to tell me what happened?"

She tells him.

"Have you *got* a quarter of a million dollars?" he asks.

"No."

"How much *have* you got?"

"About three thousand."

"So what makes them think you're rich?"

"They probably think I collected a fortune."

"How do you mean, ma'am?"

"My husband drowned eight months ago. He had a double indemnity policy with Garland."

"Is that an insurance company? Garland?"

"Yes. Garland and Rice."

"How much are you looking at?"

"Well . . . two hundred and fifty thousand, actually. When they pay it."

"You're expecting the exact sum they're asking for? I would say that's some kind of a rare coincidence. Who else knows about this big death benefit you're supposed to be getting?"

"My attorney . . . and his partners, I guess. And people at the insurance company, I suppose. But they all know it hasn't been paid yet."

"Anyone else? Have you mentioned to anyone else that you'd be coming into two hundred and fifty thousand dollars?"

"Well . . . my sister. And I suppose she told her husband."

"Where do *they* live?"

"In Atlanta."

"What's he do for a living?"

"Drives a truck. When he isn't in jail."

"That's a joke, right?"

"No, it's the truth."

"He's done time?"

"Yes. But not for anything serious."

"What was it?"

"Two dope convictions."

"Trafficking?"

"No."

"Cause that's serious, trafficking."

"This was simple possession."

"Do any of his pals know about this big insurance policy?"

"Pals?"

"Any of his former cellmates? Any of the yardbirds he buddied with? Wherever it was he did time."

"I don't know."

"Be nice to find out," Sloate says, and nods thoughtfully. He's really trying to dope this out, she thinks. But he seems so very . . . country-boy. If this were New York or some other big city . . .

But this isn't New York.

This is Cape October, Florida, and my children have been kidnapped, and at noon tomorrow a woman with a voice like a razor blade will call again and ask me if I've got the money. And all Alice can think is *I don't have the money, I don't have the money, they will kill my children.*

"How about your sister?" Sloate asks. "What does she do?"

"You're barking up the wrong tree. She loves my kids."

"Does her jailbird husband love them, too?"

"I'm telling you you're mis—"

"What does she do, your sister?"

"She works in a bank. She's straight as an arrow. Look, I really don't like the direction—"

"It wasn't *her* on that phone, was it?"

"No. Of course not."

"Mrs. Garrity said you told her the woman sounded black . . ."

"Well, she might have been black, yes."

"Does your sister have a Southern accent?"

"No."

"You said she lives in Atlanta."

"Yes, but she moved there to marry Rafe. She's originally from upstate New York, same as me."

"Rafe. Is that his name?"

"Rafe Matthews, yes. My sister is Carol Matthews."

"When's the last time old Rafe was in jail?"

"He got out two years ago."

"Been driving a truck since?"

"Yes."

"When he's not in jail, is what you said."

"Yes."

"But you don't think he'd kidnap your kids, is that it?"

"Of course not!"

"Me, I don't trust anybody who's done time. My own brother done time, I wouldn't trust him. Let's give your sister a call."

"Why?"

"Find out where old Rafe is."

"Why?"

"Man might be in Florida, who knows? Georgia's not all that far away, you know."

"Rafe doesn't have a blue car."

"Maybe the lady who called you does. Is Rafe playing around?"

"I don't know. I don't think so. My sister loves him."

"That ain't always insurance. Let's call her, okay, say hello. Would you like a drink? I have bourbon."

"No."

"Calm you down a little?"

"I'm calm."

"You don't seem calm."

"I'm just scared, is all. If anything happens to my kids . . ."

"Nothing'll happen to them. Just tell your sister you were thinking about her, decided to call. Don't mention the kids being missing," he says, and hands Alice the phone.

She dials Carol's number, and waits. One of her nephews picks up. Either Michael or Randy, she can't tell which.

"Hi, honey," she says, "this is Aunt Al. What're you doing up so late?"

"Watching TV," he says.

"Your mama know that?"

"Oh sure."

"Who's this I'm talking to?"

"Randall."

"How're you doing, Randall?"

"School sucks," Randall says.

Eight years old.

"Is she there?"

"Yeah."

"Could you get her for me, please?"

"Sure, just a sec," he says.

She waits.

"Hello?"

"Carol, hi, it's me."

"Hey, Alice, how are you, honey?"

"Fine, fine, just thought I'd check in."

"I'm glad you did. It's getting kind of lonely up here."

"How come?"

"Rafe's off on a long one. I kind of miss him stompin around. How are the kids?"

"Fine, just fine."

"Did Jamie get the *Myst* book I sent him?"

"The *what*?"

"The *Myst* book."

"What's a mist book?"

"The video game. *Myst.* M-y-s-t. It's a little booklet Randall found very useful in deciphering *Myst.*"

"Oh. No, it hasn't arrived yet."

"I sent it United Parcel, Jamie should be getting it any minute now."

"No, not yet."

"How is he, Alice?"

"He's fine."

"Is he . . . honey, is he talking yet?"

"No, not yet."

"Poor darling."

"Yes."

"Why don't you bring him up here for a while? Being with the boys might work wonders."

"Maybe so. Maybe when school lets out."

"I'd love to have him here, Alice."

"Thanks, sweetie, I appreciate that."

There is a silence on the line.

"When did Rafe leave?" Alice asks.

"Two days ago. What's today?"

"Wednesday."

"So he left Monday."

"Where's he off to this time?" Alice asks.

"Down your way, actually, was the first stop. Then it's over to Louisiana, Texas, Oklahoma, Arkansas, and back home."

"You say he's down here now?"

"Probably been and gone by now."

"Here? In Cape October?"

"No, did I say the Cape? He was heading for Jacksonville. Then Tallahassee and Mobile. I think is what he said."

"Have you spoken to him?"

"What do you mean?"

"Well . . . has he called you?"

"He never calls when he's on the road. He drives practically day and night, all he has time to do is sleep and grab a bite to eat. Anyway, he should be home by the weekend."

"That's good."

There is another silence, longer this time.

"Honey?" Carol says. "Is something wrong?"

"No, no. What could be wrong?"

"You sound . . . I don't know . . . funny."

"I'm just tired. I had a long day."

"You selling many houses down there?"

"Oh, scads."

"Maybe I'll come buy one."

"Be a good idea."

"Honey, I got to go now," Carol says. "I hear Michael screaming about something. We'll talk soon."

"Right," Alice says.

There is a click on the line. She hands the phone back to Sloate.

"Where is he?" Sloate asks.

"Mobile by now."

"Was he here on the Cape?"

"No. Jacksonville. Mr. Sloate, I don't think he came here to steal my kids. My sister would kill him, he ever did something like that."

"How about one of his jailbird pals? You think he might have mentioned to one of them that there's this beautiful widow in Florida, has two kids, and has just come into two hundred and fifty grand?"

"You're scaring me, Mr. Sloate."

"I don't mean to be doing that. I'm just trying to figure out who could've got it in his head that kidnapping your kids might be a way to get at those big bucks you're supposed to've come into. Which you haven't come into *yet,* by the way. But they don't know that, do they?"

"No, they don't."

"Come on, let's take you home. Get this thing rolling. Find out who these damn people are," he says, and rises briskly from behind his desk.

If anyone is watching the house on Oleander Street, he will see only a dark-haired woman driving a black Mercedes ML320 up the street. He will see the car pulling into the driveway and stopping to wait for the garage doors to go up. The dark-haired woman is Alice herself. The Mercedes is the car supplied to her by Lane Realty, one of the perks of being a real estate broker.

If anyone is watching the house, he will see the garage doors going up. He will see Alice driving the car in. To anyone watching, Alice seems to be alone in the car. The garage doors roll down again. After a short interval, anyone watching the house will see lights coming on in the living room. He will see the dark-haired woman—Alice again—approaching the windows, looking out at the street, and then drawing the drapes.

In the garage, Wilbur Sloate gets up from where he is lying on the floor in the backseat of the Mercedes, climbs out of the car, and comes around to the hatchback at the rear. He yanks that open, and offers his hand to Detective Marcia Di Luca, one of the sixteen detectives assigned to the Criminal Investigations Division. Marcia's specialty is communications, but she looks somewhat like a barmaid, wide in the behind, big in the chest, unruly red hair trailing to below her shoulders. She is wearing a tan skirt and a lime green blouse and a nine-millimeter Glock. Looking at Marcia, Alice gets the impression that she wouldn't particularly like to get in a catfight with her. She gets the impression that Marcia wouldn't mind shooting someone right between the eyes if the opportunity presented itself.

"What we're going to do," Sloate explains, "what *Marcia's* going to do, as a matter of fact, is place a tap on your phone before that call comes in at noon tomorrow. This way we can listen to and record any calls you get . . ."

"We call it a Tap and Tape," Marcia says.

"She's also going to set up equipment that'll be able to locate the caller's phone numbe—"

"We call that a Trap and Trace."

"And she'll put in a second line so we can call the captain direct downtown."

"That'll be Captain Roger Steele," Marcia says.

"He's in charge of the department's CID."

Alice nods.

"So, what you can do, ma'am, you can go to sleep now, while Marcia and me get started. No sense you pacing the floor all night, we're not going to hear from them again till noon tomorrow. Okay?"

"Yes, fine," Alice says.

"G'night then, ma'am."

"Good night," Marcia says, and goes out to the garage for her equipment.

The phone rings at a little before midnight.

Alice is not yet asleep. She doesn't know if she should pick up the bedroom extension or not. She throws on a robe and comes out into the living room, where Marcia and Sloate are still working.

"You ready on that trace?" Sloate asks Marcia.

"Nope," she says.

"What should I do?" Alice asks.

"Let it ring a few more times. Tell her you were asleep," Sloate says. "We can at least listen and record, get some information that way, do a voice profile later. Tell her you're selling all your stock. Tell her you'll have the money tomorrow afternoon sometime. Tell her to take a Polaroid picture of your kids holding tomorrow morning's edition of the Cape October *Trib.* Tell her to Fed Ex it to you."

"She won't do all that."

"Just keep her talking, see what she has to say for herself." He sits in front of the wiretap equipment, puts on the earphones. "Go on, pick up," he says.

"Hello?" Alice says.

"Al? It's me. Charlie."

"Charlie?"

"Did I wake you?"

"No."

"What have you heard?"

Sloate shakes his head, wags his finger at her.

"Nothing," she says.

Sloate runs his finger across his throat.

For a moment, Alice is puzzled.

Then she understands that he wants her to end the conversation.

"Charlie, I just got out of bed," she says, "can you excuse me a minute? I'll call you right back."

"Sure, honey, I'll be here."

She puts the phone back on its cradle.

"Why?" she asks Sloate.

"I wanted to brief you. I don't want you to tell him anything. Don't tell him we're here, don't tell him a thing, not a single thing. Just say we asked you a few questions downtown and let you go. You didn't tell us anything about your kids being missing."

"Charlie's my best friend. Why can't I . . . ?"

"*They* may know that, too. Nothing. Tell him nothing."

"Suppose he wants to come here?"

"Tell him no."

Alice looks at him.

"You want to see your kids alive again?"

"You're beginning to sound like *her.*"

"Better call him back," Marcia says.

"Make it short," Sloate says. "Tell him you want to keep the line clear, case anybody calls."

"He'll smell a rat."

"He'll smell a rat if you don't call back pretty damn soon," Sloate says.

Alice picks up the receiver and begins dialing.

"Hello?"

"Charlie?"

"Yes, hi. What happened with the cops?"

"They asked me a lot of questions, and then let me go."

"What kind of questions?"

"Well, you know, Rosie told them all about the kids being gone . . ."

"Yeah, so?"

"I told them they were mistaken. They said, Okay, it's your funeral, lady, and let me go."

"Were those their exact words?"

"More or less. Charlie, I hate to cut you short, but I want to keep the line free. In case they call again."

"You haven't heard from them again, huh?"

"Not yet."

"That's strange, don't you think?" he asks.

"Well, they said noon tomorrow."

"Even so."

"Charlie, I really have to—"

"I know, okay. Call me if you need me, okay? Do you want me to come over?"

"No, I don't think that would be smart. They may be watching the house."

"Right, right."

"Charlie . . ."

"I'm gone. Talk to you later."

Alice hangs up.

"Okay?" she asks Sloate.

There is an edge to her voice.

"Fine, ma'am. You did just fine."

"I hope you know what you're doing," Alice says.

"We know what we're doing, ma'am."

"I hope so. Because if anything happens to my kids . . ."

"Nothing will happen to your kids."

She looks him dead in the eye.

The look says, Nothing had *better* happen, Detective Sloate.

"Good night," she says, and goes off to bed.

Thursday
May 13

3

At 8:45 A.M., Rosie Garrity is still watching television, hoping to hear something about the kidnapping.

There was nothing on last night until she went to bed at eleven, and there's nothing on this morning, either, not on WSWF, anyway. WSWF is Cape October's own Channel 36, the "SWF" in the call letters standing for Southwest Florida. Rosie starts surfing the cable channels, one after the other, figuring a kidnapping always gets covered on the cable shows, but there's nothing there either.

She's beginning to wonder if whoever she spoke to at the police yesterday has taken any action on the case—Sloane or Slope or something like that, said he was a detective. Because if he was just sitting on this thing instead of *doing* something about it, why, he should be reported to a superior officer for disciplinary action, these were two innocent little kids out there. She is just about to dial the police again, when the phone rings, startling her. She picks up at once, thinking this might be Detective Sloane wanting further information.

Instead, it is Alice Glendenning.

"Hello, Mrs. Glendenning," she says. "Have you heard anything further from that black woman?"

"No, nothing yet," Alice says. "Rosie, the reason I'm calling . . ."

She suspects that she is going to be bawled out for having called the police. But then Alice says, "I don't think you should come in today," and Rosie immediately believes she's about to be fired.

"Why not?" she asks defensively.

"Because my children are gone, and I want to be alone here when that woman calls, if she calls."

Alone.

She has just told Rosie that she is alone.

Which means the police have *not* contacted her, as that Detective Sloane said they were going to do, which means the police are most certainly being derelict in their duty.

Well, we'll just see about that, Rosie thinks.

"I understand, Mrs. Glendenning," she says. "Just call me if there's anything you need, okay?"

"I will, Rosie. Thank you."

But there is something odd in her voice, something cool and distant. Rosie wonders just what the hell is going on here.

"Good-bye now," she says.

She hangs up, and immediately begins searching the Cape October-Fort Myers-Sanibel directory under GOVERNMENT AGENCIES.

When the phone rings at 9:10 A.M., Detective Marcia Di Luca says at once, "I'm not ready here yet, Will."

Alice can only think they've been working here all damn night, and she's still not ready. Alice can only think her children's fate is in the hands of Keystone Kops.

Sloate is putting on the earphones.

"I don't think it's her again, so early," he says. "But if it is, just let her talk, hear what she has to say."

The phone is still ringing.

"Shall I pick up?" Alice asks.

Sloate hits some buttons on his recording equipment. Reels begin spinning.

"Go ahead," he says.

Alice picks up the phone.

"Hello?"

"Alice?"

A woman's voice. She recognizes it at once. Aggie Barrows, her assistant.

"Yes, Aggie," she says.

"Did you forget your nine o'clock?"

"My . . . ?"

"With Mr. Webster."

"Oh Je—"

"He's here now. What shall I tell him? Are you coming in?"

"Let me talk to him, Agg."

She waits.

"Hello?"

"Mr. Webster, hi, I'm *so* sorry."

"That's all right," he says. "What happened?"

"I broke my ankle."

"Well, that's a new one," he says.

"I really did," she says. "I got knocked down by a car yesterday afternoon."

"I'm sorry to hear that," he says.

"I'm in a cast. I should have called you, I know, but what with the hospital and all . . ."

"Hey, that's all right, we can do it another time."

"I hope so."

There is a silence on the line.

"Is . . . everything else all right?" he asks.

Sloate glances up from his recording equipment.

"Yes, I'm fine, thanks," Alice says. "I really am very sorry about this."

"Long as it wasn't anything I said yesterday."

"No, no, I really did have an accident."

"I thought maybe I'd been out of line."

"No, no, not at all."

"None of my business, after all."

"That's okay, really. I took no offense."

"I hope not. So how shall we leave this? Will you call me? Shall I look for another broker?"

"I wish you wouldn't do that, Mr. Webster . . ."

"Webb."

"I'd love to find a home for you here on the Cape, I really would. But it may be a few days before . . ."

"I have some other business to take care of down here, anyway. Why don't we just play it by ear? Just call me when you think you'll be up and around again."

"Well, I'm able to walk now," she says. "It's just . . ."

It's just my children have been kidnapped, you see. It's just I have two detectives here in the house with me right now, one of them listening to every word you and I are saying. It's just that in less than three hours, a woman is going to call here again to tell me what I have to do next if I ever want to see my kids alive again. It's just all that, Mr. Webster, Webb, it's just I am going out of my mind with fear and anxiety, that's all it is, Webb.

"I have your number," she says. "I'll call you."

"Please do," he says, and hangs up.

She looks at the receiver. She places it back on its cradle.

"Sounds like a nice fellow," Sloate comments.

"Yes," she says.

"How you doing with that?" he asks Marcia.

"Getting there," she says.

Sloate looks at his watch.

"You've got two and twenty-five," he says.

"Thanks a lot," she says dryly.

"Just thought I'd remind you."

There is between them the easy banter of two people who have worked together for a very long time. It is almost like a good marriage, Alice realizes. Sloate isn't going to start yelling at her if she doesn't have her equipment set up in the next two hours and twenty-five minutes, and Marcia is not going to have a hysterical hissy fit if she doesn't come in under that deadline. Sloate seems confident that she will have the job done in that time. And she seems confident that she will not fail him. As he takes off the earphones, he nods assurance to Marcia, and she looks up from where her rather delicate hands—Alice notices for the first time—are twirling dials and throwing switches, and she winks at him to let him know the situation is completely under control here.

Alice wonders if it really is.

There was a time . . .

Alice was twenty-two years old, and just completing NYU's film program. Her idea was to become a famous director. That was before she met Edward Fulton Glendenning. Eddie was twenty-four, a graduate student in the business school. They met in University Park, on a bright afternoon in June.

She was sitting on a bench, crying.

He appeared out of the blue.

Tall and slender, crew-cut blond hair glistening in the spring sunshine, cherry trees in bloom all up and down the side streets surrounding the school. She saw him through the mist of her tears, standing suddenly before her.

"Hey, what's this?" he said, and sat, and took her hands in his.

His hands were soft. Delicate. She looked into his face, into his eyes. A narrow fox face, with a slender nose and fine high cheekbones, nearly feminine in its elegance, as sculpted as a Grecian mask, the eyes a pale blue, almost gray. She allowed him to hold her hands. Her hands were clasped between his own two hands, slender, a pianist's hands with long tapering fingers, everything about him so beautifully exact.

He offered her a handkerchief.

He asked her why she was crying.

She told him she'd spent all day yesterday editing hundreds of feet of film, and marking the strips with Roman numerals to differentiate this go-round from the earlier strips marked with Arabic numerals, and one of the other girls on her team—

"There are five of us altogether," she said. "We have to do this fifteen-minute film as our final project . . ."

One of the other girls came in this morning, and reedited everything she'd already done, messing everything up, getting the sound all out of synch, and replacing the Roman numerals with Arabic numerals all over again because she didn't know what Roman numerals *were*!

"Can you believe it?" Alice said. "She's twenty-one years old, she's from Chicago, that's not a hick town, and she's never heard of a Roman numeral in her *life*! She thought it was some kind of secret *code*! Can you believe it?"

"Amazing," Eddie said.

"I know. How can anyone be so . . . ?"

"You. I mean you. Amazing."

He was still holding her hands, she noticed.

"You're so very beautiful," he said.

"Oh sure," she said.

"Oh sure," he said.

They were married six months later.

The two detectives who drive into the bus loading area at Pratt Elementary at 9:30 that Thursday morning are looking for a man named Luke Farraday. Like Sloate and Di Luca, they work for Cape October's Criminal Investigations Division, and they have been sent here by Captain Roger Steele, who wants them to find out whatever they can about the blue car that supposedly picked up the Glendenning kids yesterday afternoon.

The two detectives are named Peter Wilson Andrews and Julius Aaron Saltzman. Saltzman is very large, standing at six-four in his bare feet, and weighing a good two hundred and twenty pounds when he's watching his diet. He is wearing a little blue-and-gray crocheted yarmulke fastened to the back of his head with bobby pins, this because he is very proud of his Jewish heritage and will take the slightest opportunity to discuss the impending American holocaust if nothing is done to stop the tide of anti-Semitism in this nation. Saltzman is what Andrews would call a Professional Jew, more or less, in that his Jewishness seems to dictate every move he makes and every word he speaks.

Andrews is perhaps five feet eight inches tall, very short for any cop but especially for a detective, where promotions often depend on brawn rather than brain. He is what one might generously call a redneck. In fact, he drifted down here to Florida after working on a tobacco farm in Tennessee, where his neck and his arms did grow very red indeed and then brown from hours of laboring in the hot sun, until he decided there had to be a better life somewhere for a red-blooded (and red-necked) American boy like himself.

Andrews found that better life here on the Cape, where first he worked as a bouncer in a strip joint on the Trail south of the airport, and then joined the police force as a uniformed rookie earning $28,914 a year. He is now a full-fledged detective in the CID, working with Saltzman, and thanking his lucky stars for his partner's size and raw power every time they go up against some redneck like Andrews used to be, carrying a sawed-off shotgun or a machete or even a pool cue.

They find Farraday in the school cafeteria. He tells them he came in half an hour ago after supervising the unloading of the buses, and he is just now lingering over a cup of coffee before heading home. What he does, he explains to them, is come in early in the morning to unload the buses, and then goes home until it's time to come back in the afternoon, when the kids are boarding the buses again. There's not much for Farraday at home. His wife died three years ago, he tells them. He's alone in the world, he tells them.

Farraday is wearing bifocals and a hearing aid, a man in his mid-sixties, one of a breed who come down here to retire and then discover that they have all the time in the world to do nothing but play golf and push a shopping cart up and down the aisles of a supermarket. They finally take jobs as cashiers in souvenir shops, or bank guards, or—as is the case with Farraday here—guards at school crossings or bus-loading areas, anything to keep them busy, anything to make them feel useful again. There is nothing like early retirement to make a person feel dead.

The detectives have got to be very careful here.

They have been cautioned by Steele that they are not to indicate in any way, manner, or form that a kidnapping has taken place. The Glendenning woman was warned that if she notified the police, her kids would be killed. Apparently, she is none too happy that the police are already on the job, but that's the way the little cookie crumbles, lady, and if you want your children back you don't go to a lawyer or a private eye. You go to professionals who know how to do the job. Though, to tell the truth, this is the first kidnapping Saltzman or Andrews has ever caught.

The point is, a death threat was made.

So they have to tiptoe around old Farraday here—to both Saltzman and Andrews, sixty years old is ancient—find out whatever they can about the car that picked up the kids yesterday, without indicating in any way that any sort of crime has been committed here. They have an advantage in that Farraday seems kind of stupid to them. Then again, all old people seem stupid to Andrews and Saltzman.

"These'd be Jamie and Ashley Glendenning," Andrews says. "Little boy and girl."

"You fellas want some coffee?"

"No, thanks," Saltzman says.

Andrews shakes his head no.

"Make a good cup of coffee here," Farraday says.

Old farts talk about food a lot, Andrews notices.

"Not as good as Starbucks," Farraday says, "but pretty damn good for a school cafeteria, am I right?"

"This would've been about two-thirty yesterday," Saltzman prods.

"You know who else makes a nice cup of coffee?" Farraday asks.

"Who's that?" Andrews says.

"Place called The Navigator? On Davidson? I stop there every morning on my way to work, they give you a good breakfast for a buck twenty-nine. Eggs and all. Nice cup of coffee, too."

"Would you happen to remember these kids?" Saltzman asks. "The Glendenning kids?"

"He the one can't talk?" Farraday asks.

This is the first they're hearing about the kid being a mute. The two detectives look at each other.

"Father drowned out on the Gulf one night. Probably taking a piss over the side, lost his balance, fell in. Most of these small boat drownings are guys taking a piss over the side, did you know that? It's a fact," Farraday says, and nods. "The Glendenning boy can't talk, it's some kind of post-traumatic thing, the shock of it, you know. *Won't* talk is more like it, I guess."

"That's a shame," Saltzman says. "Did you happen to see the Glendenning kids yesterday afternoon?"

"Yes, I did," Farraday says. "What's this all about, anyway?"

"Apparently, they missed the bus, and some woman was kind enough—"

"No, they didn't miss no bus," Farraday says.

"Whatever," Andrews says. "The thing is, some woman was nice enough to pick them up, and drive them home. But she left them with the housekeeper, and drove off without saying what her name was."

"That's funny, ain't it?"

"Well, she was probably in a hurry, Thing is, Mrs. Glendenning would like to thank her, so if there's—"

"But they didn't miss no bus," Farraday says. "Fact is, they were about to get *on* the bus when she called them over."

"This would've been a blue car, is that right?"

"Blue Chevrolet Impala, that's right."

"Woman driving it."

"A blonde woman, yes."

"Would you happen to know who she was?"

"Nope. Never saw her before in my life."

"A woman, though?"

"Young blonde woman, yes," Farraday says. "Hair down to here," he adds, and runs the flat of his hand along the side of his neck, about three inches above the shoulders.

Scratch a black woman, Andrews thinks. But he asks anyway. "White or black?"

"I just said she was a blonde, didn't I?"

"Well, yes, but lots of blacks these days bleach their—"

"I suppose that's true, at that," Farraday says, and nods. "But this woman was white."

"How old would you say?"

"I didn't get that good a look. Just saw a blonde leaning over to open the door for the kids."

"And the kids got right in, is that it?"

"Got right in the car, yes."

"Must've known the woman, wouldn't you say?"

"Don't know if they knew her or not. Just saw them get in the car, and she drove right off."

"You're sure it was an Impala?" Andrews asks.

"Ain't nothing wrong with my eyes, mister."

"Didn't think there was," Andrews says, and smiles. In which case, why are you wearing bifocals? he wonders.

"*Blue* Impala, right?" Saltzman asks.

"Blue as my eyes."

Which Andrews now notices are, in fact, blue. Behind bifocals as thick as the bottoms of Coca-Cola bottles.

"The year?" Saltzman asks.

"Couldn't say exactly. But it was a new car."

"You didn't happen to notice the license plate, did you?"

"Wasn't looking for it."

"Florida plate, would it have been?"

"I didn't look. I got things to do here, you know. I got a job here. I have to make sure all these kids get on their right buses. I have to make sure they all get home."

Right, Andrews thinks.

So you let two of them get in a car with a blonde woman you never before saw in your life, quote unquote.

You blind old fart, he thinks.

Special Agent Felix Forbes is here on Rose Garrity's doorstep this morning at eleven o'clock because apparently she reported a kidnapping to a detective in the Cape October PD's CID, and no action was taken on her complaint. Standing beside him on Rosie's doorstep is another federal agent named Sally Ballew, whom the Cape October cops call "Sally Balloons" because of her extraordinary chest development, which even Forbes has noticed on occasion. He does not think she knows the cops call her Sally Balloons. He is wrong. She knows. There is not much that gets by Sally Ballew.

The woman who answers the door is somewhat short and pudgy, in her early fifties, Forbes guesses, with a mop of brownish-red hair, and freckles on her cheeks and nose, and a high sheen of sweat on her forehead. This presages a house without air-conditioning, an unwelcome prospect on a day when the temperature has already hit eighty-six and the humidity is thick enough to swim in.

"Mrs. Garrity?" he says.

"Yes?"

"Special Agent Forbes," he says, "FBI," and shows his shield. "My partner, Special Agent Ballew."

"May we come in, ma'am?" Sally asks.

"Please."

The small development house is every bit as hot as Forbes expected it would be. Mrs. Garrity leads them into a tiny living room furnished with a sofa and two easy chairs slip-covered in paisley. She offers them iced tea, goes out into the kitchen to get it, and then sits opposite them on the sofa. The two agents sit on the easy chairs, facing her.

"So," Forbes says, "what's this about a kidnapping?"

He frankly finds it difficult to believe that the Cape October cops would not have acted swiftly on any report of a kidnapping. These days, however, with terrorists of every stripe and persuasion apparently slipping through the fingers of the FBI and the CIA and the INS, he would be foolish not to investigate any errant phone call, even from someone like Mrs. Garrity here, who, to tell the truth, looks a little too eager to attain her own fifteen minutes of fame by becoming the star of a little kidnapping melodrama she herself has concocted. Sally is thinking the same thing. But they are here to listen.

Mrs. Garrity tells them about being at the Glendenning house yesterday afternoon when Alice Glendenning got home from work, and then about the kids not being on their regular bus, and then about the phone call from this woman who sounded black, according to Mrs. Glendenning, anyway, who told her not to call the police or the children would die.

"Were you listening to this phone call?" Sally asks.

"No."

"Then how do you know what she said?"

"Mrs. Glendenning repeated the conversation to me."

"This woman said she had the children?"

"Yes. And she said not to call the police or the children would die."

"You didn't hear the caller's voice, is that it?"

"I did not hear it. That's correct."

"Then how do you know she was black?"

"Mrs. Glendenning said she sounded black."

"She volunteered this information?" Sally asks.

"No, I asked her was the woman white or black. She said she sounded black."

It so happens that Sally herself is black. Forbes hopes she is not about to get on her high horse here with a lot of racial attitude that has nothing to do with why they're here. If the woman on the phone sounded black, then she sounded black. There is nothing wrong with sounding black if you sound black. Which Sally herself, by the way, sounds on occasion. Like right this very minute, for example.

"So what happened after this phone call?" Forbes asks.

"I advised her to call the police. She told me no."

"Then what?" Sally asks.

There is still an edge to her voice. She is still bridling because she thinks Mrs. Rose Garrity here was doing a bit of racial profiling yesterday when she asked if the caller was white or black. It seems to Forbes that this is a perfectly reasonable question to ask in law enforcement, where a person's color or lack of it might be a clue to the person himself or herself—yes, and how about *that,* for example? For example, is it wrong to ask if a person is a man or a woman? Is that profiling, too? You can carry all this stuff just so far, Forbes thinks, and says again, "Go on, Mrs. Garrity."

"When I got home last night, I called the police. I spoke to a Detective Sloane there . . ."

"Must be Wilbur Sloate she means," Sally says. "CID."

"Was that his name, ma'am? Detective *Sloate.* S-L-O-A-*T*-E?"

"I thought he said Sloane."

"Well, maybe there's a Sloane up there, too," Forbes says.

"I thought that was what he said his name was."

"So what happened?"

"He said he'd get on it right away."

"So why'd you call us, ma'am?" Sally asks.

"Because when I spoke to Mrs. Glendenning this morning, she told me she was alone. And I figured if Detective Sloane, I'm sure his name was, had got right on it the way he said he would, then she wouldn't be alone in her house when her children are in the hands of some black woman who said she would kill them, was why I called you."

"You're sure she was alone there?"

"She told me she was alone. She told me not to come in today, said she wanted to be alone if that woman called again. I have to assume, if Mrs. Glendenning tells me she's alone in the house, that she really *is.*"

"And where *is* this, Mrs. Garrity?" Sally asks.

"Where is *what,* Agent Ballew?"

"*Special* Agent Ballew," Sally corrects. "Where is this house where Mrs. Glendenning is sitting alone waiting for a call from a black kidnapper?"

When the telephone rings, they all turn to look at the clock.

It is 11:40 A.M.

Sloate puts on the earphones.

"I think I'm ready now," Marcia says.

"Go ahead," Sloate says, and indicates that Alice is to pick up the phone.

She lifts the receiver.

"Hello?" she says.

"Alice?"

"Who's this?"

"Rafe."

"Rafe?"

"Your brother-in-law. Want to give lunch to a poor wandering soul?"

"Where . . . where are you, Rafe?"

"My rig's right outside a 7-Eleven on . . . where is this place, mister?" he shouts. "*Where?* I'm up here in Bradenton. How far is that from you?"

"Rafe, I don't think it would be a good idea . . ."

"I'll get directions," he says. "See you."

There is a click on the line.

"I thought he was supposed to be in Mobile by now," Sloate says.

"Apparently not."

"Who was it?" Marcia says.

"Rafe," Sloate says. "The jailbird brother-in-law. He's on his way over."

"We don't need him here," Marcia says.

"I don't need *anyone* here," Alice says.

The grandfather clock reads 11:45 A.M.

• • •

"Hello?"

In that single word, Christine knows intuitively that someone is in that house with Alice Glendenning. She simply senses it. The certain knowledge that the woman is not alone.

"Is someone there with you?" she asks at once.

"No, I'm alone," Alice says.

"You didn't call the police, did you?"

"No."

"Because you know that's the end of your kids, don't you?"

"Yes."

"Stay right there by the phone," Christine says, and hangs up, and goes back to the blue Impala she's parked at the curb alongside the phone booth. She begins driving at once, searching for the next pay phone along the Trail. She is not positive about how telephone traces work, but she thinks maybe they can close in on specific locations if not specific phone numbers. She called on a cell phone last night, from where the two of them are holding the kids, but they decided together that it would be safer if she called from pay phones this morning.

She pulls off the road as soon as she spots one in a strip mall. She gets out of the Impala again, walks over to the plastic phone shell, and dials Alice's number.

She looks at her watch.

12:10 P.M.

She hears the phone ringing on the other end, once, twice . . .

"Hello?"

"Have you got the money?" she asks.

"Not yet," Alice says.

"What's taking you so long?"

"There are securities to sell. It isn't easy to raise that much cash overnight."

"When will you have it?" Christine asks.

There is a silence on the line.

Someone coaching her for sure. Hand signals, or scribbled notes, whatever. She is not alone in that house.

"I'm still working on it."

"Work on it faster," Christine says, and hangs up. She looks at her watch again. The call took fifteen seconds, going on sixteen. She does not think they can effect a trace in that short a time. She goes back to the car, and drives along the Trail until she spots another pay phone. It is 12:17 when she calls the house again.

"Hello?"

"Get the money by this afternoon at three," Christine says. "We'll call then with instructions."

"Wait!"

"What? Fast!"

"How do I know they're still alive? Send me a Polaroid picture of the two of them holding today's *Tribune.*"

"What?"

"Send it Fed Ex."

"You're dreaming," Christine says.

The sweep hand on her watch has ticked off twenty seconds.

"I'll call you at three," she says.

"Are my children all right? Let me speak to Ashley, ple—"

Christine hangs up.

"Twenty-five seconds this time," Marcia says.

Sloate is already on the new phone link to the Public Safety Building downtown. Alice listens as he tells his commanding officer that they've had no luck with a trace. He tells him the woman is demanding the money by three this afternoon. The big grandfather clock in the hallway now reads twenty minutes to one.

"So what do we do?" he asks. "We've got till three o'clock."

"Let me think on it," Steele says, and hangs up.

Alice is pacing the room. She whirls on Marcia, where she is sitting behind her equipment. "Why haven't you been able to trace the calls yet?" she asks.

"She's never on the line long enough," Marcia says.

"We can put men on the moon, but you can't trace a damn call coming from around the corner!"

"I wish it *was* just around the corner. But we don't know *where* she's—"

"I don't want you here!" Alice shouts. "I want you all out of here! I'll handle this alone from now on. Just get out! None of you knows what the hell you're doing, you're going to get my children killed!"

"Mrs. Glendenning . . ."

"No! Just get out of here. Take all your stuff and leave. Now! Please. Get out. Please. I'm sorry. Get out."

"We're staying," Sloate says.

She is ready to punch him.

"I'm sorry, Mrs. Glendenning," he says, "but we're staying."

And then, infuriating her because it reminds her again of her father when he used to take a razor strop to her behind, "It's for your own good."

4

When Rafe arrives at a quarter past one that afternoon, Alice has no choice but to tell him what's going on. He looks as if he doesn't believe her. Doesn't believe these are detectives here. Doesn't believe her kids are missing, either. Thinks this is all some kind of afternoon pantomime staged for his benefit. Stands there like a big man who needs a shave and a drink both, which he tells Alice he really *does* need if all she's telling him is true. She pours him some twelve-year-old scotch from a bottle Lane Realty gave her at Christmastime. The other brokers all got bonuses, but she hadn't sold a house yet. Still hasn't, for that matter.

"What happened to your foot?" Rafe asks, noticing at last.

"I got hit by a car."

"Did you report it?" he says.

"Not yet," she says.

My kids have been kidnapped, she thinks, and everybody wants to know if I reported a goddamn traffic accident.

She takes him into the kitchen, and searches in the fridge for something she can give him to eat.

"You tell Carol about this?" he asks.

"No."

"Why not?"

"My kids are in danger."

"She's your sister."

"This okay?" she asks, and offers him a loaf of sliced rye, a wedge of cheese, and a large hunk of Genoa salami.

"You got mustard?" he asks.

"Sure."

"You should call her," he says.

"Let's see what happens here, okay?"

"She's your sister," he says again.

"When it's over," she says.

"You got any wine?"

She takes an opened bottle of Chardonnay from the fridge, hands him a glass. In the living room, Sloate is on the phone again with his captain. She wanders out there to see if she can learn anything, but there is nothing new. Three o'clock seems so very far away. When she comes back into the kitchen, Rafe is just finishing his sandwich.

"You're out of wine," he tells her, and shakes the empty bottle in his fist. "Have you got a spare bedroom? I've been driving all night."

She shows Rafe the children's empty bedroom. Twin beds in it, one on either side of the room. Rafe looks insulted by the size of the beds, big man like him. But he finally climbs into one of them, clothes and all.

Alice goes into her own bedroom, and climbs into bed, thinking she will take a nap before three, be ready for whatever may come next.

In an instant, she is dead asleep.

The nightmare comes the way it always does.

The family is sitting at the dinner table together.

It is seven-thirty P.M. on the night of September twenty-first last year; she will never forget that date as long as she lives.

Eddie is telling her he feels like taking the *Jamash* out for a little moonlight spin. The *Jamash* is a 1972 Pearson sloop they bought used when they first moved down here to the Cape. It cost $12,000 at a time when Eddie was still making good money as a stockbroker, before Bush got elected and things went all to hell with the economy. They named it after the two kids, Jamie and Ashley, the *Jamash* for sure, a trim little thirty-footer that was seaworthy and fast.

But Eddie has never taken her out for a moonlight spin without Alice aboard, and this has always required making babysitter plans in advance.

"Just feel like getting out on the water," he tells her.

"Well . . . sure," she says, "go ahead."

"You sure you don't mind?"

"Just don't take her out on the Gulf," she says. "Not alone."

"I promise," he says.

From the door, as he leaves the house, he yells, "Love ya, babe!"

"Love ya, too," Alice says.

"Love ya, Daddy!" Ashley yells.

"Love ya," Jamie echoes.

In the Gulf of Mexico the next morning, an oil tanker spots the boat under sail, moving on an erratic course, tossing aimlessly on the wind.

They hail her, and get no response.

When finally they climb down onto the deck, there is no one aboard.

Alice gets the phone call at ten that morning.

She screams.

And screams.

The telephone is ringing.

She climbs out of bed, rushes into the living room. The grandfather clock reads ten minutes to two. Sloate already has the earphones on.

"She's early," he says.

Marcia is behind her tracing gear now.

Sloate nods.

Alice picks up.

"Hello?" she says.

"Listen," the woman says. "Just listen." And then, in a stage whisper, "Tell her you and your brother are okay, that's all. Nothing else." And then, apparently handing Ashley the phone, she says, "Here."

"We're both okay," Ashley says in a rush. "Mom, I can't believe it!"

"*What* can't . . . ?"

"Do you remember Mari—?"

The line goes dead.

"Who's Marie?" Sloate asks at once.

"They're alive," Alice says. "My children . . ."

"Do you know anyone named Marie?"

"No. Did you hear her? They're both okay!"

"Or Maria?"

"I don't know. They're *alive*!"

"Fifteen seconds this time," Marcia says.

"Marie? Maria?"

"I don't know anyone named—"

"A relative?"

"No."

"A friend?"

"No. My children are alive. How are you going . . . ?"

"Someone who worked for you?"

". . . to get them . . . ?"

"Marie," he insists. "Maria. *Think*!"

"*You* think, damn it! They're alive! Do something to—"

And suddenly the knowledge breaks on her face.

"What?" Sloate asks.

"Yes. Maria."

"Who?"

"A babysitter. This was a long time ago, I'm not even sure she—"

"What's her last name?"

• • •

At two o'clock that afternoon, Charlie Hobbs, at the wheel of the Chevy pickup he uses to transport his huge canvases, drives into the bus-loading area at Pratt Elementary School, and asks to talk to Luke Farraday. It is a hot, bright, sunny day on the Cape, the temperature hovering at ninety-two degrees. Charlie is wearing jeans and a white T-shirt. Farraday is wearing a blue uniform with a square shield, and a little black plastic name tag over the left breast pocket. L. FARRADAY. Yellow school buses are already beginning to roll into the lot.

Charlie has to be careful here.

The warning from whoever has taken Alice's kids could not have been more explicit:

Don't call the police, or they'll die.

Charlie doesn't want Farraday to think anything out of the ordinary has happened here. At the same time, he hopes to get a bead on that blue car.

"I'm a friend of Alice Glendenning," he says. "She wants to thank whoever picked up her kids yesterday afternoon. Maybe you can help me."

"Cops've already been here," Farraday says. "Told 'em everything I know."

This surprises Charlie. He hopes it doesn't show on his face. Why would the cops have been here? Alice told him they let her go yesterday, so why . . . ?

"Sorry to bother you again then," he says. "She's just eager to thank the woman."

Farraday is a man maybe sixty-five, seventy, in there, one of the retirees who come down here to die in the sun. Charlie's fifty-four, which is maybe getting on, he supposes. But he knew what he wanted to be when he was seventeen. Had to leave art school when the Army grabbed him, but returned to his studies and his chosen profession the moment he was discharged. He's been painting ever since, never hopes to retire till his fingers can no longer hold a brush or the good Lord claims him, whichever comes first.

"These'd be Jamie and Ashley Glendenning," he says. "Little boy and girl."

"Yep, I know them. But like I told the detectives this morning—"

"That when they were here?"

"Round ten o'clock," Farraday says.

"And you told them what?"

"Told them a young blonde woman called the kids over to the car, drove off with them."

"What'd she look like?"

"Straight blonde hair down to here," he says, and indicates the length of it on his neck. "Slender woman from the look of her, delicate features. Wearing sunglasses and a white little-like tennis hat with a peak."

"She wasn't black, was she?" Charlie asks.

"Cops asked me the same thing."

"Was she?"

"I don't know many black blondes," Farraday says. Then, chuckling, he adds, "Don't know many blondes at *all,* for that matter. Nor too many blacks, either."

"How old would you say?"

"I couldn't say. Young, though. In her thirties maybe? I really couldn't say."

"Called over to the kids, you said?"

"Called to them. Signaled to them. You know."

"What'd she say?"

"Now there's where you got me, mister," Farraday says, and lightly taps the hearing aid in his right ear.

"Couldn't hear what she said, is that it?"

"Knew she was calling over to them, though. Waving for them to get in."

"And they just got in."

"Got in, and she drove off with them."

"In a blue car, is that right?"

"Blue Chevrolet Impala."

"Notice the license plate?"

"No. Told the cops the same thing. Wasn't looking for it."

"Florida plate was it, though?"

"Must've been, don't you think?"

"Why's that?"

"Cause it was a rental car."

"How do you know?"

"Had a bumper sticker on it. 'Avis Tries Harder.'"

Bingo, Charlie thinks.

The call from Captain Steele comes at twenty minutes to three.

"What does Oleander Street look like right this minute?" he asks Sloate.

"Empty. No traffic at all, nobody parked."

"Do you think they're watching the house?"

"No."

"If I sent somebody over right now, with those bullshit hundreds from the Henley case, can he drive right into the garage?"

"Yes. It's a two-car garage, there's only the vic's car in it right now."

The vic, Alice thinks.

She is pacing the floor near the table where Sloate sits with the phone to his ear. The vic.

"I'll call when he's on his approach. You can raise the door then."

"Got it."

"I'm sending Andrews and Saltzman to check out that babysitter," he says. "You think there's any meat there?"

"I hope so."

"Meanwhile, when your lady calls, tell her you've got the money."

"Okay."

"And set up a drop."

"Okay."

"Do you think they know we're already in this?"

"I don't think so."

"Stay in touch."

Sloate puts the phone back on its cradle.

"What?" Alice asks.

"He's sending two of our people to talk to Maria Gonzalez."

"They found her then?"

"Yes. And he's sending someone else here to—"

"No! Why?"

"With bogus bills."

"Bogus . . . ?"

"Counterfeit hundred-dollar bills."

"No. If anyone's watching the house . . ."

"He'll be driving right into the garage."

"If they smell something fishy . . ."

"They won't, don't worry."

"These are my *kids* we're talking about!"

The grandfather clock now reads 2:45 P.M.

In fifteen minutes, the woman will call again with instructions.

"When she calls," Sloate says, "tell her you have the money. That's the first thing."

"They'll know the bills are phony."

"No, they won't," he says. "These are confiscated super-bills. The Federal Reserve loaned them to us when we were working another kidnapping case down here."

"What's a super-bill?"

"All you got to know is they're so good nobody can tell them from the real thing. She won't recognize them, believe me."

"How do I get my children back?"

"That's the whole point of this phone call. You'll set up an exchange. Kids for money. No kids, no money."

"They won't go for that."

"You've got to insist on it."

"How?"

"Way we've done it before—"

"How many damn kidnappings do you *have* here in Florida?"

"One every now and then. Way we do it is this. You get out of your car with a satchelful of money. You go to her alone. She checks out the money while you're there with her. But you don't actually *give* her the money till she goes to get the kids from wherever . . ."

"Why would she do that? Once she's got her hands on that money—"

"She'll do it. That's the way we've worked it before. They need to have some assurance . . ."

"No! I'm the one who needs—"

"Mrs. Glen—"

"—assurance that I'm going to get my *kids* back! Either she has the kids with her, or I don't turn over the money. Period!"

"Well, that's what we hope will be the case."

"That's not what you said. You said she takes the money and runs. That's what you said."

"I said you don't actually *give* her the money. All you do is *show* it to her. Mrs. Glendenning . . . ma'am . . . let us try to help you, okay? Give us a chance here."

Alice says nothing.

"Let me go over it one more time, okay? One: You set up the meet."

The meet, Alice thinks.

"Two: You get out of the car, walk over to her . . ."

"Why would she risk that? Me seeing her?"

"Tell her to disguise herself however she wants, okay? We're not interested in identifying anyone at this point in time. The bills are marked, the minute they try to spend them, we've got 'em. All we want to do right now is get your kids back."

"Will I be alone?"

"No. We'll be there, wherever she says you're to bring the money."

"I'd rather go alone."

"No. We may have to move in."

"That's what I'm afraid of. These are my *kids,* damn it!"

"I know that. But these people—"

"What do you mean, you may have to move in? I don't like this. I don't like it at all."

"Can you think of a better way?"

"Yes. Leave me alone. Let me handle this alone."

"How?"

"I don't *know* how, damn it!"

Sloate looks at his watch.

"You've got ten minutes," he says. "Relax a bit till the call comes."

"I'm relaxed," she says.

He looks at her.

"I'm *relaxed,* damn it!"

"Ma'am, we're just trying to help," he says. "No one wants anything to happen to—"

"Please don't call me ma'am. My name is Alice."

"And mine's Wilbur," he says.

Alice nods. She cannot in a million years imagine calling this man Wilbur. Or any other man, for that matter. He is still standing near the table where the recording equipment is set up. Leaning against the table. Big gun holstered on his right hip. In the hallway beyond, the grandfather clock ticks noisily.

"Why do you suppose Rafe popped up here all of a sudden?" he asks.

"I don't know why. My sister said Jacksonville."

"But here he is on the Cape."

"I don't know what he's doing here."

"A coincidence probably," Sloate says.

"Probably," Alice says.

They look at each other.

"Unless they wanted an inside man at the skunk works," Sloate says. "Somebody who'd know what's going on in here."

"I don't think Rafe is involved in this," she tells him.

"Be nice to know if he told anybody about that big insurance policy, though. Be real nice to know," Sloate says. "How much longer you think he'll be snoring in there?"

"I have no idea."

He looks at her again. He's really trying to figure this out, she thinks. But he seems so very damn stupid. If this wasn't a hick town with a Mickey Mouse police force . . .

But it is.

This is Cape October, Florida, population 143,000, and my children have been kidnapped, and in ten minutes the woman who has them will call again and we will make arrangements for an exchange, kids for money, money for kids. And if it works . . .

"Try to keep her on the line longer this time," Sloate says. "Tell her you're getting confused, tell her you can't keep it straight, all this hanging up. She'll resist, but she's closer to the payoff now, so she may be getting hungry. And careless. They sometimes get careless."

With *my* children, Alice thinks.

And in that instant, the doorbell rings.

Sally Ballew recognizes Sloate at once.

"Hello, Wilbur," she says, and steps boldly into the house, taking in the living room with a single swift sweep of her dark brown eyes, knowing at once that the Garrity woman wasn't snowing them about a kidnapping. There's another dick from the CID here, too, Marcia Di Luca from their Tech Unit, which means they've already set up a wire tap and a trace; nobody's fooling around here.

"Hello, Marcia," she says. "Catch yourselves a little snatch here?"

"Who are you?" Alice asks at once.

"Special Agent Sally Ballew," she says, and shows her shield. "FBI. My partner Felix Forbes. We're here to lend a hand, ma'am."

It is three o'clock sharp.

Alice is surrounded by law enforcement people.

Yet for the first time since four yesterday afternoon, she really feels in jeopardy.

The telephone rings.

Alice's hand is trembling as she picks up the receiver.

"Hello?" she says.

"Have you got all the money?" the woman's voice asks.

"Yes," Alice says.

"Good. Now listen to what I have to say. I'll be on for thirty seconds. You can think over what I've told you before I call back again. Is that clear?"

Marcia Di Luca pulls a face. Thirty seconds again! Standing

beside her, Sally Ballew seems to grasp what's going on with the trace. She nods sympathetically.

Into the phone, Alice says, "I understand."

"There's a gas station on U.S. 41 and Lewiston Point Road. A Shell station. Do you know it? Yes or no?"

"Yes," Alice says.

"Bring the money to the ladies' room there. Ten o'clock tomorrow morning. Have you got all the money?" she asks again.

"Yes," Alice says. "But—"

"Just listen. There's only one stall in the ladies' room. Leave the money in the stall. Ten o'clock. Come alone."

"I will. But how do I—?"

"I'll call back," the woman says, and hangs up.

Sally Ballew thrusts out her chest as if to assert female superiority. It is some chest. All the men in the room are impressed. So is Alice. But she does not need the FBI here now, not when her children are out there someplace with a strange woman and whoever may be her accomplice. Too many cooks, she thinks. Too damn many cooks.

"How long does he stay on the line, average?" Sally asks.

"*She,*" Marcia corrects. "Twenty, thirty seconds."

"You'll never get her."

"We might," Marcia says dryly.

The two women do not like each other. This is very clear to Alice.

My children will die, she thinks.

"What are you hoping to accomplish?" Sally asks Sloate.

"Who invited you here?" Sloate asks. "I wasn't aware a state line had been crossed."

"I'm asking what you hope to accomplish, allowing this woman to talk directly to the—"

The phone rings again.

Sloate nods to Alice. She picks up. It is going to be the same routine again. On again, off again. Except that this time, she is caught in the crosshairs of inter-agency rivalry.

"Hello?" she says.

"Do you understand everything I told you?" the woman asks.

"Yes."

"Repeat it to me."

"Ten tomorrow morning."

"Yes?"

"Shell station at Lewiston and the Trail."

"Yes, that's right."

"The stall in the ladies' room."

"Yes. You'll leave the money there," the woman says.

"No," Alice says.

There is a brief silence.

"No?" the woman says. "Listen to me, girlfriend. You ever want to see your children alive again—"

"We make an exchange," Alice says quickly. "Right then and there."

Sloate is already shaking his head. Sally doesn't know what's going on. Neither does Forbes.

"I hand over the money, you hand over the kids," Alice says. "A simultaneous exchange."

"Stay by the phone," the woman says, and hangs up.

"Thirty seconds on the nose," Marcia says.

"You just blew it," Sloate tells Alice.

Charlie gets to the airport Avis desk at ten minutes past three that afternoon. A woman with voluminous blonde hair greets him with a cheery smile, but the moment he asks about who might have rented a blue Chevrolet Impala sometime recently, she tells him she's not allowed to give out such information.

Charlie tells her what the problem is.

Using the same open infectious smile and innocent guile he used while talking countless susceptible Japanese maidens into bed on R & R in Tokyo during the Vietnam War, he says that he is an artist, and here he shows her several postcard-sized samples of his work from his gallery in Naples. He tells her that his gallery in New York informed him that they were sending an independent contractor down to pick up some of his paintings, but the person never showed up. So when he called New York this morning, they told him a blue Chevrolet Impala from Avis had been rented by the contractor sometime recently . . .

"What is this man's name?" the Avis lady asks.

"Woman. It's a woman. A blonde woman. Hair about to here," Charlie says, and with his finger shows her the length on his neck. "She's supposed to pick up four of my paintings," he says. "I sure wish you could help me, miss," once again flashing his Come-Hither Lieutenant B. F. Pinkerton smile.

"What's her name, this woman?"

"I have no idea," Charlie says. "She's just an independent contractor the gallery sent down."

"Don't *they* know her name?"

"It was arranged down here."

"Where down here?"

"I don't know."

"Well, where'd they *send* her from? If she rented a car here at the airport, she had to be coming in on a plane, am I right?"

"I would guess so. Yes, you're absolutely right."

"Well, where was she coming *from*? How can I locate a rental if I don't have her name, which besides I'm not supposed to give out such information, anyway."

"I know that, and it's very kind of you to give me all this time. But if you could check your records for any blue Impalas you may have rented yesterday or the day before, anytime recently . . ."

"You know how many blue Impalas we rent every day?"

"How many?" Charlie asks.

"Plenty," she says. "Also, these look like very big paintings here on these postcards. I doubt—"

"You can keep those if you like."

"Thank you, they're very pretty. But I doubt if they'd even *fit* in an Impala," she says. "Four of them, no less. Are you sure she rented an Impala?"

"That's what they told me. Miss, I'm gonna lose this sale unless I can locate her."

"Don't know how I can help you," the Avis lady says.

Just try a little harder, Charlie thinks, but she has already turned away and is starting to talk to the next customer in line.

Rafe comes out of the bedroom at three-thirty.

"Don't believe we've met," he tells Sally, his glance idly coveting her chest.

"Who's this?" she asks Sloate.

"The brother-in-law," Sloate says.

"Rafe Matthews, nice to meet you."

Sally merely nods. "What's your plan?" she asks Sloate.

Sloate tells her. Show her the money. Send her for the kids. Make the exchange. Kids for money.

"She won't go for it," Sally says. "She'll take the money and tell you they'll let the kids go later, such and such a time, such and such a place. That's the way they work it."

"Well, we've worked it this way before," Marcia tells her.

"When?"

"The Henley case. Three years back."

Rafe is listening to all this.

"Must've been before our time," Forbes tells Sally.

"One-on-one exchange," Sloate says. "Money for the kids, kids for—"

"You sending Mrs. Glendenning out there alone?" Sally asks.

"We'll be covering her."

"You really going to hand over the ransom?"

"A cool two-fifty large," Sloate says. "Supers," he explains.

"They'll tip," Sally says.

"They didn't three years ago."

"That was three years ago. What if they tip now?"

The telephone rings.

"Keep her on," Sloate says.

"Hello?"

"No deal," the woman says. "Your kids die."

And hangs up.

"She'll call back in a minute," Marcia says.

But she doesn't.

She does not call back until four-thirty.

"Do you want to see your kids alive ever again?" she asks.

"Yes. But please . . ."

"Then don't try to make deals with me!"

"I'm not. I'm just trying to set up a reasonable exchange."

"Who told you to say that?"

"Nobody."

"Who gave you those words to say?"

"Nobody."

"Who's there with you?"

"Nobody, I swear."

"I hear movement there."

"No, you—"

"You're lying!" the woman says, and hangs up.

"Shit!" Marcia yells.

The woman calls back again at five minutes past five.

"I'm getting confused," Alice tells her. "If you keep hanging up, I can't follow—"

"Because you're trying to trace my calls!"

"No."

"I hear clicking."

Marcia shakes her head. No. There's no clicking she can possibly hear. No.

"No one's here with me," Alice says. "No one's trying to trace your calls. I have the money you asked for. I want my children back. Now let's arrange a reasonable—"

"You're on too long," the woman says, and hangs up again.

Alice is on the edge of tears.

"You should never let a vic negotiate," Sally says.

"They threatened to kill her children," Sloate says.

"They always do," Forbes says.

"But they hardly ever," Sally adds.

Hardly ever, Alice thinks.

"These are not your children!" she shouts. "Nobody invited you into this house. You have no right—"

The phone rings again.

"Ask *her* to work out the exchange," Sally says. "See what *she* has to suggest."

Alice looks at her.

"Put the whole thing on her," Sally says. "She's the one wants the money."

Their eyes meet.

"Believe me," Sally says.

Alice picks up the phone.

"Will you be there at ten tomorrow or what?" the woman asks at once.

"How do I know I'll get my children back?"

"You've got to take that chance."

"Give me some way to trust you."

"What do you want, girlfriend? A written guarantee?"

"Tell me what you'd suggest."

"I suggest you leave the goddamn money in that stall!"

"Please help me," Alice says. "I think you can understand why I can't just hand over that kind of money without some sort of—"

"Then you want them dead, is that it?"

"I want them *alive*!" Alice screams.

But the woman has hung up again.

The backup from downtown arrives some twenty minutes later, driving directly into the garage and then coming into the house with a small black airline carry-on bag.

He is a soft-spoken black man who introduces himself as "Detective George Cooper, ma'am, excuse the intrusion." He is carrying $250,000 in counterfeit money, and he asks her at once if she has her own bag to which he can transfer the bogus bills.

"What do you mean, bogus?" Rafe asks him.

"Who's this?" Cooper asks Sloate.

"The brother-in-law," Sloate says.

"Bogus, phony, false," Cooper says. "Super-bills. Counterfeit."

"I'll be damned," Rafe says.

Alice is back with a Louis Vuitton bag Eddie bought her for Christmas one year. Cooper is beginning to transfer the bills when someone knocks at the back door.

"Who the hell is *that*?" Sloate asks, and looks at his watch.

"Is the captain sending another backup?" Marcia asks.

Cooper shakes his head no. He is busy moving bills from one bag to the other.

"I don't want any more policemen here," Alice says. "Tell them to go away."

Sloate is already in the kitchen, unlocking the back door. A uniformed man is standing there.

"Sheriff's Department," he says. "Got a call from a neighbor saw the garage door going up and down, strange car pulling in, big truck parked outside. Everything all right here?"

"No problem, Sheriff," Sloate says, and takes a leather fob from his pocket, and opens it to show his detective's shield.

"What is it that's happening?" the sheriff asks, puzzled, trying to peek into the living room, where there seems to be a lot of activity and some kind of electronic equipment set up.

"Minor disturbance," Marcia explains. "No sweat, Sheriff."

If anyone's watching the house, Alice thinks, what they'll see now is a sheriff's car out there in the drive. They'll think I've notified every damn law enforcement agency in Florida.

"What happened to your leg, lady?" the sheriff asks.

"I got hit by a car."

"You report the accident?"

"Yes, I did," she tells him, even though she still hasn't.

"Well," the sheriff says, "if everything's all right here . . ."

"Everything's fine," Sloate assures him. "Thanks for looking in."

"Just checkin," the sheriff says. "Like I say, a neighbor saw the garage door goin up, strange car movin in, big truck parked outside, wondered just what was goin on here."

Everyone in the state of Florida is calling the police on my behalf, Alice thinks. First Rosie sticks her nose into this, and now some neighbor . . .

"G'day, ma'am," the sheriff says, and tips his hat to her.

"Good day," Alice says.

Sloate closes and locks the kitchen door behind him. Alice goes into the living room and peers out through the drapes. Big red dome light flashing on top of his car. People coming out of their houses all up and down the street. He's alerted half the damn neighborhood. If anyone is watching the house . . .

They'll kill the children, she thinks.

Maria Gonzalez was fifteen years old the last time she babysat for Alice and Eddie Glendenning. At the time, she was a somewhat chubby little girl who had come over from Cuba many years ago in a boat with her mother, her father, and her older brother, Juan. Well, fifteen *years* and three months ago, actually, since Maria was inside her mother's belly at the time. Agata Gonzalez was six months pregnant with her unborn baby daughter when she and her family undertook the perilous journey from Havana in a rickety boat with thirty-one other brave souls.

Maria Gonzalez is now seventeen years old, and even chubbier than she was two years ago. That is because she is now seven months pregnant with a child of her own. Maria's father, a cabinetmaker who earns a good living down here where people are constantly buying and remodeling retirement homes, is not very happy to see two police detectives standing on his doorstep at six-thirty on a Thursday night, when he is just about to sit down to supper. When it turns out that they are here to talk to his daughter, he is even more displeased.

Maria quit her job at McDonald's two weeks ago, when she started to get backaches, and now what is this? Trouble with the police already?

The two detectives who are here to see her are Saltzman and Andrews. Saltzman is still wearing a yarmulke, which is appropriate to his religious beliefs, but which makes him look very foreign and strange to Anibal Gonzalez, who himself looks foreign and strange to a lot of people on the Cape, even though he's an expert cabinet-maker. He does not look at all strange to Saltzman or his partner Andrews, who run into a lot of Cuban types in their line of work, and who would not be at all surprised if this fellow with the mustache here, about to sit down to dinner in his undershirt, turns out to be somehow involved in the kidnapping of the two Glendenning kids. They would not be surprised at all, and fuck what anybody thinks about profiling.

The girl turns out to be as pregnant as a goose, but this doesn't surprise them, either, these people. Wide-eyed and frightened, she sits down with the detectives in a small room just off the dining room. There is a sewing machine in the room, and Maria's mother explains that she does crochet beading at home, a fashion that has come into style again. Neither Andrews nor Saltzman knows what the hell crochet beading is, nor cares to know, thank you. All they want to know is why little Ashley Glendenning asked her mother if she remembered Maria Gonzalez. All they want to know is what Maria Gonzalez has to do with this kidnapping. So they politely ask Agata Gonzalez to get lost, please . . .

Actually, Saltzman says, "I wonder if we could talk to your daughter privately, Mrs. Gonzalez."

. . . and then they explain to the girl that she is in serious trouble here, which is a lie, and that it would be to her best advantage to answer all of their questions truthfully and honestly, which are the same thing, but Maria doesn't make the distinction, anyway.

"Do you know where Ashley Glendenning is right this minute?" Saltzman asks.

"Who?" Maria says.

"Ashley Glendenning," Andrews says. "You used to babysit her."

"I don't know anybody by that name," Maria says.

"Ashley Glendenning," Saltzman says. "Ten years old. She was eight or so when you used to babysit her."

"Out on Oleander Street," Andrews says.

"Oh," Maria says.

"You remember her now?"

"Yeah, I think so."

"Has a little brother."

"Yeah, Jimmy."

"Jamie," Andrews says.

"Jamie, right. What about them?"

"Well, you tell us," Saltzman says.

"What do you want me to tell you?"

"Where they are."

"How would I know where they are?"

"Ashley brought up your name."

"*My* name? Why would she do that?"

"Asked her mother if she remembered you."

"Why would her mother remember me? That was a long time ago, I sat for those kids."

"Two years ago," Saltzman reminds her.

"I was a kid myself," Maria says.

"We think she was trying to tell her mother something."

"What was she trying to tell her?"

"Your name."

"Look, what the fuck is this?" Maria asks, and then realizes her father is probably listening to all this in the next room, and hopes he hasn't heard her say "fuck," and suddenly wonders why he doesn't throw these two cocksuckers out of the house.

"It's all about Ashley Glendenning asking her mother if she remembered Maria Gonzalez," Andrews says.

"So what's so unusual about that? That it brings the cops here?"

"She's been kidnapped, Maria."

"Who?"

"Little Ashley. You remember little Ashley? Cause she sure as hell remembers you."

"I don't know nothing about no kidnapping," Maria says.

"Then why'd she ask her mother . . . ?"

"I don't know why she asked her mother nothing. I'm pregnant, I'm seven months pregnant, why would I kidnap anybody?"

"How does two hundred and fifty thousand dollars sound?"

"What?"

"That's how much little Ashley and her brother are worth to whoever kidnapped them."

"I didn't kidnap nobody. Look, this is ridiculous. Did Ashley say I kidnapped her? Why would she say that?"

"You tell us."

"I *am* telling you. I haven't even *seen* Ashley since, it has to be at least two years now. If I kidnapped her, where is she? *More* than two years. Do you see her here? We're just about to have supper, do you see her here?"

"Where is she, Maria?"

"How the hell do I know where she is?"

"Has your husband got her someplace?"

"I don't have a husband."

"Your boyfriend then?"

"I don't have a boyfriend, either."

"Whoever knocked you up then. Is he in this with you?"

"Santa María, me estás poniendo furioso con todo esto!"

"English, Maria."

"My baby's father is in Tampa. He found a better job and a blonde girlfriend there."

"A blonde, huh?" Saltzman says, and glances at Andrews. Both men are suddenly alert.

"That's what he told me on the phone."

"Nice that gallantry's still alive here in Florida," Andrews says.

"What?" Maria says.

"What's his name, this hero of yours?"

"Ernesto de Diego. And he's no hero of mine."

"Would you happen to know his address in Tampa?"

"No."

"When did you see him last?"

"February twelfth," Maria says.

But who's counting? Saltzman thinks.

The phone rings again at a little past eight o'clock. Alice picks up the receiver. Sloate and Marcia are ready to do their useless thing, he with the earphones on, she behind her worthless tracing equipment.

"Hello?" Alice says.

"Alice, it's me, Charlie."

"If that's Carol," Rafe says, "tell her hello for me," and goes off into the kitchen.

"Who's that?" Charlie asks.

"My brother-in-law."

"Have you heard from them yet?"

Alice hesitates. This is her best friend in the entire universe. Sloate is already shaking his head. No. Tell him nothing. Rafe comes out of the kitchen with a coffee cup in his hand. He begins wandering the room, idly observing. Sloate is shaking his finger at her now. No, he is telling her. No.

"Yes," Alice says. "I've heard from them."

Sloate grabs for the phone. She pulls it away, out of his reach.

"The police and the FBI are here with me, Charlie."

"Oh Jesus!" he says.

"They've been trying to trace her calls . . ."

"The blonde's?" Charlie says.

"What blonde?"

"I went over to Pratt a little while ago, talked to the guard who saw the kids get into that Impala."

"Tell him to keep out of this!" Sloate warns.

"Who's that?" Charlie asks.

"Detective Sloate."

"Same one who called you at my house?"

"Yes."

Rafe is at the living room drapes now. He parts them, looks out into the street.

"Did he tell you to lie to me?" Charlie asks.

"Yes. What blonde?"

"The guard told me a blonde woman was driving the Impala. Is that who you've been talking to?"

"I don't know."

"She still sound black to you?"

"She could be black. Or simply Southern. I don't know."

"What does she want?"

"Quarter of a million dollars."

"Jesus!"

"By ten tomorrow morning. I'm supposed to leave the money—"

Sloate is out of his chair. He starts to say, "You're jeopardizing your own—" but just then Rafe turns away from the drapes.

"Red convertible pulling into the driveway," he says. "Blonde at the wheel."

"Who . . . ?" Alice starts, but she hears a car door slamming outside. "I have to go," she tells Charlie. "I'll call you back," and hangs up and goes instantly to the front door. Looking through the peephole, she sees Jennifer Redding loping from the driveway to the walk, still wearing the white bell-bottom pants she had on yesterday, still showing her belly button and a good three inches of flesh, but with a blue cotton sweater top this time.

"Who is it?" Sloate asks.

"The woman who ran me over yesterday."

"Get rid of her."

Alice opens the door, and steps outside. Bugs are flitting around the light to the left of the entrance steps. Jennifer stops on the walk, looks up at her in surprise.

"Hi," she says. "How's your foot?"

"Fine," Alice says.

"I brought you a little get-well present. I hope you like chocolate."

"Yes, I do. Thanks."

"Everybody likes chocolate," Jennifer says, and hands her a little white box imprinted with the name of a fudge maker on The Ring. "In fact, I wouldn't mind a piece right now," she says, smiling. "If you're offering, that is."

"Sure, help yourself," Alice says, and breaks the white string holding the box closed. The aroma of fresh chocolate wafts up past the open lid of the box. Jennifer delicately grasps a piece of fudge between thumb and forefinger, lifts it from the box.

"Wouldn't mind a cup of coffee, either," she says. "If you've got some brewing."

"Gee, I'm sorry," Alice says. "I'd ask you in, but I have company."

Jennifer looks at the truck parked at the curb and gives Alice a knowing look. She pops the square of fudge into her mouth, chews silently for a moment, and then swallows and says, "That's too bad. I was hoping we could talk awhile. Get to know each other a little better."

She is looking directly into Alice's eyes. Searching her eyes. Alice remembers what Charlie just told her on the phone. *A blonde woman was driving the Impala.*

"Some other time maybe," she says.

"Anyway, I wanted to thank you for not calling the police," Jennifer says.

She is still studying Alice's face intently.

"Or did you?" she asks.

"No," Alice says. "I never got around to it."

"I think it would look much better if I reported the accident, don't you?"

"Probably."

"Since I was driving the car and all."

"I guess so. But I think there's no-fault insurance down here, isn't there?"

"I don't know," Jennifer says. "I'm a recent import myself."

"Jennifer," Alice says, "you have to forgive me . . ."

"I'll call my insurance people when I get home, ask their advice."

"I think that's a good idea."

"I'll let you know what I find out," she says, and hesitates. "Alice," she says, her voice lowering, "I'm sorry for what happened, truly." She offers her hand. Alice takes it. "Later," Jennifer says, and smiles, and swivels off toward her red Thunderbird convertible.

Alice watches as she pulls out of the driveway.

Jennifer waves good-bye.

"Sweet chassis," Rafe says. "The car," he adds, and grins.

Alice says nothing.

"Who is she?" he asks.

"Woman named Jennifer Redding. She's responsible for the foot."

He takes her elbow, leads her away from the door. Across the room, the law enforcement people are gathered in a tight little knot, conferring.

"You think these people know what they're doing?" he whispers.

"No, I don't."

"I gather they're planning to pay the ransom with counterfeit money, is that right?"

"That's the plan, yes."

"You gonna let them do that?"

"I want my kids back."

"Seems like a sure way *not* to get them back."

"What else can I do, Rafe?"

"Give them what they want. Go to the bank and—"

"And *what*? Where am I supposed to get a quarter of a million dollars?"

Rafe looks at her.

"You told Carol there was insurance," he says.

"They haven't paid yet."

"It's been eight months, Alice."

"Don't you think I know how long it's been? They haven't paid yet."

"Well . . . when will they pay?"

"Rafe, do me a favor, okay? Get in your truck and go wherever you have to go. You're not doing any good here."

"I'm just trying to help," he says, almost plaintively, but she has already moved away from him to where a wall phone hangs over the kitchen counter. She picks up the receiver.

"Who are you calling?" Sloate asks at once.

"Charlie."

"He's done enough damage already. Asking questions . . ."

"He found out she's a blonde!" Alice snaps. "You sit here with your earphones on, and your expensive equipment, twiddling dials, while a fifty-six-year-old artist—"

"We already *know* she's a blonde," Sloate says.

"What?"

"We already—"

"Then why didn't you tell me?" she says, slamming the phone onto the hook. "These are my children! Why isn't anyone *telling* me anything?"

She realizes she is screaming at him. She clenches her fists, turns away. She wants to punch Sloate. She wants to punch anyone.

"I'm calling Charlie," she says, and picks up the phone again.

"This is a mistake," Sloate says.

But she is already dialing.

"Hello?"

"Charlie? It's me."

"What does the blonde want you to do?"

"Bring her the money."

"Have you got it?"

"Phony bills, yes."

"That's dangerous."

"I know, but . . ."

"They're not locals," Charlie says. "The blonde was driving a rental car."

Sloate's eyes open wide.

"How do you know?" Alice asks.

"Guard saw an Avis bumper sticker. I went to the airport, checked on it—"

"Jesus!" Sloate says.

"—they wouldn't tell me anything. But now that the cops are all over you, maybe *they* can find out who rented that Impala."

"Maybe."

"Where'd that woman ask you to leave the money?"

"Don't tell him!" Sloate warns.

"The Shell station on Lewiston and the Trail."

"What time?"

"Don't . . ."

"Ten tomorrow morning."

"Good luck, Alice."

"Thanks, Charlie."

She hangs up, looks Sloate dead in the eye.

"Think you can find that car now?" she asks.

Sloate turns to Sally Ballew.

"Make yourself useful, Sal," he says. "We're looking for a blue Impala, maybe rented from Avis by a blonde in her thirties."

"Piece of cake," Sally says dryly.

As she and her partner leave the house, the grandfather clock in the hallway reads 8:30 P.M.

When they first moved down here, the kids thought they'd died and gone to heaven. Before they bought the boat, Eddie and Alice used to take them to the beach on every sunny weekend. After they owned the *Jamash,* it was day trips up and down the Intercoastal or out onto the Gulf when the seas weren't too rough. At the beach one day . . .

She remembers this now with sharp poignancy.

Remembers it with an immediacy that is painfully relevant.

Jamie is three years old, and fancies himself to be an interviewer on one of his favorite kiddie TV shows. One hand in his sister's, the other wrapped around a toy shovel he pretends is a microphone, he wanders up the beach, stopping at every blanket, thrusting the shovel-mike at each surprised sunbather, asking in his piping little voice, "What do you want to be when you grow up?"

Tirelessly, he parades the beach with his sister, a relentless, pint-sized investigative journalist.

What do you want to be when you grow up?

One day . . .

Oh God, that frantic day . . .

They know they are not to go anywhere near the water. The waves that roll in here are usually benign, even at high tide, but the children know that they are not to approach the water unless Eddie or Alice is with them. They know this. And usually, they wander up the beach for . . . oh, ten minutes or so . . . Ashley inordinately proud of her little brother's interviewing technique, Jamie grinning in anticipation as he holds out his microphone to ask even sixty-year-olds, "What do you want to be when you grow up?"

The beaches here on the Cape are not too terribly crowded, even in high season, so Alice or Eddie can keep the children in sight as Jamie conducts his "interviews." But on this day . . .

They are discussing something important. Beaches tend to encourage deep discussions about important matters.

She doesn't remember now what they were discussing. Perhaps buying a boat. Perhaps deliberating whether they can afford to buy even a used boat; they always seem to be discussing money, or the lack of money, when suddenly . . .

"Where are the kids?"

This from Eddie.

Alice looks up.

"Where are the kids?" he asks again. "Do you see them?"

She looks up the beach. She cannot see them anywhere. She is on her feet at once. So is Eddie.

"Did they come back this way?" he asks.

"No, I don't think so."

"Did we miss them?"

Alice's heart is racing now.

"They didn't go in the water, did they?" she asks.

"You go that way!" he says, and points, and she immediately begins running up the beach. Eddie is off in the opposite direction.

"Ashley!" she yells. "Jamie!"

Running. Her eyes scanning the water. She does not see them anywhere in the water. Nor does she see them anywhere on the beach. What . . . ? Where . . . ?

"Excuse me, did you see a little boy pretending to be a television reporter?"

Coming toward this end of the beach, the bathers and baskers thinning out now, still no sign of the children, oh dear God, please say they haven't gone in the water, please say they haven't been carried out to sea! She turns, comes running back down the beach, her eyes darting from sand to sea, and suddenly . . .

There.

Coming out of the tan brick building near the parking lot.

"Ashley!" she yells.

She rushes to the children, hugs them close.

"You scared me to death!" she says.

"Jamie had to pee," Ashley says.

"What do you want to be when you grow up?" Jamie asks, grinning, and holds out the shovel to Alice.

The woman calls again at a few minutes before ten. "Listen to me carefully," she says. "All you have to remember is that we have your children. If you don't come to that gas station alone, your children will die. If you don't have the money with you, your children will die. If anyone tries to detain me, your children will die. If I'm not back where I'm supposed to be in half an hour, your children will die. That's all you have to know. See you tomorrow at ten."

She hangs up.

"Twenty-three seconds," Sally says.

The grandfather clock strikes ten P.M.

In exactly twelve hours, Alice will be delivering the ransom money.

But the woman's words keep echoing in her head.

Your children will die, your children will die, your children will die.

Friday
May 14

5

The Tamiami Trail may once have been a dirt road hacked out through the palmettos and palms, but that was long before Alice moved down here.

Today, U.S. 41 is a four- (and sometimes six-) lane concrete thoroughfare lined for miles and miles with fast food emporiums, gift shops, car washes, gasoline stations, pizzerias, furniture stores, nurseries, carpet salesrooms, automobile dealers, shopping malls, movie theater complexes, and a variety of one-story cinder-block shops selling plaster figurines, citrus fruit, discount clothing, rattan pool and garden furniture, cigarettes and beer (free ice if you buy a case), stereo equipment, lamps, vacuum cleaners, typewriters, burglar alarms, swimming pools, and (the only such shop in all Cape October) adult marital aids, games, and related reading material.

Alice is familiar with the Shell station on Lewiston Point Road because the road itself dead-ends at the ferry landing where you catch the boat to Crescent Island, not a thousand yards off the southern end of Tall Grass. Crescent is the least developed of the Cape's offshore keys. Accessible only by water, the island has on it a small, eccentric boater's paradise known as Marina Blue, some thirty minutes away and 10,000 miles distant from U.S. 41. Some four or five years ago, the family spent a long, cherished weekend on Crescent, and the memories of that happy time are still with her.

She parks the black Mercedes truck in a space for about five or six cars, near the air hoses, gets out—and hesitates.

For a fleeting instant, she wishes she'd taken with her the snub-nosed .32-caliber pistol Eddie gave her as a birthday present the year they moved down here. Instead, it is resting under her lingerie in the top drawer of the bedroom dresser back home.

But they have the children, she thinks.

The children will die, she thinks.

She shakes her head, pulls back her shoulders, walks briskly into the convenience area. The guy behind the counter there gives her a look as she limps past toward the rear of the building, following the sign that indicates RESTROOMS. He does not appreciate cripples limping in here to use the toilets without buying either gas or food. Alice is carrying the small Louis Vuitton bag, decorated with its repeated LV monogram, and stuffed at the moment with 2,500 fake hundred-dollar bills "so good nobody can tell them from the real thing"—she hopes.

A black woman is at the coffee machine, filling a cardboard container. She is some five feet seven inches tall, Alice guesses, as tall and as slim as a proud Masai woman. Wearing a very short green mini and a white T-shirt. Good firm thighs and shapely calves tapering to slender ankles in strappy flat sandals. Oversized sunglasses and a wide-brimmed straw hat that hides half her face. Wide gold bracelet on the biceps of one dark, rounded arm. Alice wonders if this is the woman she's been talking to on the phone.

"Morning," the woman says, and smiles.

Alice does not recognize the voice.

"Morning," she answers, and goes to the door marked WOMEN, and tries the knob.

"Occupied," the woman says.

Alice still does not recognize the voice.

"Are you waiting?" she asks.

"Nope," the woman says.

The door to the ladies' room opens. A fat woman in a flowered dress comes out, smiles at both of them, and then goes toward the front of the building. The black woman is now putting sugar into her coffee. Alice goes into the ladies' room.

The room is an entirely gray entity. Gray tile floors, gray Formica countertop, gray porcelain sink, gray door on the single stall in the room.

She throws the bolt on the entrance door. The click sounds like a minor explosion in the small confines of the room.

She approaches the gray door. She enters the stall—the fat woman has forgotten to flush—puts the bag down alongside the toilet bowl.

For a moment, she stands alone and silent in the small cubicle. Then she leaves the stall, and leaves the ladies' room. The black woman is still there at the coffee machines, sipping from the cardboard container.

Alice walks over to her.

"Are you the one?" she asks.

The woman appears startled.

"Are you the one who has my children?"

The woman says nothing.

"If you are, then listen to me," Alice says. "If you don't let my kids go, I'll find you and kill you."

"Gee," the black woman says, and goes immediately to the ladies' room door. She grabs the doorknob, turns to face Alice, looks her dead in the eye. "Be gone when I come out," she says. "Do anything foolish, and they die. We'll call you." She nods. "You understand what I'm saying?" she says, and stares at Alice a moment longer before opening the door and entering the ladies' room.

Alice hears the click of the bolt.

"I hope *you* understood me!" she shouts to the closed door.

But her threat is an empty one.

They have the children.

There is nothing she can do.

Nothing at all.

• • •

The three detectives have positioned themselves outside the Shell station in a classic triangular surveillance pattern, ready to pick up on the perp the moment she comes out of the convenience area, if indeed she's in there. They have to assume she's in there. They haven't spotted a blue Impala in the station area itself or parked on any of the surrounding side streets, so they can only think she walked from wherever she parked the car, if in fact she drove the blue Impala and not some other vehicle here to the station. But she has to be inside there. Nobody in her right mind would leave a satchelful of hundred-dollar bills in a public ladies' room for longer than five minutes.

The detectives know they are not quite as Mickey Mouse as Alice Glendenning believes. They have already ordered backup from Captain Steele, and four unmarked CID cars are waiting to pick up the perp's trail the minute she steps into a car, if she steps into a car. One of them is parked facing the distant Gulf, its nose pointed toward the Crescent Island ferry, in case she decides to head out that way. The other is parked facing east on Lewiston, in case she decides to go for I-75. The other cars are facing north and south, on either side of 41, should she decide to go either north to downtown Cape October, or south to Fort Myers. All four cars are within reach of easy radiophone contact if/when Sloate, Di Luca, or Cooper, on foot, have any information to relay.

From all three vantage points, they each and separately see Alice Glendenning come out of the convenience area and walk rapidly to her black Mercedes. She is no longer carrying the Louis Vuitton bag. Good. That means the perp now has the evidence money in her possession, which further means they can arrest her without a warrant. Arresting her is not what they wish to do, however. What they wish to do is follow her to wherever she and her blond accomplice are holding the kids. That is their hope and their plan.

Mrs. Glendenning is in the car now.

The Mercedes engine kicks into life.

Sloate figures she will now be heading home.

Good, he thinks. Just stay out of our hair.

We've got the situation under control here.

From where Christine is crouched beside the small window in the ladies' room, she can see the black Mercedes backing out of its space, and then circling past the gas pumps, and making a left turn on the corner, heading north on 41, toward downtown Cape October.

She looks into the Louis Vuitton bag.

All that money in there looks so sweet and beautiful.

She comes out of the ladies' room, walks past the coffee machines and the counters bearing fast food junk food, and then stops at the counter to pay for her coffee. In a moment, she is out the front door, walking across the asphalt pavement past the gas pumps.

Almost jauntily, she steps out into the balmy morning.

The three detectives are right behind her.

The girl is very definitely black.

Some five-seven or -eight, Sloate imagines, sporting a short green skirt and a busty white T-shirt. Good-looking girl. Splendid legs, sweet ass. Gold bracelet on her right arm, the one carrying the Louis Vuitton bag.

She struts off 41 and begins walking west toward Citrus, a cell phone to her ear now, supremely sure of herself, the bag full of bogus bills bouncing on her right hip. She knows that as long as she's got those two kids tucked away someplace, no one's going to touch her.

Sloate is on point.

Cooper is across the street from him, and several yards behind, in case she decides to turn right.

Marcia Di Luca is on the other side of the street, should the girl decide to hang a Louie.

She is approaching Citrus now, will she go right or left? Cooper wins. She makes the right turn, and he assumes point at the A position, picking up at once, allowing Sloate and Di Luca to fall back into new locations at the B and C corners of the triangle. They have done this sort of surveillance many times before, but never when the lives of two children were at stake.

They are far enough back from the girl to avoid suspicion. Moreover, Di Luca is wearing rayon tailored slacks and a floral-patterned, short-sleeved blouse, whereas Cooper is wearing jeans and a striped T-shirt, and Sloate is wearing a wrinkled linen suit with an open throat sports shirt. They hardly look related by class, status, or profession. They are merely three disparate citizens out for a morning stroll, nothing more on their minds than enjoying the brisk breezes that suddenly sweep the streets, presaging rain.

The girl seems to be enjoying her stroll as well. Her step is brisk. Sloate cannot see her face, but he's willing to bet she's smiling. He'd be smiling, too, a bag full of hundred-dollars bills in the kip, he'd be laughing all the way to the bank. They are quite some distance from the Shell station now, still heading north on Citrus, and still no Impala or any other kind of pickup vehicle. By radiophone, Sloate has already informed the unmarked mobile units of the detectives' present location, and has advised two of the cars to move into position at the eastern end of Citrus, where it rejoins 41. He has asked the remaining two cars to stay far behind the ABC team on Citrus, ready to move in to pick them up should the blue Impala surface. He is hoping that will be soon.

It is Di Luca who first spots the car.

It is parked in a side street a block ahead of where the girl now steps out with a longer stride. She knows she's almost home free, Di Luca thinks, and quickens her own step. "Suspect vehicle on Citrus and Graham," she says into her radiophone. "Nose pointing east."

"Adam and Boy, stand by to pick up," Sloate says into his radio.

The girl has almost reached the corner now.

Sloate looks over his shoulder to see one of the unmarked cars approaching, either Adam or Boy, he can't tell which just yet. The other car is just behind it. In less than a minute, the black girl will enter the Impala, and the following detectives will split up into the two cars, one maroon, one green, hoping she'll lead them straight to where the kids are stashed.

She is turning the corner now.

A flash of lightning illuminates the western sky.

Big one coming in off the Gulf.

In that instant, an orange-colored garbage truck makes a left turn onto Graham, braking when the driver spots the Impala. Sloate can no longer see the girl as she gets into the car. A maroon Buick pulls up to the curb alongside him. Through the windshield, Sloate recognizes Danny Ryan at the wheel. Adam car then. He pops open the front door, climbs in.

"Don't lose her," he warns. "She's just ahead of that garbage truck."

Behind him, Di Luca and Cooper climb into Boy car, the green Olds. The Cape October PD favors GM products.

The blue Impala is moving away from the curb.

As Ryan makes his right turn from Citrus onto Graham, Sloate catches a quick glimpse of the slender woman driving the car, long blond hair trailing almost to her shoulders.

The garbage truck is in motion again.

It blocks the street completely, parked cars on either side of it.

Ryan leans on the horn.

But by the time they pull around the truck, the street ahead is empty.

The blue Impala has vanished from sight.

And so have the black girl and the blonde who picked her up.

Reginald Webster is sitting on the front-stoop steps when Alice gets back to the house at eleven-thirty. He is wearing white slacks and white leather loafers without socks. A blue blazer with brass buttons is open over a white linen shirt. The house behind him is still and dark. Rafe's rig is nowhere in sight. Webb's own rented Mercury convertible is parked out front, the top down. The hasty rain has come and gone. The late morning is still. She pulls the Mercedes truck into the driveway, and gets out. Webb rises the moment he sees her.

"Thought I'd missed you," he says.

She merely nods.

She does not need Reginald Webster here this morning. Or any morning, for that matter. An hour and a half ago, she turned over a bag full of hundred-dollar bills to the woman who has her children. The cops seem to have deserted her after promising they'd do all they could to get her kids back, and now the money is gone, and her kids are still gone, and apparently those jackasses from the FBI are gone, too, and so is Rafe. So Alice is all alone here, except for Mr. Reginald Webster, standing here on her doorstep and looking as if he's dressed for a regatta at the local yacht club.

"Want to have lunch with me?" he asks.

"How'd you find me here?" she asks.

"Looked up your name in the phone book. You're listed, you know."

"I don't usually . . ."

"I'm sorry . . ."

". . . mix business with . . ."

"I just thought."

". . . pleasure."

"Yes, I'm sorry. Really. I just thought . . . your accident and all . . . your foot . . . you might be feeling down . . . you might want to go out for a quiet lunch in . . ."

"No."

". . . a good restaurant . . ."

"No, I'm sorry."

"That's okay," he says.

"I have other things to do today."

"Sure. Just thought I'd . . ."

"And in any event . . ."

". . . drive by, see if you were free or not."

". . . I don't date."

He looks at her.

"Not since my husband died. I haven't dated anyone. I doubt if I'll ever date anyone ever again, as long as I live."

"I'm sorry to hear that."

"That's the way it is."

"Although this wouldn't be a date, you see."

"Then what would it be?"

"Not in that sense."

"In what sense would it be what?"

"I guess in a sense it would just be two lonely people talking and perhaps enjoying each other's company. Is what I thought it might be."

"I'm not lonely," she says.

"In that case, I was mistaken, and I sincerely apologize," he says. "Good day, Alice, I'm sorry if I disturbed you."

He turns, and is starting toward where he parked the Mercury at the curb when she says, "Wait."

The street is still and silent.

Webb stops, turns to face her again.

"I'll find some other houses for you to look at," she says.

"Please do."

"When . . . this is resolved."

He looks into her face.

"When what's resolved, Alice?"

"This . . . this thing I'm going through."

"What is it?" he asks.

She almost tells him.

But her children are still in danger out there.

"Nothing," she says.

He nods.

"Okay," he says. "Call me when you have some houses to show."

"I will," she promises.

Alice doesn't know anyone who was a stockbroker during the eighties who is not now a millionaire. The eighties were when you could make a killing on the Street. Eddie got into the game a little too late. After he earned his master's, he worked too long in the business office of a Madison Avenue advertising agency, missing out on all those big downtown opportunities. He didn't join the esteemed brokerage firm of Lowell, Hastings, Finch and Ulrich until after Jamie was born. That was eight years ago. By then the ship had sailed, and though Eddie made a very good living, and the family never wanted for anything, his chances of striking it rich on the Street were gone. He told her once that he regretted ever having gone to business school at all.

"What would you rather have done?" she asked.

"Be a pirate," he said, and laughed.

Some pirate; he was thirty years old when they moved down here to the Cape, still wearing a crew cut, still looking like a fresh-faced bumpkin from Kansas—which impression was false, even back then when she'd first met him. Eddie was originally from Greenwich, Connecticut, son of a judge in the lower circuit court, now deceased. His mother was gone, too, both the victims of a terrible automobile accident some seven years ago. This was the main reason Eddie insisted on changing his death benefit policy to one with a double-indemnity clause, even though the yearly premiums would cost more.

"You never know what might happen," he said.

You never know, she thinks now.

You never know that your husband will sail out into the Gulf alone like a pirate, you never know there'll be ten-foot seas that night, and a wind blowing out of the east. You never know that your husband, an expert sailor, will drown in the waters of the Gulf of Mexico, you never once in your life imagine something like this can ever happen to you.

Until it does.

She has often imagined him alone on that sloop, battling the waves that eventually washed him overboard. She has often thought if only she'd been there with him, the two of them together might have conquered whatever seas came at them, together they might have brought that boat back to shore, back to safety.

You never know what might happen.

When he left the house that night, he was wearing jeans and a paler blue shirt, a yellow windbreaker, a peaked white captain's hat. He was wearing his hair longer. A loose shock hung boyishly on his forehead.

Had they remembered to say they loved each other? Before he left forever, had they remembered . . . ?

Yes.

Love ya, babe.

Love ya, too.

Yes, they had not forgotten.

The phone begins ringing almost the instant she enters the house; she rushes to it, out of breath when she gropes for the receiver. Outside, she can hear Webb starting the Mercury and pulling away from the curb.

"Hello?" she says.

"Alice, it's Charlie. I've been trying you for the past fifteen minutes. What happened? Have you got the kids?"

She tells him what happened. Tells him the cops left here the same time she did this morning, tells him she saw the woman who—

"You *saw* her?"

"Yes. She's black, Charlie."

"She let you *see* her?"

"They have the kids, Charlie."

And that says it all.

"She told me to go home. Said they'd call me."

"Anybody there with you now?" he asks.

"No one. I'm alone."

"Where the hell are the cops?"

"I don't know."

"I can come over this afternoon," he says. "Shall I do that?"

"Do you want to?"

"Yes. You shouldn't be there alone, Al."

"All right, come," she says.

"I'll see you later," he says, and hangs up.

She replaces the receiver on its cradle, and goes into the kitchen to prepare a pot of coffee for when Charlie gets here. There is a note on the refrigerator door, held there with a magnet in the shape of an ear of corn:

> Alice—
>
> Sorry I have to run. The open road calls.
>
> Thanks for your hospitality. I spoke to Carol. She will be calling you.
>
> Rafe

She looks at her watch. The coffee is taking forever to perk. It suddenly begins bubbling, and in that instant she hears a car pulling into her driveway. She goes to the drapes, parts them. A red convertible is there, the top down, a blonde at the wheel.

Jennifer Redding is here again.

This time, she lets her into the house.

All the wiretap and tracing equipment is still sitting on the long table in the living room. Alice wonders if the police will be coming back for it. Jennifer looks at the black boxes, the dials, the switches, the trailing wires, the earphones.

"I'm having a new phone system installed," Alice says.

"I hate new phones," Jennifer says, peering around the room appraisingly now. "Cute," she says at last.

"Thanks."

"How's the foot?"

"Beginning to itch. And throb a little."

"Have you been driving?"

"Yes."

"Maybe you shouldn't."

"The doctor said I could drive."

"Doctors don't know," Jennifer says. "I once had poison ivy all over, they said I could drive."

Alice wonders what poison ivy has to do with driving a car.

"I called the police," Jennifer says. "I told them what happened. They said I should have reported the accident at the scene."

"Yes, you should have. I told you."

"I told them I had to rush you to the hospital. They said next time I should be more careful. They thought I was a ditz. Everyone thinks I'm a ditz."

Alice says nothing.

"It's because I'm a blonde. Do you still have any of that fudge left?" she asks.

"I think so," Alice says, and opens the fridge door, and looks inside for the white box she put in there earlier today. When she opens it, half the fudge is gone. Good old Rafe, she thinks.

"And you do have coffee this time, I see," Jennifer says, and helps herself to a mug on the drain board. Sipping at the coffee, nibbling on a piece of fudge, she says, "Something's going on here, right?"

"No. What do you mean? No."

"Big truck outside when I came here the other day. What was that?"

"My brother-in-law drives a truck."

"Was he the company you said you had?"

"Yes."

"And that's why you wouldn't invite me in? So I wouldn't meet your brother-in-law?"

"We had a lot to talk about."

"Was it a lover instead?"

"What?"

"Was he your lover? Instead of your brother-in-law? Your truck-driver lover?"

"Don't be ridiculous!"

"It just seemed funny, your not letting me in the house when the only person here was your brother-in-law."

"Look," Alice says, "I hardly know you. You run me over the other day . . ."

"Run you *over,* come on!"

"Well, what would you call it? You come barreling around the corner . . ."

"What is it, Alice?" she asks suddenly. "Tell me. What's happening here you're trying to hide?"

Her blue eyes hold Alice fixed in a steady gaze.

Alice is remembering that the woman who was seen picking up her children was a blonde. Hair down to here, just about the length Jennifer Redding wears it.

"I want to help you," Jennifer says. "I'm very smart about some things."

"You're not being smart now," Alice tells her. "Look, I'm sorry I have to rush you out of here . . ."

"There *is* something, I know it," Jennifer says, narrowing her eyes, and Alice realizes that she is involved here with one of those people who watch too much television and who think they are world-class snoops on the order of Miss Marple or Jessica Fletcher. Either that or she is the blonde accomplice who drove that car on Wednesday.

Alice does not for a moment believe this is even remotely possible. A blonde exists; Alice is sure of that. The woman in that Shell station was definitely black and no one has yet described the driver of the Impala as a black woman. So there *is* a blonde, yes, but Alice doesn't believe Jennifer Redding is that blonde. She believes Jennifer Redding is just a meddling pain in the ass, and she wants her out of here before that phone rings again, whenever it rings, *if* it rings, with instructions on when and where she can pick up her kids.

"I'll find out, you know," Jennifer says, and nods sagely, like a woman who is accustomed to solving all sorts of heinous crimes when she is not out in her red T-bird knocking down real estate brokers. She swallows what's left of her coffee, sets the mug in the sink as if she lives here, says, "I can help you if you'd let me," gives Alice an unexpected hug, and then marches out of the house like a model on a runway.

Alice shakes her head in amazement.

The phone rings.

She looks at the clock.

It is now almost ten past twelve. It can't be the black woman calling, can it? Not so soon. Or can it? She yanks the receiver from its cradle.

"Hello?"

"Al? It's Carol. Rafe just called me. Are the kids back?"

"No."

"What are you going to do?"

"Wait. Hope they call me. She told me to go home. She said they'd call. I'm hoping—"

"Who, Alice? Who said that?"

"The woman who has them."

"Is it some kind of crazed person who doesn't have kids of her own?"

"I don't think so. She didn't look crazy."

"You *saw* her?"

"Yes."

"She let you *see* her?"

Same thing Charlie asked. And she gives the same answer now.

"They have the kids, Carol."

And again, this says it all. They have the kids. If I do or say anything that will compromise their position, they will kill my children. That is the simple truth of the matter.

"They?" Carol asks. "Who's *they*?"

"These two women."

"There are *two* of them?"

"Apparently."

"Did you give them money?"

"Yes."

She doesn't wish to discuss with her sister the strategy the Cape October Police used, or *are* using, if in fact they're doing a damn thing now. She can only hope that the $250,000 in false currency is truly so good nobody can tell it from the real thing. Otherwise, she has signed her own children's death warrant.

"Are the police there now?" Carol asks.

"I don't know where they are."

"Well . . . what are you *doing*, Alice?"

"Waiting," Alice says. "Just waiting."

"Who's helping you there?"

She does not know who's helping her here. She has never felt so completely alone in her life.

"Have you called the FBI?" Carol asks.

"They've been and gone."

"I'm coming down there," Carol says. "Right this minute."

"No, that's not—"

"I'm getting in my car and driving down."

"Carol . . ."

"Look for me, honey," she says, "I'm on the way."

And she, too, is gone.

They do not want to get the Tampa PD involved in this because in Captain Steele's view, there are enough law enforcement people on the scene already. He didn't like the FBI sticking its nose in this uninvited and unannounced, and he certainly doesn't want any fresh representatives of the law marching in now.

The computer kicks up an Ernesto de Diego recently released from prison and regularly visiting a parole officer in Tampa, but he's forty-three years old, and Maria told the detectives that her former boyfriend was only eighteen. So that rules him out, unless Mr. de Diego has a namesake son, which would make him Ernesto de Diego, Jr., but the computer has nothing at all on such an offspring.

In the Tampa phone directory, they find listings for a Dalia de Diego, a Godofredo de Diego, a Rafael de Diego, and a Ramon de Diego, but alas, no Ernesto. On the off chance that one of these de Diegos might be a relative of the Ernesto they're looking for, they go down the list and hit pay dirt on the second call they make. A woman named Catalina de Diego tells Detective Saltzman that she is Godofredo's wife, and that his brother Ernesto is presently living with them until he can find a place of his own. Belatedly, she asks, "What's this about, Officer?"

At a quarter to one that afternoon, Detectives Saltzman and Andrews are on the de Diego doorstep, talking to Catalina again, in person this time. She tells them her husband and her brother will be home for lunch around one o'clock, and invites them in to wait. She serves them strong coffee and these tasty little cookies sprinkled with sugar. She tells them that both her husband and her brother-in-law work at an auto repair shop not far from here. "My husband got the job for Ernesto," she says. She introduces them to her three-year-old son, Horacio, who immediately tells the detectives he knows how to "go potty." Detective Andrews tells him, "That's nice, son."

So far, this does not look like a bunch of desperados who've kidnapped the Glendenning kids, but who knows? The quietest guy on the block is always the one who turns out to have killed his whole family and the goldfish, too, isn't that so? Besides, Ernesto can't be such a sweetheart, can he? Leaving a pregnant girlfriend back on the Cape?

The brothers get home at a little before one.

The detectives can hear them laughing up the front walk to the small house. They are both light-skinned, with brown eyes and curly black hair. Ernesto is a little taller than Godofredo. They look like a pair of hardworking guys who've just put in a long morning, and are ready now to wash up for lunch, but who knows?

The detectives tell them they'd like to talk to Ernesto privately, if that's okay. They go out together into the yard behind the small house. There is a coconut palm in the yard, and several bird-of-paradise plants. There is a shell walkway and wooden lawn furniture painted pink. A nice cool breeze is blowing. Inside, they can hear Godofredo and his wife talking in Spanish.

"So what is this?" Ernesto asks. "Is she claiming the kid's mine?"

"You mean Maria?" Andrews asks.

"Is that why you're here?"

"You tell us," Saltzman says.

"What's there to tell? She fucked everybody in that high school, not only me. So now she says the baby's mine. That's a crock of shit, man."

"She says you have a new girlfriend now, is that right?"

"What's that her business?"

"It's just what she told us."

"It's none of her business, what I have or I don't have."

"*Do* you have a new girlfriend?"

Ernesto gives them a long hard look.

He is suddenly suspicious. Suddenly tipping to the fact that this has nothing to do with Maria's baby.

"You come all the way up from the Cape to ask me do I have a new girlfriend?" he says.

"Do you?"

"Yes. Why?"

"She doesn't happen to be a blonde, does she?"

"What?" he says.

"Your girlfriend. Is she a blonde?"

"Is that what Maria told you?"

"That's what she told us."

"She should learn to keep her mouth shut."

"Well, you knock her up, you disappear . . ."

"I *didn't* knock her up! And I didn't *disappear,* either! My brother got me a job here, so I moved up. I even called Maria to tell her where I was."

"Nice of you."

"I don't owe her a fuckin thing!"

"Does she drive a blue Impala? Your blonde girlfriend?"

"What?"

"Your new girlfriend. Does she happen to drive a blue Impala?"

"No, she drives a white Jag."

"What's her name?"

"Why do you want to know?"

"What's her name?"

"I can't tell you that."

"Why not?"

"Because she's married."

"Oh?" Saltzman says.

"Well, well," Andrews says.

"Anyway, what is this? Is she in some kind of trouble?"

"Tell us her name, Ernesto."

"Jesus, what did she do?"

"Tell us where she lives, Ernesto."

"She's married, I can't—"

"You want to take a ride to the Cape, or you want to give us your little married girlfriend's name and address? Which, Ernesto?"

"Judy Lang," he says at once.

Charlie Hobbs pulls into the driveway at twenty minutes past one that afternoon. Alice greets him at the front door, taking both his hands in hers and leading him into the house.

"Are you okay?" he asks.

"I'm glad you came."

"She call yet?"

"Not yet. Charlie, I'm scared silly."

"Don't be. She'll call."

"You think?"

"I know she will."

Charlie looks around the living room, takes in all the police equipment.

"So where are the masterminds?" he asks.

Alice shakes her head.

"Tell me everything that happened," he says.

"Here's what we've got," Sally Ballew is telling her boss.

The agent in command of the regional FBI office is a man named Tully Stone, bald and rangy and mean as dog shit. It is rumored that shortly after the disputed Gore-Bush presidential election, Stone single-handedly rounded up a ring of anti-government protestors right here in the sunny state of Florida. Broke a few heads and cracked even more ribs, or so the story went, before all those bleeding-heart liberals decided it wasn't right to go against the Supreme Court decision that made Bush president of these United States.

Sally Ballew feels that black people—*her* people—in the state of Florida were disenfranchised in that election, but she has never mentioned this to her boss, whose role model is John Ashcroft. She is reporting to him now on the number of blue Chevrolet Impalas that were rented from Avis at the Fort Myers airport during the past two—

"I don't understand," Stone says. "Is this our case?"

"That depends," Sally says.

"On what?"

"On do we want it."

"Why would we?"

"Might become high-profile."

"How?"

"Woman's a widow. Pretty woman, two good-looking kids—the ones who got kidnapped, sir. Eight and ten years old, little boy and girl."

Stone does not seem impressed.

He is pacing his office. In one corner of the room, an American flag rests furled in an ornate wrought-iron stand. The wall behind him is adorned with a big replica of the FBI seal with its thirteen stars and its laurel leaves, and its red-and-white-striped shield. On the upper rim of the predominately blue seal, the words DEPARTMENT OF JUSTICE are lettered in white. On the lower rim, FEDERAL BUREAU OF INVESTIGATION, again in white. Just below the striped little shield with its engraved blue scales, there is a flowing white ribbon upon which the words *Fidelity, Bravery,* and *Integrity* are lettered.

There was a time, Stone reflects, when those words meant something.

Now he's standing here with a woman who can't contain her tits, and they're debating whether or not they should step into a case merely because it might become high-profile, in which event the Bureau will be able to bask in the cleansing light of some much-needed glory, if/when they ever arrest the sons of bitches who took two little kids from their mama.

"What'd be our justification for butting in here?" he asks.

"Reasonable presumption that the perps crossed a state line."

"They're already out of Florida?"

"We don't know that, sir."

"Then how's a state line been crossed?"

"We think they may have come down from New York."

"Oh dear, we're dealing with big-city sharpies, eh?" Stone says, and almost grins in anticipation. There is nothing he likes better than to bust the ass of a city slicker. That ring of liberal rabble-rousing ruffians was based in Chicago. Came down here to raise a fuss and cause six kinds of trouble. He has not mentioned to Sally Balloons here that the leader of *that* little band was black as the ace of spades. Some of these people can get touchy, even if they work on the side of the law.

"You got proof of that?" he asks.

"No, sir. Not quite proof."

"There's no such thing as not quite proof," Stone says. "There's evidence, or there's lack of evidence. Nobody can be just a little bit pregnant."

"Well, sir, we think we may have found whoever rented the Impala described by the school guard," Sally says. "And she's from New York City. Which means a state line may have been crossed in anticipation of committing a future crime. At least, her driver's license gives an address in New York City."

"Anticipation of a *future* crime? What the hell is this, a Tom Cruise movie? Do you know for certain that this woman has in *fact* committed the crime of kidnapping?"

"No, sir, we do not. But, as I was about to say—"

"She the only person rented an Impala like the one this school guard described?"

"No, sir. Twenty-six blue Impalas were rented at the Fort Myers airport within the past two weeks, sir. Twenty of them have already been returned, and the renters long departed. Six of the cars are still out, we've got the license plate numbers for all of them, and in some instances local addresses for the renters."

"Isn't that obligatory? Giving a local address?"

"Some people just don't know where they'll be staying. They drive around the state, they stop here, they stop there . . ."

"Have you got a local address for this woman you say crossed a state line in *anticipation* of committing a future crime?"

"No, sir. She's one of them who didn't know where she'd be staying."

"If I was about to kidnap some kids, I'd make damn sure I didn't tell Avis where *I'd* be staying, either."

"Yes, sir."

"What's her name, this woman?"

"Clara Washington."

Stone almost asks, "Black?"

He doesn't.

But a name like Washington?

Has to be black, doesn't it?

"Avis rep who rented the car to her says she was black," Sally says, beating him to the punch. "Woman in her thirties, about five-eight, five-nine, good-looking according to the Avis person. Showed a New York driver's license as ID. Charged the lease to an American Express credit card."

"So what's the problem?"

"We checked with American Express; they do not have any card holder named Clara Washington in the city of New York. We checked with the New York State Department of Motor Vehicles; they did not issue a driver's license to anyone named Clara Washington in the city of New York. It would appear that both pieces of ID are false, sir."

"Dime a dozen nowadays."

"Dime a dozen, sir."

"So you don't really know if a state line *has* been crossed. If that driver's license came in a Cracker Jack box . . ."

"That's what I meant by 'not quite proof,' sir."

"If the driver's license is queer, the woman could have come from anywhere. Could've got off a bus from Jacksonville or Tallahassee, could've walked over to the airport from downtown Fort Myers, no state line crossed, no reason for the FBI to come into the case, end of story."

"*Except,* sir—"

"Except what?"

"Except if we find her, and she really *is* from New York, and we nail her for the kidnapping, then we had good reason all along to assume the case fell within federal jurisdiction. And we become the heroes, sir."

"Heroes," Stone says.

"Yes, sir. And *not* the Cape October PD."

"Heroes," Stone repeats.

There was a time when a hero was someone who single-handedly charged a Vietcong machine-gun nest with a hand grenade in each hand and a bayonet clenched between his teeth. Now you were a hero if you tracked down a little colored girl—well, not so little, five-eight, five-nine—who may or may not have crossed a state line in *anticipation* of committing a crime that would get your name and your face all over television if you caught her.

"So what do you suggest, Ballew?"

He almost called her "Balloons."

"We have the license plate number, sir. I suggest we do a sweep of all the area motels, hotels, B & B's, what-have-you, see if we can't find that car and that woman."

"Declare ourselves officially in this thing?"

"Not until we're sure we'll be making an arrest, sir. Otherwise, we let the local cops take the heat."

Stone is wondering how many of his people he will need for a sweep of all these area dwellings. But if he doesn't grant Special

Agent Ballew's simple request, will she then file a report to division headquarters later on, claiming she went to her superior with information about a kidnapping, and he swept it under the carpet the way certain flight-school information was swept under the carpet prior to the 9/11 attacks?

Stone is tempted to tell Special Agent Sally Ballew here to take a walk, they have no jurisdiction.

But the entire nation is ready to reward whistle-blowers of every stripe and persuasion nowadays, a far cry from the scorn heaped upon one of the country's true heroes, Linda Tripp.

"Set up the sweep," he says. "Full team, twenty-four-seven, the whole nine yards. But find this woman fast, or back off."

Sally can almost see herself on television already.

"I'll find her, sir," she says.

The little digital clock on Stone's desk reads 1:47:03.

The phone call comes at two o'clock sharp.

By then, Charlie has figured out the wiretap equipment and is sitting with the earphones on his head. He flicks a switch and nods for Alice to pick up.

"Hello?" she says.

"We've got a problem here," the woman says. Alice's heart leaps into her throat. Charlie is suddenly attentive, as if he's listening for incoming mail at Khe Sanh.

"Somebody followed me," the woman says.

"Let me talk to Ashley."

"No, your daughter's got a big mouth, you don't have to talk to her again," the woman says. "My partner spotted them behind us. Two men in a maroon Buick. It wasn't for a garbage truck, we'd be in serious trouble here."

Alice says nothing.

My partner, she is thinking. Does this mean her partner in this ambitious little enterprise of theirs? Or does it mean her *sexual* partner? Is this a pair of lesbians she's dealing with?

"Were they cops?" the woman asks.

"I don't know who they might have been," Alice says. "I don't know anything about it."

"Are they there with you now?"

"No one's here with me," Alice says.

"I'll call you back, anyway," the woman says, and hangs up.

"That's her pattern," Alice explains. "She's afraid we'll be tracing the call."

"Is she right about that Buick?"

"I have no idea."

"How damn stupid can these people be?"

"I told you, Charlie. They deserted me this morning . . ."

"Putting a clumsy tail on—"

The telephone rings.

"There she is," Charlie says.

Alice picks up.

"Hello?" she says.

"Why'd you call the police?"

"I didn't."

"Then who were those men in the Buick?"

"I don't know. I came there alone. I don't know anything about anyone following you. Let me talk to my daughter."

"Forget it."

"You said—"

"Never mind what I said. You went back on your word."

"I did *not* call the police!" Alice screams into the phone.

Even Charlie almost believes her.

The woman is silent for a moment.

Then there's another click on the line.

"Damn her," Alice says, "I could *kill* her!"

"When she calls back, get right to the point. Tell her she's got the money, ask her when and where you can pick up the kids."

Alice nods.

"Okay?"

"Yes."

"Don't let her rattle you. If the kids have been harmed already—"

"Oh Jesus, Charlie, don't even—"

"—they wouldn't be calling you, don't you see, Alice? The kids are still all right."

The phone rings.

"Remember. Stick to the point. When, where? Stay calm."

"Okay."

"Pick it up."

He throws the LISTEN switch. Alice picks up the receiver.

"Hello?" she says.

"We can't give you the kids today," the woman says.

"You promised . . ."

"We have to check out the money first."

They'll discover it's fake, Alice thinks. They'll—

"Give us time," the woman says, and suddenly her voice softens. "Your kids are okay, just give us a little time here."

And she is gone again.

6

It is ten past two by the time Carol gets to I-75 South. Big rigs like the ones Rafe drives are roaring at her on the other side of the divider.

She figures it will take her some ten to twelve hours to get to Cape October. According to her map, it's a good hour or more to Macon, some sixty-five miles or so, before she has to turn off at the Valdosta exit to merge with I-475 South. Just now, she feels wide awake and peppy, but she plans to stop at a motel for the night, get to the Cape in time for breakfast tomorrow morning. The longest stretch of road will be the four-hundred-plus miles between Macon and St. Pete, but she's made the trip before—with kids screaming in the backseat, no less—and she knows she can make it this time, too, with no sweat.

She cannot possibly imagine how Alice must feel, her kids gone and a passel of fools handling the case. She can remember times when the two of them were growing up in Peekskill, Carol the older sister and constantly getting Alice out of jams. But nothing as serious as this had ever—

Well, Eddie drowning that way.

Carol had taken the first plane down out of Atlanta. She thought her younger sister would never get through it; God, how she loved that man. Held her sister in her arms, sobbing, Alice clutching a photo of Eddie with his shining blue eyes and crooked grin and pale unruly hair.

Carol wonders what it's like to love a person that much. Here alone behind the wheel of the Ford Explorer, trucks coming at her like attacking Martian spaceships, she wonders if in fact she really loves Rafe at all, really ever loved him at all.

Unlike her sister, Carol never went for the slight slender type, oh no, it was always the big brawny college football hero or the wrestling team champ. Though Rafe is neither, Rafe never even graduated from high school; no wonder he got in trouble with the law those two times. Well, dope. Everybody's into dope these days, she hopes some damn dope fiends haven't got their hands on those two adorable kids, what on earth is *wrong* with the cops down there, handling this so damn stupidly?

Her foot is pressed hard to the accelerator.

A glance at the speedometer tells her she's hitting seventy, seventy-five, the needle wavering. She doesn't want to get stopped by the Georgia Highway Patrol, but neither does she want to drive along too slowly, risk lulling herself to sleep that way. Rafe told her once that he averages ninety miles an hour on his long hauls; he was probably lying to her, ninety is really too fast.

His call this morning was . . . well, peculiar.

Broke the news to her about the kidnapping, told her Alice was already on the way to meet whoever it was had the kids, carrying a bag full of funny money, he sure hoped those people would accept it.

"What do you mean?" Carol said.

"Otherwise, there might be trouble."

"You mean if they . . . ?"

"If they tip to the money being fake," Rafe said.

"Well, you just told me it's very good stuff."

"Is what the cops told Alice, yes."

"So how can they tip?"

"These people ain't fools, you know," Rafe said. "You can't be a moron and figure out something like this."

"That's right, it takes a rocket scientist to grab two kids and ask for ransom."

"I mean, the way they've been handling it, Carol. I've been right here, you know, I see how the woman hangs up every two, three seconds, I see how carefully they've worked this whole thing out. All I'm saying is I hope they don't realize Alice brought them counterfeit money. I worry about them kids, Carol."

She wonders now if he really worries about Alice's kids, or anybody's kids, for that matter. Or anyone but his own self.

Carol has long suspected that her husband plays around on these long trips of his. Never calls her when he's on the road—today was an exception, but it's not every day your sister's kids get kidnapped. Gone sometimes three, four weeks when he's hauling to the West Coast, you think he'd call every few days, tell her he loves her, whatever. Never does. That's either a man who's in tight control of his emotions, or else it's a man fooling around with whatever comes his way on the road, she wouldn't be at all surprised.

Something else he said continues to bother her.

It was just before Christmas. Carol had invited Alice and the kids up to Atlanta, but she said she had to stay down there on the Cape, where Jamie's speech therapist was, he had already stopped talking by then. Rafe told Carol that he'd read something in the *Atlanta Constitution* about some insurance company paying any accident-related claims within a week of filing, even without death certificates.

"So when's this insurance company of *Alice's* gonna pay *her* that two-fifty?" he asked.

"I'm sure Alice is asking that very same question along about now," Carol said.

"Be nice to get *our* hands on some of that, wouldn't it?" Rafe said.

"What makes you think . . . ?"

"Be *real* nice," he said.

Carol wondered about this at the time. She knew her sister would be coming into $250,000 as soon as that insurance claim was settled, and she knew she and Rafe still had a big mortgage on the house, and payments on the Ford to make each and every month, and it would certainly be helpful if Alice decided to be generous with a little of that money. But Carol would never ask, and Rafe knew that, and so it was funny that he'd brought up the insurance money, and she'd wondered about it at the time.

She is still wondering about it.

She keeps her foot pressed hard to the accelerator.

"How do we know they didn't rent a condo?" Forbes asks.

"That's another possibility," Sally says.

"People come down, rent a condo for a week or two," Forbes elaborates.

"I know that."

"What I'm saying, this could turn into a wild goose chase," Forbes says.

In fact, he doesn't like the way this whole damn thing is shaping up.

First off, they are putting those children in harm's way. That is the plain and simple truth of the matter. Stone knows that, and so does Sally. You go knocking on someone's door, ask did they rent a blue Impala at the airport, if they've got the kids inside there with them, they're going to panic and maybe blow the kids away. That is a fact that should be evident to any law enforcement officer. That is the first thing that stinks to high heaven here.

The second thing is that this is once again turning into a footrace with the local fuzz, everybody grabbing for the gold ring, never mind the welfare of the vics. It's who's gonna bring home the bacon, who's gonna end up the glory boys and girls. There's no question but that the FBI can use a little praise these days, the way we fouled up before and after 9/11, none of us has yet found whoever it was mailed that anthrax around, now have we?

So jump on the merry-go-round, boys and girls, and let's see who can find that blue Impala first, us or the local yokels, and pray to God nobody behind one of those hotel, motel, B & B, what-have-you doors won't start blasting away the minute we say those words "FBI" and show the shield, just pray to God, boys, just pray to God.

The FBI has not shared with the Cape October PD's Criminal Investigations Division the information it gathered from the Avis desk at the airport. So Captain Roger Steele does not know that the person who rented a blue Impala four days ago showed identification bearing the name Clara Washington.

Steele knows only that a blue Impala driven by a slender blonde picked up a good-looking black girl some five feet seven inches tall—close enough to the five-eight or -nine described by the Avis woman, but that's another thing he doesn't know. He does know that the girl was carrying Alice Glendenning's Louis Vuitton bag full of Monopoly money, and he further knows that the car was subsequently obscured by an orange Cape October Department of Sanitation garbage truck, thereby eluding their grasp this morning. He also knows that the blue Chevy has got to be out there someplace because, as Detective Wilbur Sloate put it to him, "*Ever'body* gotta be someplace, boss."

So Steele has put out an all-points bulletin for the car, and meanwhile, his entire CID team is out checking every hotel and motel in town, hoping to locate the blue car and consequently the black girl and her blonde girlfriend.

Cape October is a city of 143,000 year-round residents, 90 percent of them white, 8 percent of them Cubans who have drifted over to the West Coast from Miami, 2 percent of them black, and the remainder a tiny spattering of Asians. There are twenty-four churches of varying denominations on the Cape, ranging from Catholic to Baptist to Jewish (Orthodox and Reform) to Presbyterian to Lutheran to Seventh-Day Adventist and including two for the Mennonite sect, its followers identified by the black clothing and beards worn by the men, and the plain dresses and simple white caps worn by the women.

And because the Cape is a tourist destination, there are also fifty-two hotels, motels, small inns, and cottages in this town, not to mention a few dozen more bed-and-breakfast places.

Roger Steele does not think the kidnappers would risk taking those two kids to any of the bigger hotels or even to one of the resorts out on the keys. But there are small motels all up and down the Trail, and even some out on Grosse Bec. These are the ones his team of sixteen CID detectives are checking. Sixteen detectives. That's all Steele has. This is a very small number of detectives for such a mighty number of venues, even assuming the perps are still in the state of Florida.

And besides, it is starting to rain again.

The manager of the Shell station on U.S. 41 and Lewiston Point Road is not happy to see three detectives from the Cape October Police Department coming out of the rain at two-thirty that Friday afternoon.

One of the cops, a burly black man named Johnson, tells the manager they're investigating an automobile theft.

"The thief may have used the ladies' room sometime this morning. So we'd like to go in there and look around, if that's okay with you."

"What kind of car was it?" the manager asks.

"Cadillac Saville," Johnson lies, without batting an eyelash.

"We get lots of Savilles in here," the manager says.

"Yeah," Johnson says. "So if you'll unlock the ladies' room for us, we'll just go about our business."

"It's unlocked as it is," the manager says.

"Well, fine then, we'll just get out of your way."

The three Mobile Crime Unit cops have been sent by Captain Steele to get everything they can from the ladies' room where Mrs. Glendenning dropped the ransom money, and where an as-yet-unidentified suspect picked up the bag and managed to elude a successful surveillance. Steele's game plan, such as it is, is to find out if the black girl who sashayed off with two-fifty large in supers has a record of any kind. From what his detectives have told him, Steele has a pretty good inkling that Mrs. Glendenning isn't too happy about the continued presence of the Cape October Police in this case. So he intends to send Sloate and Di Luca back to her with some real information, as soon as he *gets* some real information, before she goes blabbing on television that the cops in this neck of the woods don't know what they're doing.

Unfortunately, the two suspect women—the blonde and the black girl—have thus far eluded pursuit, and so far none of the Cape October uniforms have spotted the suspect blue Impala. So he figures if the MCU can come up with real meat, then he can go back to the Glendenning woman and calm her down regarding the procedure they've been following, a perfectly sound procedure, by the way, that resulted in a capture and conviction in the Henley case three years ago, even though the little boy was dead by the time they got there.

The three MBU cops know how important this case is to the captain, so they go over the ladies' room with more devotion to detail than they might normally lavish at any crime scene. They vacuum the place top to bottom for stray hairs or fibers, they dust the sink faucets and knobs for latent fingerprints, and the paper towel dispenser, and the hand drier, too, and the doorknobs—inside and out—on the entrance door, and the turn bolt lock on the entrance door, and the latch on the door to the one stall in the room, and the flush handle on the toilet, and the toilet seat, and the toilet-paper holder, and the windowsill, and the little pulls on the window sash, and the window itself, and anything and everything in that room. It is almost two-thirty by the time they leave the place.

The manager tells them he's had a lot of complaints from ladies who had to pee.

Johnson, the detective/first heading up the team, tells him he should have directed them to the men's room.

"Shoulda thought of that," the manager says.

It is still raining.

• • •

In Cape October, during the rainy season—but May is not the rainy season—you can expect a thunderstorm along about three or four every afternoon, at which time the humidity and the heat have combined to leave the suffering citizenry virtually limp. The rain, when it comes, mercilessly assaults the sidewalks and the streets, but only for an hour or so. During that short while, the torrential downpour brings at least a semblance of relief. But once the rain stops, you'd never know it had been there at all. Oh, yes, the gutters are running with swift-flowing muddy water, and there are huge brown puddles everywhere, and here and there a truly flooded street—but the heat and the humidity follow as closely behind the brief storm as does a rapist his victim. Within minutes you are sweating again.

This is not the rainy season; this is May.

But by three o'clock that afternoon, the rain is coming down in buckets.

Detectives Wilbur Sloate and George Cooper have been driving in the pouring rain from motel to motel ever since two o'clock. Following the Cape October city and county grid supplied to them by Captain Steele, they have already visited twelve motels, and when they spot an Impala in the courtyard outside the Tamiami Trail Motor Lodge, they can hardly wait to get out of the maroon Buick they're driving.

"Go!" Sloate shouts, and both detectives burst out of the car and into the rain, dashing across the courtyard to the motel office, where—in his soft-spoken, seemingly subservient black way—Cooper tells the clerk behind the desk that they are looking for a person driving an Avis-rented blue Impala, and they've just noticed that there is such a vehicle parked outside, sir.

"Yeah?" the clerk says.

"Want to tell us who's driving that car?" Cooper asks.

"Let me see your badges," the clerk says.

They both flash the Cape October PD tin.

The clerk studies the shields as if they were freshly minted. He is not sure how he feels about cops on the property. He is sure his boss won't like learning about it when he comes in tomorrow morning. But there's nothing he can do about their being here, he supposes, unless . . .

"You got a search warrant?" he asks.

"Mister," Cooper says, "let's just see your damn register, okay?"

This turns out to be academic because Sloate is already turning the register so they can read it. They have no trouble finding the license plate number from the car outside, or matching it with the name alongside it, Mr. and Mrs. Arthur Holt from Cleveland, Michigan.

"This the room they're in?" Cooper asks. "3B?"

"It's a cabin. We don't have rooms here, we have cabins," the clerk says.

"This the cabin then?"

"That's the one."

"They happen to be black, these people?"

"Man was white. Didn't see the woman, she stayed in the car. Lots of them stay in the car while the man registers. Specially if it's raining."

"Was it raining three days ago, when it says here they checked in?"

"I don't know what it was doing three days ago," the clerk says.

"Then you want to show us where 3B is?" Sloate says.

"It's right across the courtyard," the clerk says. "What's this all about, anyway?"

"Just checkin on a car, is all," Cooper says.

The clerk figures they're looking for either a wanted desperado or an al-Qaeda terrorist, but he points them in the right direction, and hopes there won't be any gunplay here.

The white man who opens the door is wearing a bathrobe over pajamas. This is a quarter to four in the afternoon and he's ready to go to bed. Meanwhile, the two detectives are standing in the rain.

"Mind if we come in, sir?" Sloate asks.

"Well, gee, I don't know," Holt says.

He has a little Charlie Chaplin mustache. Behind him, the television set is on with a rerun of a cop movie. The detectives have just showed him their shields, but Holt seems more interested in the movie than in the real live cops standing in front of him. They can hear a shower running behind a closed door they assume leads to the bathroom. Mr. Holt's wife, no doubt, if indeed she is his wife. Quarter to four in the afternoon, he's ready for bed. Can it be his wife? They are still standing in the rain. He still hasn't asked them to come in.

Sloate steps in, anyway, guidelines be damned. Cooper comes right in behind him. Holt still doesn't know what they want, but to play it safe he tells them he's from Cleveland, Michigan—which they already know from the register—and that he has been coming down to Cape October ever since 1973, when he caught bronchitis and his doctor advised him to go someplace warm for the winter. He tells them that he is here with his wife, Sophie, who is at this moment taking a shower, and he tells them that tomorrow he will be taking her to Disney World in Orlando.

"Been coming down here for more 'n thirty years now, never been to Disney World, can you imagine?" he says.

"Is your wife black?" Cooper asks.

"Black?" Holt says. "No. What kind of question is that? Black? I'm from Cleveland. What do you mean, black? My wife? What's this all about, anyway?"

He does not look or sound like the sort of person who has kidnapped a pair of little kids, but then again not many rapists look like rapists or bank robbers like bank robbers, at least not in the experience of these two cops. In any case, there is just this one room here, and the bathroom beyond, where they can still hear the shower going, so they have to assume—until they can check out the bathroom, at any rate—that since there are no little kids in evidence, this is not the man and woman who kidnapped the Glendenning children. Unless Mrs. Holt—if she is Mrs. Holt—turns out to be the black Sheena of the Jungle they followed strutting up Citrus Avenue with the expensive French luggage bouncing on her hip and the wide gold bracelet on her arm.

"We'd like to have a look in that bathroom whenever Mrs. Holt is finished in there," Sloate says.

"I don't suppose you have a search warrant, do you?" Holt asks.

"No, we don't, Mr. Holt," Sloate says. "Do you want us to go all the way downtown to get one?"

Holt decides he would rather not have them do this.

For the next five minutes or so, they stand around awkwardly, waiting for Mrs. Holt to finish her shower. At last, she turns off the water. Holt goes to the bathroom door, knocks on it, and says, "Hon, there're some police detectives here. You'd better put something on before you come out."

"There are some *what* here?" a woman's voice answers.

She does not sound black.

She comes out a moment later, wearing a pink robe and a bemused expression that says, Gee, there really *are* two people who look like detectives standing here with my husband!

She is definitely not black.

She is, however, blonde.

But not the slender blonde with hair to her shoulders Sloate saw at the wheel of the Impala. Instead, she is in her late forties, a somewhat stout little woman, her short hair still wet and straggly, her face shiny bright from the shower.

"Sorry to bother you, ma'am," Sloate says, and they both go into the bathroom to look around, though neither of them now believes there are any kids here in this motel room.

"Sorry to bother you," Sloate repeats as they come out of the bathroom. "Just had to check out something."

"What is it you're looking for?" the woman asks.

"Routine matter," Cooper says in his shuffling, soft-spoken way, and they thank the Holts for their time, and then leave the room, and drive out of the motel grounds, on their way to the next place on their list.

"Now what do you make of that?" Holt asks his wife.

• • •

Judy Lang is perhaps five feet seven inches tall, and slender, and quite beautiful in a fox-faced way, her blonde hair cut so that it falls loose and straight to just above her shoulders. When she opens the door to the tenth-floor condo, she is barefoot and wearing a brown mini and a short pink cotton sweater that exposes a ring in her belly button. Her blue eyes open wide when she spots the yarmulke on the back of Saltzman's head. Her first thought is that somebody has told the rabbi she's been dating an eighteen-year-old Cuban.

Dating isn't quite the proper word, either, since she and Ernesto haven't yet *gone* anywhere together, except the backseat of his brother's big roomy Oldsmobile. Judy knows that her husband will kill her for sure if he ever finds out about what she's been doing in that car every day of the week except Saturday and Sunday, with a Cuban teenager, no less. So here's this big tall guy with a yarmulke, standing on the doorstep, here to read her passages from the Talmud, she feels certain. Instead, he flashes a badge that has the initials COPD on it, which—it immediately becomes clear—stand for Cape October Police Department.

"Detective Julius Saltzman," he says. "My partner, Detective Peter Andrews."

The shorter guy with him mumbles something Judy doesn't quite catch. At least they aren't here from the synagogue.

"May we come in, please?" Saltzman asks.

"Well . . . my husband isn't home," she says.

"It's you we want to talk to," Andrews says. "If you're Judy Lang?"

"Well . . . yes, I am," she says. "But why?" Despite the exuberant breasts in the snug sweater and the lissome hips in the tight-fitting mini, there is a certain adolescent gawkiness about this woman. Both detectives suddenly wonder if Ernesto de Diego hasn't nailed himself another little teenager here, instead of the thirty-something housewife Judy Lang actually is. They follow her into a living room that overlooks the wide green expanse of a golf course below, and take seats on a sofa opposite her. All they want to know is whether or not

Judy Lang might have been the blonde who picked up the Glendenning kids yesterday afternoon. Being cops, however—and small-town cops at that—they can't come right out and ask her if she happened to kidnap two kids. Instead, they go at it in a more subtle manner, they think.

"Do you drive a car?" Andrews asks.

"Yes, I do," she says.

"What kind of car is it?"

"A white Jag. My husband gave it to me for my thirty-fifth birthday."

Thirty-five then. Going on thirty-six.

"Ever drive a Chevy Impala?"

"I don't think so. No. Why?"

"Blue Chevy Impala?"

"No."

"You weren't driving a blue Chevy Impala this past Wednesday afternoon, were you? Down in Cape October?"

"Not this past Wednesday or *any* Wednesday," Judy says. "I've never been to Cape October in my life."

"But your boyfriend's from the Cape, isn't he?"

"What boyfriend?" she says. "I'm a married woman. What are you talking about, boyfriend?"

"Do you know a girl named Maria Gonzalez?"

"No. Did somebody run her over with a Chevy Impala?"

"Ever hear of a woman named Alice Glendenning?"

"No. Who is she?"

"Did Maria Gonzalez ever mention the Glendenning children to you?"

"I told you I don't know anybody named Maria Gonzalez."

"Judy?"

A voice from the front door. They all turn to look at the arch leading to the entrance foyer.

"Is someone here, dear?" the voice asks.

He is wearing sandals, khaki slacks, and a lime green shirt. He is a man in his fifties, they guess, bald, tanned, with a dead cigar in his mouth. Putting his keys back into his pants pocket, he enters the living room, his eyes squinching in puzzlement when he sees the two men sitting on the sofa.

"Yes?" he says.

"Darling," Judy says, and rises, and goes to him and takes both his hands in hers. "These gentlemen are from the Cape October Police Department."

"Oh?" he says.

"Detective Saltzman," Saltzman says.

"Detective Andrews," Andrews says.

"Murray Lang, what can I do for you?"

His manner is abrupt and hostile. He is not used to finding policemen in his luxurious condo, even if one of them is wearing a yarmulke, and his attitude clearly wants to know what the hell they're doing here. Judy's eyes are darting all over the place, from one detective to the other. Just a few minutes ago, they mentioned a boyfriend, which means they know about Ernesto. She is sensing imminent disaster here. She is thinking of throwing herself out the window before her husband finds out what's been going on. Her eyes have a desperate pleading look. They are saying, "Please, officers, don't tell him about Ernesto, okay? Please."

The detectives don't want to cause any trouble here. All they want to know is whether or not Judy Lang and some black woman—

It suddenly occurs to Saltzman that they may have real meat here. However unlikely might seem the menage à trois formed by a married Jewish lady in her thirties, a teenage Cuban boy, and a black woman also in her thirties, the possibility exists that Judy Lang, Ernesto de Diego, and the nameless woman on the telephone are all in this together. A coalition of the willing, so to speak.

"We're trying to locate a blue Chevy Impala," he says.

"Why?" Murray Lang asks. "And what's it got to do with us?"

"A woman who fits your wife's description—"

"Am I going to need a lawyer here?"

"Not unless you want one, sir."

"Because I have lawyers coming out of my wazoo, you want lawyers."

"We want to know where your wife was at two-thirty P.M. Wednesday afternoon, sir. Is all we want to know."

"Tell them where you were, Judy. And then you can get the hell out of here," Murray tells the detectives.

Judy can't tell them where she was Wednesday afternoon at two-thirty because at that time she was on the backseat of an Oldsmobile parked behind A&L Auto Repair, where Ernesto and his brother work, and where everybody else who works there knows that Ernesto fucks the nice Jewish lady at two-thirty every afternoon on the backseat of his brother's car. A&L Auto is where Judy first met Ernesto when she brought the white Jag in for a tune-up a month ago, little realizing that Ernesto would soon be giving her regularly scheduled tune-ups the likes of which she has never before had in her life. But she can't tell the detectives any of this, not while her beloved husband Murray is standing there glowering with a dead cigar in the corner of his mouth. She thinks again that throwing herself out the window might not be such a bad idea.

"Ma'am?" Saltzman prods.

"Wednesday afternoon," she says, thinking hard.

"Yes, ma'am. At two-thirty."

"Why do you want to know this?"

"Were you in Cape October Wednesday afternoon at two-thirty?"

"No, I was not. I told you. I've never been to Cape October in my entire life."

"At Pratt Elementary?" Andrews says.

"Is that a school down there?" Murray asks.

"It's a school, yes, sir. Were you at Pratt Elementary—"

"I told you I've never been to Cape—"

"—behind the wheel of a blue Chevy Impala?"

"Did some schoolkid get run over?" Murray asks. "Is that it?"

"Were you, ma'am?"

"No, I was not."

"Then where were you?"

"Tell them where you were, Judy."

"Shopping," she says.

This Murray can believe. His wife knows shopping. Boy, does she know shopping!

"Shopping where?" Saltzman asks.

"International Plaza."

"Is that a shop, ma'am?"

"No, it's a mall."

"Where's it located?"

"Near the airport," Murray says. "Everybody knows International Plaza."

"We're not that familiar with Tampa," Saltzman says. "Can you tell us where it's located?"

"Boy Scout and West Shore."

"Are those cross streets?"

"They're boulevards. Boy Scout Boulevard, West Shore Boulevard."

"Where in the mall did you shop?" Andrews asks Judy.

"Different shops."

"Which ones?"

For a moment, she hesitates. But she's been to the mall often, and she's familiar with all the stores there.

"Neiman Marcus," she says. "Arden B. Lord & Taylor. St. John Knits. Nordstrom. A few others."

"Must've bought a lot of stuff," Andrews says.

"No, I didn't buy anything at all."

This causes Murray's eyebrows to go up onto his forehead. The detectives look surprised, too.

"I didn't see anything I liked," Judy explains.

"What time did you leave the mall?"

"Around three-fifteen."

Which is about when she was pulling up her panties and rearranging her skirt on the backseat of Godofredo's Olds.

"Spent about forty-five minutes there, is that it?"

"Little bit longer," Judy says.

"Came right back home, did you?"

"No, I stopped for a small pizza at the California Pizza Kitchen."

"Where's that?"

"In the mall. On the first floor. Right by Nordstrom."

"Had a pizza there, did you?"

"A *small* pizza, yes."

"See anybody you know in the Pizza Kitchen?"

"*California* Pizza Kitchen. No."

"Or anyplace else in the mall?"

"No."

"So we just have your word for where you were."

"Her word is good enough for me," Murray says, smiling, and goes to her and takes her hand, and pats it.

"We'll be checking all those shops you went into," Andrews says.

"See if anybody remembers anyone answering your description," Saltzman says.

"*Was* it a kid got run over?" Murray asks.

In the hallway outside, Andrews says, "She's lying."

"I know," Saltzman says.

"We really going to check out all those stores?"

"I don't think so, do you?"

"No, I don't think so."

"Cause if she kidnapped those kids, I'll eat my yarmulke."

Andrews looks at his watch.

"We're gonna hit traffic going back," he says, and sighs heavily.

Back at the lab—which is a very modern lab for a town the size of Cape October—the boys print the latents they lifted at the Shell station, and run them first through their own Bureau of Criminal Identification, but they come up with nothing on the multitude of stuff they gathered. So they try the Automated Fingerprint Identification Section next, and come up blank with them as well. Having exhausted their own BCI and the nationwide AFIS, and having no other letters in the alphabet to turn to, they inform Captain Steele that the black woman Mrs. Glendenning met outside the toilet has never been in the armed forces, has never held a state or federal position, and has never been arrested for any criminal activity whatsoever, otherwise her prints would be on file someplace.

This is now almost five-thirty in the afternoon.

"So what are we dealing with here?" Steele asks Johnson. "Amateur night in Dixie?"

He is commenting about the kidnappers, Johnson hopes.

"We do have some nice hair and fiber samples," he says. "We ever get anything to compare against."

Rosie Garrity is at home that evening when the local news comes on at six P.M. Her husband, George, is a waiter at the Unicorn Restaurant up in Sarasota, and he's already left for work, so she's alone, sitting in the genuine-leather recliner/easy chair he bought for her at Peterby's Furniture on the Trail.

The television news anchor is a man named Taylor Thompson, handsome as homemade sin, with a voice as deep as an Everglades swamp. He is giving them the headlines of the stories he will discuss at greater length later. Rosie likes Taylor Thompson even better than she likes Tom Brokaw.

". . . raging out of control in downtown Fort Myers," Taylor is saying. "A pair of housewives foil a holdup attempt in a Sanibel supermarket. And in Cape October . . ."

Rosie leans forward in her recliner.

". . . a cat in a jacaranda tree is rescued by heroic firemen. This is Taylor Thompson, back to you in a moment with all the news in the Fort Myers area."

"Not a word about those poor little darlins," Rosie says aloud.

• • •

More and more, Alice is beginning to believe that the two women who kidnapped her children are lunatics. They *have* their goddamn money, why haven't they called yet?

"And what is it Ashley couldn't believe?" she asks Charlie, as though he's been reading her thoughts. "That they were even letting her *talk* to me?"

She is pacing the room. The steady ticking of the grandfather clock is a constant reminder that they still haven't called.

"Were they treating her so badly that just allowing her to talk to her own *mother* . . ."

"Don't go there, Al," Charlie warns.

"She sounded so *amazed,* Charlie! 'Mom, I can't believe it!'"

In her mind, she goes over the entire conversation yet another time.

Tell her you and your brother are okay, that's all. Nothing else. Here.

We're both okay. Mom, I can't believe it!

What *can't . . . ?*

Do you remember Mari—?

And she was cut off.

So . . . well, of course . . . she'd been about to say "Maria." And that had to be Maria Gonzalez. What other Maria could it possibly be? Alice doesn't *know* anyone else named Maria. Or even Marie. So, yes, the black woman grabbed the phone because she didn't want Ashley saying Maria's name.

But what is it that Ashley found so goddamn unbelievable?

Maria surfacing again after almost two years, *more* than two years, however long it was? Maria returning to *kidnap* her?

Well, yes, that's unbelievable.

To Alice, it is *utterly* unbelievable that this mild-mannered, soft-spoken, chubby little girl who still spoke English with a Spanish accent would come to kidnap her children all this time after she'd babysat them, that is totally and completely unbelievable to Alice—but apparently not to Captain Steele, who has sent his Keystone Kops chasing after her.

We're both okay. Mom, I can't believe it!

And then, immediately: *Do you remember Mari—?*

Even before Alice completed her sentence, even before she possibly could have known that Alice was about to ask "*What* can't you believe, honey?"

Do you remember Mari—?

And silence.

A dead line.

"Something's missing," she tells Charlie.

And the phone rings.

It is ten minutes past seven.

Charlie immediately puts on the earphones.

"Hello?" Alice says.

"Mrs. Glendenning?"

A male voice. No one she's ever heard before.

"Yes?" she says.

Her heart is suddenly beating faster. Is this another accomplice? The blonde, the black woman, and now . . .

"This is Rick Chaffee, night editor at the Cape October *Tribune*?"

"Yes?"

"I hope I'm not—"

"What is it?" Alice says.

"We got a call from some woman . . . we get many such calls, Mrs. Glendenning, especially since Iraqi Freedom. You have no idea how many people see anthrax bubbling in their toilet bowls, or hear bombs ticking in their closet . . ."

Charlie is already shaking his head in warning.

"But this woman—"

"What woman?" Alice asks.

"Woman named Rose Garrity, does that name mean anything to you?"

"Yes?"

"Said she's your housekeeper, is that correct?"

"What's this about, Mr. . . . Jaffe, did you say?"

"Chaffee. C-H. *Is* she your housekeeper, ma'am?"

Charlie is shaking his head again.

"Yes, she is," Alice says.

"Well, ma'am, she called here some ten minutes ago to say she informed the police and then the FBI that your children were—"

"No," Alice says.

"—kidnapped the other day . . ."

"No, that isn't true."

"It isn't, huh?"

"It isn't."

"Claims there's been no action from either the local police or the—"

"Perhaps that's because nothing's happened here. Mrs. Garrity is mistaken."

"She seemed pretty sure some black woman—"

"I just told you she's wrong," Alice says, and slams the receiver down onto its cradle. She picks it up again at once, begins dialing a number by heart. Her eyes are blazing.

"Hello?"

"Are you trying to get my kids killed?" she yells into the phone.

"Mrs. Glen—?"

"Stay away from this, do you hear me?"

"I'm so worried about them . . ."

"Shut up!" Alice yells.

The line goes silent.

"Do you *hear* me, Rosie?"

"I was only trying to—"

"*No!* Don't try to help, don't try to do anything at all. Just keep your damn nose *out* of it!" she yells, and slams the receiver down again.

"Wow," Charlie says.

"Yeah, wow," Alice says.

But she knows the damage has already been done.

7

The three men meet in a roadside joint that calls itself the Redbird Café. Not far from the Fort Myers airport, the Redbird is a shack adjacent to a gasoline station, open only for breakfast and lunch on weekdays, but also for dinner on weekends. This is now seven-thirty on a Friday night, and the three men are eating dinner.

Rafe has ordered the broiled catfish dinner with green beans and fries. The other two men are eating fried pork chops with mashed potatoes and the green beans. All three men are drinking coffee. They're dressed casually, these three, Rafe wearing the blue jeans and denim shirt he always wears when he's driving, the other two also wearing jeans and what look like Western shirts with those little darts over the pockets. The two men are wearing boots. Rafe is wearing loafers, which are easy to drive in. His rig is parked outside, alongside the Plymouth both the other men arrived in.

All three men did time at Rogers State Prison in Reidsville for violation of Code 16-13-30 of the Georgia State Statutes. That's where they met, each serving what the three of them called "bullshit narcotics violations." The prison facility was a small one, housing only twelve-hundred-some-odd inmates, some of them pretty odd, as the old joke went. It was easy for the men to make each other's acquaintance in the yard, especially since their so-called crimes were similar in nature.

The Redbird is almost empty at this hour, but the men are speaking softly, anyway. Hell, they're discussing big bucks here. It makes them feel important to be discussing $250,000 in hundred-dollar bills, even if the bills are counterfeit, even if their voices are low.

"Super-bills, huh?" Danny Lowell says.

"Is what the cops called them."

"You ever hear of super-bills, Jimbo?"

"Never in my life."

"So good you can't tell 'em from the real thing," Rafe says, and picks up some fries with his fingers and shovels them into his mouth.

"Is what your sister-in-law said, right?"

"Is what the *cops* said."

"Two-fifty large, right?"

"Is how much they turned over to this black chick."

"What makes me nervous," Jimmy Coombes says, "is there's a kidnapping involved here. I don't know what the law is here in Florida, but back home, you do a kidnapping, you're looking at the 'Seven Deadly Sins,' man. That means life without parole. I ain't eager to do that kind of time."

"I don't think it's the same in Florida," Rafe says. "Besides, we wouldn't be involved in no kidnapping."

"I tend to agree with James," Danny says. "We'd in effect be sharing in the proceeds of the crime, and that might be cause to link us to the crime as co-conspirators or whatever. If Florida has as tough a kidnapping law as Georgia, we could be looking at the long one, Rafe."

Jimmy hates it when Danny sounds like a fuckin jailhouse lawyer. He also hates to be called either James or Jimbo, when his fuckin name is Jimmy. At the same time, Danny is agreeing with him. They have to be careful here. Doing time for kidnapping ain't no walk in the park.

"There is no way we could be linked to the snatch," Rafe says. "We don't even know who these people *are*. How can we possibly get linked to a conspiracy?"

"Conspiracy to commit kidnapping," Danny says reasonably, and looks to Jimmy for confirmation.

"Which is another thing that bothers me," Jimmy says. "Our not knowing who they are."

"That's why we're here," Rafe says.

"Are your chops okay?" Jimmy says.

"Yeah, they're fine," Danny says. "Why?"

"Mine are a little overdone."

"They have to cook pork that way. Because of trichinosis," Danny says.

"They don't have to *burn* the fuckin things," Jimmy says.

"Mine are fine," Danny says, and shrugs.

"I got a cholesterol problem," Jimmy says, "I eat red meat—"

"Pork is white meat."

"Yeah, bullshit," Jimmy says. "I eat beef, pork, maybe once a month, twice if I wanna live real dangerously. So when I order pork chops, I don't expect to get burnt shoe leather. I mean, this is a *treat* for me, eating pork."

"So send them back if they're not the way you want them," Danny says.

"I'm almost finished with them already."

"Then finish them already."

"I'm just saying," Jimmy says, "this is supposed to be a fuckin *treat* here. Instead, they're burned to a crisp."

The men eat in silence for several moments.

"Also," Danny says, "there's more than one of them. That's what you said, right, Rafe?"

"Yeah, but one of them's a chick. Maybe both of them, for all I know," Rafe says. "Maybe these two chicks got it in their heads to steal my sister-in-law's kids. They know she's coming into big money . . ."

"You're sure about that, huh?"

"Positive. It's a double indemnity policy. It'll pay two-fifty."

"*When* it pays," Danny says.

"*If* it pays," Jimmy says.

"It'll pay," Rafe assures them. "Besides, who cares about the policy? We're talking about the *fake* money here. We're talking about two-fifty large *already* in the hands of whoever's got the kids. We're talking about *retrieving* that money."

"Who we don't even know who they are," Danny says.

"Miss?" Jimmy says, and raises his hand to the waitress. She signals that she hears him, finishes taking the order at a table across the room, and then comes over to them.

"Freshen it?" she asks.

"Please," Jimmy says. "Also, my chops were overdone."

"Gee, I'm sorry about that," she says.

She's maybe eighteen years old, little blonde girl in a yellow uniform, big tits and frizzy hair, Southern accent thick as molasses.

"You'da told me, I'da ast the chef to do them all over again," she says. "You want me to do that now?"

"No, that's okay," Jimmy says.

"Won't take a minute," she says.

"I'm fine, thanks," Jimmy says.

"Y'all want more coffee, too?" she asks the other two men.

They both nod. Danny, in fact, lifts his cup and puts it on her tray, smiling. He fancies himself a ladies' man even though he's ugly as homemade sin. That's another thing Jimmy doesn't like about him. His vanity. Vanity just ain't appropriate on a man. The waitress fills their cups, returns Danny's smile even though he's ugly, and leaves the table. Jimmy is having very serious doubts here about going into an enterprise with a man like Danny, who calls him Jimbo and James and who thinks he's handsome as hell when he ain't. Also, kidnapping is a serious offense.

"Also," he says, thinking out loud, "suppose there's *more* than just the two chicks? Or suppose it's just the black chick your sister-in-law knows about, plus some *guys,* let's say. Maybe some hardened *criminals,* let's say, and not some small-time drug shits like the three of us. We go after that money . . ."

"He's got a point, Rafe. We could be walking into a hornet's nest here."

"Or not," Rafe says. "Instead, we could be walking away with two hundred and fifty thou in bills that look so real you can lick them off the page."

"If it's true."

"It's what the cops said."

"Cops," Jimmy says.

"You trust what cops say?" Danny says.

"The bills *have* to look good," Rafe says. "You think they'd endanger those kids' lives? Come on, be reasonable."

"He's got a point, James," Danny says.

"So let's say, for the sake of argument," Jimmy says, "these bills *do* look like the real thing . . ."

"Exactly my point," Rafe says.

"And let's also say, for the sake of argument, that we manage to somehow get our hands on these bills . . ."

"And split them three ways, don't forget."

"What does that come to?" Danny asks.

"Eighty-three K for each of us."

"Comes to a big thousand bucks a year," Jimmy says.

"I don't follow."

"Assuming Florida's as tough on kidnapping—"

"We don't know that for sure."

"—and assuming I live to be eighty-three years old," Jimmy says.

"Behind bars," Danny says, nodding in agreement.

The table goes silent.

"So what are you saying here?" Rafe asks.

"I'm saying count me out," Jimmy says.

"Me, too," Danny says.

Rafe sits alone at the table long after his so-called friends have got into their car and driven off. Man, he thinks, you can't count on a fucking soul these days. Asshole buddies in the lockup—well, not literally—they get a taste of fresh air and then chicken out of the sweetest little setup anyone could ever want. Two-fifty large sitting out there someplace in the hands of two dizzy chicks, just waiting to be ripped off. Well, he can't do it alone, that's for sure, everybody needs their back covered, man.

He drinks a second cup of coffee, checks the cash Danny and Jimmy left on the table as their share of the bill and tip, adds his own share to it, and then calls the little blonde waitress over.

"S'pose I oughta get out of here, huh?" he says with a grin. "Before you start charging me rent."

"Oh, don't let that worry you none," she says. "We got plenty to do here 'fore we close."

"What time would that be?" he asks.

"We're usually out of here by ten."

The clock on the wall reads five minutes to nine.

"What do you do then?" he asks. "After you get out of here?"

She knows at once he's putting the moves on her. She takes a deep breath to fill out the uniform chest, rolls her big blue eyes, and says, "Well, usually, my boyfriend picks me up here."

"How about tonight? Is he picking you up tonight?"

"I reckon," she says, without a trace of regret. "Did you want me to take this now?" she asks, and lifts the plate with the cash and the bill on it.

"Sure," he says. "Thanks."

Her rejection annoys him even more than his so-called pals' did. Telling him, in effect, she prefers a pimply faced kid who probably slings burgers at McDonald's to a sophisticated thirty-five-year-old man who's been around the block a few times, sweetheart, and who can teach you some tricks you never learned here at the old Redbird Café. He's beginning to regret having left a fifteen percent tip on the plate. Ten percent would've been enough. More than she'd see down here in a week. Pay for a fuckin two-week vacation. He leaves the table before she comes back.

His rig is parked outside.

He settles himself in the cab, starts the engine, and then turns on the cell phone. Nothing he can do down here anymore, he might as well head back home. He dials his home number, lets it ring three times, and is surprised when a voice he doesn't recognize answers.

"Hello?"

"Who's this?" he asks.

"It's your nickel, mister," the woman says. "Who's *this*?"

"This is Rafe Matthews, and I *live* there, ma'am! Now who the hell . . . ?"

"Oh, golly, Mr. Matthews," the woman says, "I'm sorry, this is Hattie Randolph. I'm sittin your kids while your missus is gone."

"Gone? Gone where?"

"Down to Florida. To see her sister."

"Cape October?"

"I reckon, sir. She gave me the number there, if you'd like it."

"I have the number. When did she leave?"

"Early this afternoon. Said she should be there by tomorrow morning sometime."

"Okay," Rafe says.

He is already thinking.

"Did you want me to tell her anything? If she calls?"

"No, I'll get in touch with her myself, Hattie, thanks. How are the kids?"

"Fine. I just put them to bed."

"Well, give them a kiss for me in the morning, okay?"

"Yes, sir, I'll do that."

"Good night, Hattie."

"Good night, Mr. Matthews," she says.

He turns off the phone, and sits alone in the cab, in the dark, thinking. He doesn't like the idea that Carol just picked up and left for Florida without first consulting him about it. On the other hand, the fact that she's on the road and doesn't expect to get down here in Florida till tomorrow morning means that she'll be stopping at a motel to sleep over, which further means he's free as a bird till morning, when he'll give her a call to bawl her out.

Rafe doesn't realize this about himself, but his usual way of dealing with disappointment or frustration is to look for female companionship. His rejection by first his former jailhouse cronies and next the big-titted little blonde waitress might have remained just mere annoyance if Carol had been home where she was supposed to be. Instead, he calls and gets some black woman he never heard of, while his wife is driving alone in the dark and sleeping Christ knows where on the road, and this pisses him off further, this truly pisses him off mightily.

Suddenly—

Or at least he thinks it's suddenly.

He remembers the blonde who ran over Alice's foot.

He activates the phone again. Dials Information. Presses the SEND button.

"Cape October, Florida," he says.

"Yes, sir?"

"Jennifer Reddy," he says. "That's R-E-D-D-Y. I don't have an address."

He waits.

"I'm sorry, sir," the operator says. "I don't have a listing with that spelling."

"What *do* you have?" he asks, about to get angry all over again.

"I have a Ready-Quik Car Wash, and a Ready-Serv Rental . . ."

"No, this is a residential listing. And it's not Ready, it's Reddy. R-E-D-D-Y."

"Could it be *Redding,* sir? R-E-D-D-I-N-G? I have a J. Redding on Mangrove Lane. Could that be it?"

"It might," he says.

Redding, he thinks. Jennifer Redding.

"I'll try it for you, sir."

He hears the operator dialing. Hears the phone ringing on the other end.

"Hello?"

A woman's voice. A Jennifer Redding voice. Crisp and young and sensual.

"Miss Redding?" he says.

"Yes."

"This is Rafe Matthews?"

"Who?"

"I was at Alice Glendenning's house when you stopped by yesterday."

"Alice . . . ? Oh. Yes."

There is a silence on the line.

"So . . . uh . . . what is it?" Jennifer asks.

"I happened to notice you. Through the drapes."

Another silence.

"I wouldn't intrude this way," he says, "but I know you're a friend of Alice's . . ."

"Well, actually, I ran her over," Jennifer says.

"Yes, so I understand."

"Is that what this is about?"

"No, no. Not at all."

"Then why . . . ?"

"Point is, I'm still in the neighborhood, more or less, and I was thinking you might like to meet me for a cup of coffee. Or something."

"What do you mean by 'more or less'?"

"Actually, I'm in Fort Myers. Near the airport here. Or we could meet for a drink. If you'd prefer a drink."

"Why should we meet at *all*?" Jennifer asks. "For *anything*?"

"Well, like I said, I happened to notice you through the drapes . . ."

"And so?"

And so I'd like to fuck your brains out, he thinks, but does not say.

"If you're busy," he says, "I'm sorry I bothered you."

"I'm not busy," she says. "And you're not bothering me. It's just . . . I don't know you at all."

"Well, that's the idea," he says.

This is getting too difficult, he thinks. Fuck it. I'll go back inside and hit on the waitress again.

"Get to know each other a little better," he says.

"Well, now, why would I want to do that?"

It suddenly occurs to him that she may be flirting.

"Friend of Alice's and all," he says.

"I told you," she says. "All I did was run over her foot."

"Glad it wasn't *my* foot," he says.

She laughs.

"I'll bet," she says.

"So what do you think?" he asks. "Coffee? A drink? Or get lost?"

She laughs again.

"Can you be at the Hyatt by ten?" she asks.

"I'm not dressed for the Hyatt," he says.

"What are you wearing?"

"I'm driving a rig. I've got on jeans and a denim shirt."

"Casual, huh?"

"And loafers," he says.

"Okay, drive out to the end of Willard Key. There's a place out there on the water, it's called Ronnie's Lounge, which sounds gay but it isn't. You're not, are you?"

"No, ma'am, I am not."

"Who shall I look for?"

"Big handsome guy in jeans and a denim shirt."

"Modest, too," she says.

But she laughs again.

"Ten o'clock," he says.

"See you," she says, and hangs up.

Hot *damn*! he thinks.

Actually, Rafe has done this sort of thing many times before. The trick is to make it look as if he's never done it before. In the past, he's never blatantly flashed his wedding band—nor is he doing that tonight—but if the subject happened to come up, he never denied he was married, either. The way the conversation is going here in

Ronnie's Lounge, it looks as if the subject might come up any minute now.

Jennifer Redding is wearing a little black fuck-me dress that's cut high on the thigh and low over what Rafe considers an exuberant set of lungs. She is wearing strappy black sandals with a stiletto heel, and her legs are crossed, and she is jiggling one foot, which always makes him think a woman is about to come. She looks overdressed for the kind of place this is—especially after he told her on the phone he was in denim and jeans—but she doesn't seem uncomfortable here. In fact, some of the other women draped here and there around what is essentially a wooden shack hung with fishing nets and buoys are also dressed to the nines whereas the guys look like they just got off either a boat or a horse.

Jennifer is drinking a Cosmopolitan, which he never heard of before tonight, and which she earlier explained is a cocktail composed of four parts vodka, two parts Cointreau, one part lime juice, two parts cranberry juice, a dash of orange bitters, and an orange twist.

"You're supposed to set fire to the oil from the orange peel before you drop it in the glass, but I never saw any bartender down here do that," she told him.

But now the conversation has moved toward more basic matters, as for example how he happens to know Alice Glendenning. This is the moment of truth.

Rafe lifts his glass. He is drinking Wild Turkey bourbon on the rocks. He takes a sip, puts the glass down again. Looks across the table at her.

"She's my sister-in-law," he says.

Jennifer doesn't seem at all surprised.

"I knew that," she says. "I was testing you."

"Did I pass the test?" he says.

"Is she your brother's wife?"

"No. My wife's sister."

"Ah," Jennifer says.

"Yeah," he says, and lifts the glass again, and takes another sip.

"So what are you doing here with me?" she asks.

"I told you. I thought we might get to know each other better."

"The way you know your wife's sister better?"

"No, no. Hey, *no*! Definitely not. There's nothing going on between me and Alice."

"Then what were you doing there yesterday?"

"I happened to be in the neighborhood, so I stopped by to see her. She's my *sister*-in-law, for Christ's sake!"

"Okay," Jennifer says, and nods again.

She sips at the Cosmopolitan. He sips at the bourbon. The table is silent for several moments. Somewhere across the room, the jukebox is playing some kind of country-western song about a guy leaving home in his pickup truck with his hound dog.

"So what are we supposed to do now?" she asks. "You being married and all?"

"That's entirely up to you," Rafe says.

"I'm not the one who's married," she says. "Being married is your problem, not mine."

"I don't see it as a problem. How do you see it as a problem?"

"Well, gee, let me think," Jennifer says. "Being married means there's a *wife* someplace, right?"

"Yeah, but not here," Rafe says.

"Then where?"

"Right now, I guess she's in a motel somewhere on the interstate."

Jennifer looks at him, puzzled.

"Driving down from Atlanta to see her sister," Rafe explains. "Won't be here till tomorrow morning sometime."

"Which means you're alone for the night, is that it?"

"It would appear so, yes," Rafe says.

"Is this what you do all the time? While your wife's on the interstate?"

"First time," he says.

"I'll bet."

Jennifer nods again, thinking it over. She is still jiggling her foot.

Rafe moves his glass around on the tabletop, making wet rings. He is sure her shoe will fall off.

"So what do you think?" he asks.

"I think I'd like another Cosmo," she says.

Alice has just brought a pillow and a blanket into the living room when car headlights splash across the drawn blinds. Both she and Charlie turn at once toward the windows. Outside, they hear a car engine quitting. A car door slamming. Moments later, the front doorbell rings.

The grandfather clock reads 10:45 P.M.

"I'll get it," Charlie says, and motions for Alice to move back. She steps away from the door. Charlie glances over his shoulder to make certain she cannot be seen from the outside, and then he says to the closed door, "Who is it?"

"Dustin Garcia," a man's voice says.

"Who's Dustin Garcia?"

"Cape October *Trib.* Could you open the door, sir?"

"Send him away," Alice whispers.

"Only make it worse," Charlie says, and motions again for her to stay out of sight. He unlocks the door, opens it, peers out through the mesh of the screen door. Bugs are clattering around the porch light.

The man standing there is short and slight. He is wearing a tan suit with a dark brown sports shirt, no tie. He is also wearing a brown snap-brim straw hat and brown shoes. He holds up a card with his photo on it and the word PRESS in green across its face.

"Sorry to bother you this time of night," he says. "My editor says he talked to you earlier . . ."

"Yes, what is it?" Charlie says.

"Rick Chaffee, do you remember him calling?"

"Yes, I remember."

"You are, sir?"

"Charlie Hobbs."

"Nose for news, Rick has," Garcia says. "He thought I ought to stop by and talk to you."

"Is that what he thought?"

"Yes, sir. All right for me to come in?"

"Sorry," Charlie says. "No."

"Awfully buggy out here."

"Then go back to your car," Charlie says. "Bet it's not buggy there."

"Rick seems to think somebody's been kidnapped here."

"Rick's wrong."

"Two little kids, Rick seems to think."

"Look, Mr. Garcia, it's late . . ."

"I'd like to come in and talk to Mrs. Glendenning."

"She's asleep."

"Do you live here, sir?"

"No, I don't."

"Where are the Glendenning children, Mr. Hobbs?"

"Asleep. Where are *your* children this time of night?"

"I don't have any children."

"I don't, either," Charlie says. "Mr. Garcia, it was nice of you to stop by, but nothing's happened here, and you're wasting your time."

"Then let me talk to the kids."

"No."

"I'll talk to someone at Pratt first thing tomorrow morning, you know," Garcia says. "That's where they go to school, isn't it?"

"School's closed tomorrow," Charlie says.

"I'll find somebody."

"Good night, Mr. Garcia," Charlie says, and closes and locks the door.

Rafe realizes that it might not be provident to ask a lady if she'd mind your parking a truck and trailer weighing some forty thousand pounds empty in front of her house overnight. He suggests that she follow him to a truck stop he knows near the airport—which is a good half hour away from Ronnie's Lounge out on Willard—and she tells him to go park the truck there all by himself, thanks, and then catch a cab to her house if he's still interested. He does not get to Mangrove Lane until eleven-thirty.

The only light burning in any of the houses on the street is a little blue one in the house next door to hers. Someone watching television. Otherwise the street is dark. He pays and tips the cabby, goes to the front door, and rings the bell. Jennifer answers it a moment later.

She is wearing red silk lounging pajamas, a black silk robe, and the same strappy black sandals she had on earlier tonight.

"Thought you'd never get here," she says.

"The last flight came in from Tampa at nine," he says. "Not a taxi in sight. I had to phone for one."

"But you're here," she says.

"It would appear so, yes."

"That's a verbal tic," she says.

"What's a verbal tic?"

He doesn't know what a verbal tic is. But she thinks he's asking her to clarify exactly which words constitute the verbal tic, whatever it may be.

"Saying 'It would appear so, yes.' You said the same thing when I asked if you were alone for the night."

"Then it must be true," he says. "I am in fact alone for the night, and I am also in fact here."

"While your wife is in a motel on the interstate."

"That's where I guess she is."

"What does she look like, your wife?"

"She's about five-six, and she has brown hair and blue eyes."

"But you prefer blondes, is that it?"

"I prefer blondes who look like you," he says.

"Do you have any children?"

"Two."

"You should be ashamed of yourself, fucking around this way."

"Well," he says, "so far I'm not doing much fucking around, am I?"

Jennifer laughs. Her laugh is raw and sexy. He hopes this doesn't turn out to be a false alarm here, because he's already getting hard in his jeans and he doesn't want to have to call another cab.

"Would you like a drink?" she asks.

"I think I've had enough to drink."

"I'm going to have another drink," she says, and crosses the living room to where the drop-leaf front of a wall unit is hanging open. The black silk robe flutters about her like the wings of a butterfly. He wonders if she's wearing anything under those red silk lounging pajamas. He's never seen Carol in lounging pajamas. Do women wear anything under lounging pajamas? He sure as hell hopes she doesn't turn out to be a cock tease.

"Sure?" she says, and turns from the bar to hold up a glass.

"Positive," he says.

She shrugs, pours vodka for herself into a short fat glass, and screws the cap back onto the bottle. Leaving the glass on the open bar top, she moves to the audio equipment in the wall unit, slides a couple of CDs into the player, and presses a button. A female singer whose voice he can't recognize begins singing a bluesy number. Jennifer picks up her glass and dances over to him, arms wide, robe fluttering, floating again to where he is still standing across the room. She takes a swallow of her drink, looks at him over the rim of the glass, smiles, and kisses him on the mouth. She pulls away just as he starts getting hungry.

"How do I know you're not fucking Alice?" she asks.

"Nobody's fucking Alice," he says. "Her husband drowned eight months ago. She's still grieving."

"Did you try?"

"I knew better," he says.

"How come you didn't know better with me?"

"Did your husband drown?"

"I don't have a husband."

"Then let's go to bed," he says.

"No, let's dance," she says, and sips at the drink again, and goes into his arms.

They move about the floor slowly. His hand slides from the small of her back to the swell of her ass under the silk garments. She backs away from him, raises her eyebrows like a virgin, and then moves out of his arms completely to sip at her drink again. Her nipples are puckered under the silk. Jesus, he thinks, please don't let this be a false alarm.

"What time will your wife be getting down here tomorrow?" she asks.

Back to the wife again.

"Around breakfast time, I'd guess."

Is she building up to kicking him out of here? Once, in St. Louis, he made the mistake of hitting on a flight attendant staying at the same Holiday Inn he was, but it turned out she was a friend of the flight attendant he'd fucked two weeks earlier. Gave her the same line. Only she *knew* the line already because her friend had told her all about him. So she let him buy her dinner and walk her back to her room, even invited him in for a drink, where he kept giving her the same jive he'd given Gwen—that was the first girl's name—two weeks earlier. She finally told him he should change his line at least as often as he changed his underwear, and showed him the door. Couldn't even remember her name now, the bitch, but was this the same thing here? Was Jennifer getting him all hot and bothered only to turn him out into the night?

"Aren't you afraid she might see your truck where you parked it?"

"She won't be going near the airport. Anyway, what I do is my business."

"Oh? Is that right? Have you got some kind of arrangement or something?"

"No, but I'm my own man."

"Oooo, big macho man," she says.

"Look," he says, "if you're not—"

"Be still," she says.

"I mean, I'm married, okay? If that—"

"I said be still."

She moves away from him, glides to the bar, sets her empty glass down in front of the bottles arrayed there, and then lifts the folding top, closing the bar. As she turns back to him, she lets the black silk robe slide from her shoulders. And then she is fiddling with the silken cord at her waist, loosening it, untying it, allowing the pajama bottoms to slide down over her thighs and her knees, bunching at her ankles, stepping out of them in her high heels and taking a stride toward him, the palms of her hands flat on her naked thighs now.

Her pubic hair is black.

"Are you sure you prefer blondes?" she asks, and when he doesn't answer, she says, "Why don't you just come on over here and eat me, hmm?"

Saturday
May 15

8

By midnight, they have already fucked once and are lying naked on Jennifer's king-sized bed in a bedroom overlooking a small lagoon in her backyard, getting ready to have another go at it, from the look of things. Rafe feels no guilt whatever; he has done this many times before, with many different women. In fact, he feels exhilarated. She is more spectacularly beautiful than he could have prayed for, lying beside him now with her Miss Clairol Blondest Gold hair spread on the pillow, her legs spread below where her unbleached coal-black hair tufts in crisp anticipation, one hand lying palm up on the pillow above her head, the other hand already stroking his cock again.

The combination of black and blond is somehow very exciting. My head may be fake, it seems to declare, but, baby, what you get down here is the real thing. Moreover, his being able to *witness* the disparity brings a sense of greater intimacy to their nakedness. Here I am, her bush is saying, this is what I'm really like, and you alone are privileged to see it. Me alone, and ten thousand other guys, Rafe thinks, but he's not one to look a gift horse in the mouth or any other open orifice.

What she's doing now is positioning herself so that she can maneuver the head of his cock against her nether lips. She does this with total disregard for his own needs or desires. It is as if his cock isn't even attached to him. She uses it like a dildo, pushing the head this way and that until she finds her clitoris and then rubbing herself against it gently at first and then more vigorously and then straddling him completely and sliding herself onto him, wet and open and savage and totally absorbed with pleasuring herself alone. She seats herself firmly and deeply, grabbing her breasts in both hands, working the nipples with thumbs and forefingers, head thrown back, blonde hair above, black below, it is almost like having two women in bed with him.

She keeps him deep inside her, insistently moving her clitoris against his shaft, locked onto his cock, lost in herself, tossing her head, murmuring cunt and fuck and cock and yes and do it and fuck me, and then pulling herself back just on the edge of orgasm, and gliding up to the head of his cock again, almost losing it, capturing it again at the very last moment, and then sliding down deep again, repeating the action, over and over again and again and again, his hands clutching her ass, yes, fuck me, she says, and then screams aloud and hangs above him in agonizing orgasm and flings herself onto him, breasts crushed against his chest, mouth seeking his, tongue lashing, oh jesus, she murmurs, oh jesus.

This is what's nice about fucking a stranger, Rafe thinks.

She doesn't bring up the wife again until half an hour later. They always bring up the wife after they've been royally fucked, Rafe thinks. Never miss an opportunity to bring up the wife. It's like they're thinking, Well, you son of a bitch, now that you've had your way with me, let's discuss this small matter of the little woman back home. They never put it quite that way, of course, he has never met a woman that stupid. Actually, there's no woman on earth who will ever say exactly what she means. With women, you've always got to decode what they're saying. If a woman says, "Do you think Hawaii is really as nice as they say it is?" what she really means is "I've booked a room for two weeks at the Royal Tahitian." That is the way women talk. The only time women talk straight is when they're fucking. But that's not the woman talking, it's the cunt. The cunt is saying fuck me, not the woman.

That was half an hour ago.

Now it's the woman talking.

"So tell me," Jennifer says, "is Atlanta a nice place to live?"

Meaning, "So tell me about this goddamn wife of yours in Atlanta."

"It's okay, I guess," he says.

"Did you ever live anyplace else?"

He almost tells her he spent a year and four months in Reidsville, Georgia, at the correctional facility there.

Instead, he says, "Born and raised there."

"Your wife, too?"

Here it comes, he thinks.

"No, she's originally from Peekskill. That's upstate New York."

"So how'd she end up in Atlanta?"

Meaning "So how did you meet this fucking wife of yours?"

"She was going to college in Athens. University of Georgia. That's about sixty miles northeast of Atlanta."

"So what'd you do? Meet at a prom or something?"

"No, my sister was going to school there, too."

"Ah."

"Yeah."

She nods. She is sitting beside him on the bed, cross-legged, still naked. Her lips are only a trifle pursed. She is thinking this over. About to get pissed off that she went to bed with a married man. And enjoyed it. All of this is beginning to eat at her.

"You are so beautiful," he says.

Rescue operation.

"Mmm," she says, and nods again, and pulls a little face.

He is about to get kicked out of here in the middle of the night unless he says something very smart very soon. He knows she won't believe him if he tells her he doesn't love his wife, which isn't true, anyway, or at least he doesn't think it's true. He has been to bed with a lot of different women since he met Carol, but never once has he ever stopped loving her, he supposes, although he has to admit that never once has he ever felt like this in bed with another woman. Just lying here beside Jennifer, he is beginning to get hard again. And this is without touching her again or anything, this is just remembering what happened half an hour ago, thirty-five minutes ago. He wonders if he should call her attention to the fact that he is getting hard again, give a wink in the direction of old Willie there, who has a mind of his own, and who certainly isn't thinking about Carol in a motel someplace on I-495.

"Let me tell you something," he says.

"Sure, tell me something," she says.

Meaning, "But make it fast because you're going to be out of here in ten minutes flat."

"The minute I saw you . . ."

She is already rolling her eyes in disbelief.

". . . I knew you were going to mean more to me than any woman I'd ever met in my life."

Meaning what? he wonders.

She seems to be wondering the same thing. A moment ago she was turned slightly away from him, sitting there like a doubting Indian maiden with a black bush but incongruous blue eyes and blonde hair, legs crossed at the ankles, head erect and staring straight ahead, hands palm up in her lap, but now she turns her head to him and looks him directly in the eyes, wanting to know—though not asking—what he means by what he just said. Is this some bullshit line he gives to small-town girls all over the south and southwest? What exactly does he mean when he says she will mean more to him than any other woman he's ever met, or words to that effect?

"That's why I called you," he says. "I couldn't let you just walk out of my life," he says. "I had to see you again, Jennifer. And as it turns out, I was right, wasn't I?" he asks rhetorically. "I have never in my life felt this way with another woman."

Meaning exactly *what*? her eyes are still asking.

"I mean *about* someone," he says. "I've never felt this way *about* another woman," he says. "The way I feel about *you,*" he says.

"And how exactly is it that you feel?" she asks.

She almost sounds prim. Almost sounds like a schoolteacher. He wonders if she's a schoolteacher. He realizes that he knows hardly anything at all about her, and here he is telling her he's never felt this way about another woman, whereas even he himself doesn't know what the hell that means. But she's waiting for an answer.

He is tempted merely to nod at old Willie down there, who is now standing erect after merely hearing Rafe's feeble attempt at describing how he feels, present the evidence of a rock-hard cock to the court not forty minutes after he and Jennifer fucked for the second time, I mean what does *that* have to say about how a man feels about a woman, huh, Jennifer?

"Does anyone call you Jenny?" he asks, and places the tip of his forefinger on one rounded knee.

"No," she says, and brushes his hand aside.

"Jenny," he says, "I feel as if—"

"Don't call me Jenny," she says. "My name is Jennifer."

"I'm sorry, Jennifer," he says.

"Yes," she says, and nods.

"What do you want me to say?" he asks.

"You're the one doing the talking."

"I'm married," he says, "I'm sorry about that. I didn't expect to meet you, I didn't expect to fall in love with you, I'm sorry all to hell, but these things—"

"You *what*?" she says.

He blinks at her. What was it he just said?

She seems to notice his cock. At last. She glances at it slyly, but does not reach to touch it.

"Say it again," she says.

"I've never felt this way before in my life," he says.

"That's not what you said."

"What did I say?"

"You said you didn't expect to fall in love with me."

"That's true, I didn't."

"Say it again."

"I didn't expect to fall in love with you."
"*Are* you in love with me?"
"I think I'm in love with you, yes."
"Think?" she says, and seizes his cock.
"I'm in love with you, yes," he says.
"Say it."
"I love you."
"Say 'I love you, Jennifer.'"
"I love you, Jennifer."
"Say it again."
"I love you, Jennifer."
"Again."
"I love you, Jennifer. I—"
"What about your wife?"
"Fuck her," he says.
"Fuck me instead," she says, and rolls onto him.

Afterward, he begins to learn a little bit about her. She's been divorced for a year and a half, she tells him, used to be married to a lawyer who still practices in Sarasota. Was married for three years before she discovered he was playing around with this redhead in his office, another lawyer, who wore minis shorter than Ally McBeal ever did.

"Which is one of the reasons I didn't want to start up with you," she says.

"Because I'm a redhead?" he asks, which he isn't. "Or because I wear minis?"

"Because you're a married man who plays around," she says.
"All married men play around."
"You'd better not ever cheat on *me,*" she says.
"We're not married," he says.
"But you love me, right?" she says.
"It would appear so, yes."
"There's that tic again."

"I love you, yes," he says.

He's beginning to believe it himself.

She tells him that she's been working in a jewelry boutique out on Willard, which is how she happens to know Ronnie's Lounge, but that she's been thinking of maybe starting her own business, if she can get her wonderful ex to make his damn alimony payments when he's supposed to . . .

"I'm supposed to get a thousand dollars a month, but he's always late with his check," she says.

"Yeah," Rafe says.

He's thinking the one thing he doesn't need in his life is paying alimony to an ex-wife, no matter how much you love another woman, *if* in fact you do love her, now that Willie has shrunken back into his shell again. She does indeed have a splendid rack, though, and a lovely ass, and he can't get over the blonde hair and black bush, which he still thinks is entirely trusting of her to expose herself that way. He is beginning to think he's never been quite this intimate with another woman in his life, which is perhaps what he meant when he said he'd never felt this way about another woman, which maybe is being in love, after all. He is beginning to get a little confused.

"Did you ever go to bed with Alice?" she asks out of the blue.

This is now three o'clock in the morning. Around three in the morning, they all ask you out of the blue to start cataloging all the women you've ever slept with. He's almost forgotten this about women. You have to know this about women if you ever hope to survive. He's glad he's remembering it now. Before it's too late. Too late for what? he wonders. And feels confused again.

"No, hey," he says, "what kind of a bounder do you take me for?"

"Bounder, huh?" she says, and giggles.

It pleases him that he can make a beautiful woman like this one giggle. Not that Carol isn't beautiful. It's just that she doesn't giggle much, anymore. Well, two growing boys, who would giggle anymore?

"A bounder and a rounder, too," he says, pressing his luck, and damn if she doesn't giggle again. "But I would never hit on my own sister-in-law."

"Then what was your truck doing parked outside her house?" she asks.

"I told you. I stopped by to see her. I do that all the time. She's my sister-in-law!"

"Then why wouldn't she let me in?"

"Because . . ."

"Because the two of you were alone in there. And if I know you . . ."

"No, no, we weren't alone."

"Then who was there?"

"The police."

"The police? Why?"

So he has to explain that his little niece and nephew were kidnapped . . .

"Get out!"

. . . and that the people who kidnapped them asked for two hundred and fifty thousand dollars in hundred-dollar bills, which the police supplied for Alice to drop off Friday morning . . .

"That poor woman!" Jennifer says.

"Yeah, and she *still* hasn't got the kids back," Rafe says.

"What do you mean the police supplied it? Where'd *they* get that kind of money?"

So he has to explain that the Treasury Department supplied the bills for another kidnapping down here a couple of years ago, and that the bills were these counterfeits called super-bills . . .

"Get out!" she says again.

. . . which are so good it's impossible to tell them from the real thing.

"Which is what I tried to explain to these former business associates of mine," Rafe says, "but they wouldn't buy into it."

"Wouldn't buy into what?"

"Well, these people are criminals, am I right?" Rafe says. "The ones who kidnapped Alice's kids?"

"So?"

"So what harm would it do if someone *took* that money from them? I mean, they're *criminals,* am I right? Serve them right, am I right?"

"I'm still not following."

"And also, the money is fake besides."

She shakes her head, totally bewildered.

"What we've got," he explains, "is a pair of chicks sitting out there on two hundred and fifty grand in fake money so good you can't tell it from the real thing. So what if some enterprising souls *relieved* them of that money? It's fake, anyway, am I right? And they're criminals in the bargain. So where's the harm?"

"Two chicks, huh?" Jennifer asks.

"It would appear so, yes."

"All we have to do is find them," she says.

"That's all, baby," he says.

For some reason, he's getting hard again.

Alice's phone rings at 8:45 A.M.

Charlie is still asleep on the living room sofa. She grabs for the receiver at once.

"Hello?"

"Alice, it's Frank. How are you?"

Her boss at Lane Realty.

"Fine, Frank."

"How's your foot?"

"Okay."

"Are you able to get around?"

"Pretty much so."

"Do you think you'll be coming in today?"

"I don't think so."

"Still in pain, are you?"

"No, Frank, it's just . . . the foot's in a cast, you know . . ."

"Yes, so I understand."

". . . and it's a little clumsy driving. Maybe Aggie can handle any appointments I have for today . . ."

"Is that what you'd like me to do?"

"Yes, Frank."

"Give these various listings to Aggie?"

"I'm sure she can handle them."

"When do you think you'll be coming back to work, Alice?"

"I'm not sure."

"Sundays are big, too."

"Yes, I know."

"O-kay, Alice," he says, and sighs heavily. "Let me know when you're ready to come back, will you?"

"I'll let you know, Frank."

"Thanks," he says. "Get better."

And hangs up.

They know the blue Impala was followed yesterday, but they do not yet know that Avis has given up the license plate number. Even so, they are reluctant to drive the car again, or even to leave it where they've parked it on the mainland. They check the Yellow Pages under CAR RENTAL AGENCIES, find the nearest location for a Hertz place, and call to reserve a car for Clara Washington. It is Christine who arrives at the Henderson Grove outlet in a taxi that morning.

She shows the clerk behind the counter the same fake driver's license, and charges the car rental to the same fake American Express card. The man from whom they purchased the credit card in New Orleans told them it was a "thirty-dayer," his exact words, meaning it would be good for thirty days before Amex recognized it as a phony. He assured them that the driver's license, however—which also cost them a sizable bundle—would never be challenged. Christine doesn't know that the FBI has already flagged both the license and the credit card. But in any event, the Hertz people say nothing about her credentials, and she drives off in a sporty new red Ford Taurus.

There have been a lot of bank holdups in the state of Florida during the past year or so, and a big sign at the entrance to Southwest Federal cautions all customers to remove hats, sunglasses, or kerchiefs before approaching any of the tellers' windows. Christine takes off her own sunglasses the moment she steps into the lobby. A uniformed guard at the door gives her the once-over, but she surmises he's scrutinizing her boobs rather than her potential as a bank robber.

She chooses a black teller, a woman like herself. HENRIETTA LEWIS, her little name plaque announces in white letters on black. Sometimes choosing a sister backfires. You get a black with attitude, she'll give another black more grief than any white person in the whole wide world. But this one greets Christine with a cheery smile.

Christine is carrying $5,000 in hundred-dollar bills, five of them in the bill compartment of her wallet. The cab driver who drove her to the Hertz place accepted one of those bills with a pained expression not half an hour ago, when he nonetheless made change for her. For his trouble, she gave him a big tip and a leg show as she got out of the taxi. She now removes three more of those bills from the wallet, slides them onto the marble counter, and says, "May I have these in tens and twenties, please."

Henrietta smiles, and picks up one of the bills.

She notices at once that this is not one of the new hundreds with the oversized picture of Benjamin Franklin on it. There are still many of these old hundreds in circulation; it will in fact take years before they're all replaced by the Federal Reserve. Henrietta checks these older bills more carefully than she does the Big Bens because she knows there are a lot of fakes out there. The American hundred-dollar bill is the most widely used piece of currency in the world, and hence the most counterfeited.

She holds it to the light to check the security strip along its edge, sees the repeated USA100USA100USA100USA100, picks up the second bill to perform the same check and then something catches her eye in the sequence of serial numbers, and she frowns slightly—which Christine catches even though it lasts for less than maybe five seconds.

"Excuse me one minute, miss, okay?" Henrietta says, and leaves the teller's window, and goes to where a bald-headed white man wearing a blue seersucker suit is sitting behind a desk near the vault. Christine sees her handing one of the bills across the desk to him. She wonders if she should run. The white man looks over to where she's standing. Henrietta is handing him the second bill now. Let's get out of here, Christine thinks. Just walk slowly to the door, smile at the uniformed guard there, go out to where she's parked the red Taurus, and split, sister!

The bald-headed manager, or whatever he is, gets up from his desk, smiles at Christine where she is still standing at the teller's window, and goes to a paneled walnut door. He disappears from sight behind it. Henrietta walks back to the teller's cage.

"Sorry, miss," she says, "but Mr. Parkins has to run those bills through the machine."

"What machine?" Christine asks.

"To verify them."

"Oh dear," Christine says. "Did someone pass me some fake money?"

"It happens," Henrietta says, and smiles. "These supers are hard to recognize with the naked eye. But the machine will tell us."

"Supers?"

"Super-bills. They're made in Iran on intaglio presses the U.S. sold to the old shah. They print the bills on German stock. They're really *very* good."

"I see," Christine says.

Her eyes are on that closed walnut door.

"But the Fed installed these machines in all our branches. Just like the ones they've got in D.C. I guess after 9/11, they're more worried about people using fake money to do mischief."

"I'll bet," Christine says.

"Did you read about all those bank accounts the terrorists had? Right here in Florida! Opened them with fake social security cards, can you imagine? You can buy all sorts of fake ID nowadays, no wonder there's so much trouble in the world. Ah, here he comes now."

Run, Christine thinks.

But something keeps her rooted to the spot.

The bald-headed man is smiling behind the bars of the teller's cage.

"Miss," he says, "I'm sorry, but these bills are counterfeit. We'll have to confiscate them."

"What does that mean?" Christine asks.

"By law, we're required to send them to the Federal Reserve in Washington. I'm sorry."

"Yes, but what do you mean, *confiscate*? Will I be out three hundred dollars?"

"I'm afraid so, miss. The bills are counterfeit."

"I guess I should've cashed them someplace that doesn't have a machine," Christine says, and pulls a face.

"I'm sorry, miss."

"I just don't see why I have to suffer for somebody else passing phony bills."

"I'm sorry, that's the law. We can't allow counterfeit currency to stay in circulation. I'm sorry."

"Well, I don't think it's fair," Christine says.

Her heart is pounding in her chest.

She turns away from the teller's cage, walks past the guard at the front door and the sign asking patrons to please not wear hats, kerchiefs, or sunglasses, puts on her sunglasses, and walks out to where she parked the Taurus.

What Henrietta and Mr. Parkins neglected to do this morning was check the Cape October police list of marked bills that was circulated to every bank and merchant in the state of Florida.

On that list were the hundred-dollar bills Christine just now tried to cash.

Luke Farraday is beginning to wonder why so many people are so suddenly interested in who picked up the Glendenning kids on Wednesday afternoon. The one here now is from the Cape October paper, on Luke's day off, no less, and he's given Luke some cock-and-bull story about one of the kids, he doesn't know which one, having a party, he doesn't know what kind of party, and wanting to put an announcement about it in the social calendar, but he needs to have a cute little story to go with it. He thinks the story about them getting picked up after school and their mother thinking they missed the bus might be just the sort of human interest thing that would tickle his paper's readers. Then again, Garcia looks like a Cuban to Luke, and maybe Cubans have different senses of humor than Americans have.

"What kind of car was it, would you remember?" Garcia asks.

It suddenly occurs to Luke that maybe there's a bit of change to be made here.

The job he holds at Pratt Elementary is what the Cape October Department of Education officially calls a School Loading Area Director, a Level-4 position that pays $8.50 an hour, not a hell of a lot more than he could earn at the local Mickey D's, if they were hiring anything but teenyboppers these days. Way Luke looks at it, the entire state of Florida is run by teenagers, if not the entire United States of America. So if there's a few extra bucks to be picked up here for providing information to a journalist, well, why not take advantage of the situation? There were women who'd been raped by Martians who sold their stories to the tabloids for thousands of dollars.

"Why's this of such importance to you?" he asks, and Garcia immediately recognizes that he's about to be hit up.

"Give the story some interest," he says.

"Get your facts right, you mean."

"Kind of car, all that."

"How much would your newspaper pay," Luke asks straight out, "to give the story some interest? Get the facts right?"

"Let's say that depends on the facts."

"How much do you usually pay for facts of this sort?"

"Twenty bucks? Thirty?"

"How about fifty?" Luke says.

"Fifty's cool."

"The kids were picked up by a blue Impala driven by a blonde woman," Luke says. "Avis sticker on the right rear bumper."

"Thanks," Garcia says.

In Cape October, because the police force is so small, the Radio Motor Patrol officers ride one to a car. The single officer in the car usually hangs his hat on the back rest of the passenger seat, so that it looks as if there are two cops patrolling instead of just one. Everybody in town knows there's just that one cop in the car, however, so the effect is somewhat diminished.

The RMP officer patrolling Charlie Sector of the Pecan Street Division hung his hat beside him when he started his tour of duty at 7:45 A.M. this morning, and it is still there at 9:15. Like Tom Hanks talking to the volleyball in *Cast Away,* Officer Searles has begun talking to his own hat of late, a good argument perhaps for putting a second officer in the cars. Searles considers this good police work, however. Talking things out loud, so to speak, checking out the scene with someone else, even if the someone else is only your own hat.

"Narrow it down to blue cars," he tells his hat. "No sense checking the tag on a red car, for example."

He is slowly cruising the parking lot of the Pecan Street Mall. The mall opened at nine, and there are already plenty of parked cars in the lot.

"Weekend shoppers," he tells his hat.

He is coming around the northern end of the long mall building, making a turn past the new Barnes & Noble that just came in last week, when he spots a pale blue four-door sedan parked some four ranks back from the front doors of the store.

"Hey!" he tells his hat. "A blue one! But is it a Chevy?"

The car is a Chevy.

It is, in fact, a four-door full-size sedan that Searles identifies at once as an Impala. On the right rear bumper there is a sticker that reads WE TRY HARDER. Searles takes out his pad, studies the notes he took this morning at roll call.

"We may have just won the lottery," he tells his hat.

He pulls up alongside the blue Impala, engages the parking brake of his own vehicle, leaves the engine idling, and gets out of the car. He bends over, takes a look through the left rear window of the Impala. Empty. He drapes a handkerchief over his right hand, tries the back door. Locked. He tries the front door on the driver's side. It opens to his touch. He leans into the car.

There is a red baseball cap on the backseat.

Christine is afraid to go tell him what happened.

Phony bills! Super-bills! What the hell is this, some kind of science fiction? Bills printed in Iran? He'll never believe her. He'll think she's trying to pull a fast one, he can be so damn suspicious sometimes.

She has stopped for breakfast in a diner on U.S. 41, not far from the bank where she tried to cash the counterfeit bills. Can you imagine them just taking the money from her like that?

We'll have to confiscate them.

What does that mean?

By law, we're required to send them to the Federal Reserve in Washington. I'm sorry.

Yes, but what do you mean, confiscate? *Will I be out three hundred dollars?*

I'm afraid so, miss. The bills are counterfeit.

I guess I should've cashed them someplace that doesn't have a machine.

She guesses she should've.

Fuckin thieves.

Worse than a stickup in a dark alley.

But what was she going to tell him?

Never mind being out three hundred dollars. If the bills are phony—well, they *have* to be phony, the bank has a damn machine! So, yes, let's say the bills are very definitely phony. Which means they are out not three *hundred* dollars but two hundred and fifty *thousand* dollars, which further means the whole damn scheme has gone up the chimney. Unless he can come up with another idea, he's never been short of ideas, it was his idea to do this thing in the first place.

She is afraid to go tell him.

"More coffee, miss?"

The waitress.

"No, thanks," she says. "Just a check, please."

What do we do now? she wonders.

Here we are with two hundred and fifty thousand dollars in perfectly fine-looking fake money we can wipe our asses with, and we've got two kids on our hands we won't know what to do with now that—

"Here you go, miss."

"Thank you," she says, and takes the check, studies it. Six dollars and twenty cents for an orange juice, a cup of coffee, and a toasted English. At least on the Cape, they didn't get you by the food. All they did was get you by the bills.

Smiling in spite of herself, she leaves a dollar tip on the table, and then walks to the cash register. She has a ten-dollar bill in her wallet, and she can just as easily pay for her breakfast with that. But suddenly . . .

I guess I should've cashed them someplace that doesn't have a machine.

. . . the thought comes to her.

She opens her wallet and takes out another of the hundred-dollar bills.

"I'm sorry," she tells the cashier. "I don't have anything smaller."

The cashier looks at the bill, snaps it sharply between both hands, the bill making a crisp little cracking sound, holds it up to the light to check the security strip, and then rings open her register and begins counting out change . . .

"Twenty-five, fifty, seven dollars," she says, placing the coins on the countertop. And then three singles, "Eight, nine, ten."

Watching her counting out more bills now.

"Twenty, forty, sixty, eighty, a hundred. Thank you, miss, have a nice day."

Christine picks up the cash.

"You, too," she says, and walks out of the restaurant and across the parking lot to where she left the red Taurus.

"Are you okay?" Charlie asks.

Alice looks at him across the breakfast table. It occurs to her that she has not sat at this table with anyone but her kids since Eddie's death.

"Yes," she says. "I'm okay, Charlie."

"We'll get them back, don't worry," he says.

There is something confident and comforting about his manner. It reminds her of Eddie's self-assurance when first they met. But Eddie was very young then, and Charlie, of course, is fifty-six, though there is about him the vigor of a much younger man. She finds this strength reassuring, and realizes all at once that if she were facing a dozen hungry lions, she would rather have Charlie at her side than a hundred Wilbur Sloates.

"Something?" he says, and smiles.

"No," she says, and returns the smile. "Nothing, Charlie."

He hears a sound outside, and turns toward the living room windows. A car is pulling into the driveway. Alice has begun dreading the appearance of anyone here at the house. Every new appearance seems to bring her children closer to greater peril. A car door slams. A moment later, the front doorbell rings.

"Want me to get it?" Charlie asks.

But she is already on her way. She looks through the peephole, and then immediately unlocks the door and throws her arms open wide. The sisters embrace. Carol looks up into her face.

"Hey, honey," she says.

"Hey," Alice says.

She leads Carol in, locks the door behind them. Charlie is standing now, a napkin in one hand.

"Charlie," she says, "this is my sister, Carol."

"Never would've guessed," Charlie says, and extends his free hand. "Damn if you don't look like twins."

"I'm a year older," Carol says.

"Have you had breakfast, hon?"

"Could eat a bear."

Alice goes to the stove, pours a cup of coffee for her sister, carries it to the table. She realizes she is smiling. For the first time since Wednesday afternoon, she is smiling. She cuts a few slices of rye bread, pops them into the microwave. Charlie is asking Carol how the trip down was. She's telling him there was a lot of traffic, but it was moving fast. Alice carries the bread, a slab of butter, and a jar of raspberry jam to the table. Carol digs in.

"So what's happening here?" she asks.

Alice suddenly hugs her close.

"Hey, what?" Carol asks. "What?"

Christine figures one of the malls is the best place to go. No need to go driving all over town, all the shops are in one location here. In a Barnes & Noble, she buys the two latest Nora Roberts novels, and pays for them with one of the hundred-dollar bills. The man behind the counter doesn't even bother to check the bill's security strip. He makes change for her, smiles, and looks up at the next customer in line.

At a Victoria's Secret, she buys two Balconette push-up bras at $19.99 each, one in the black hydrangea, the other in the cheetah print, and a pair of low-rise thongs, both in the leopard print at $5.99 each, and a black lace garter belt at $7.99, for a total of $59.95 before tax. She hands the salesperson a hundred-dollar bill and then wanders over to look at the sleepwear collection, choosing a red sequin-lace baby-doll nightgown and carrying it back to the cash register.

"Can you add this to the bill?" she asks, and the salesperson smiles and says, "Of course, miss," adding $29 to the earlier total, for a grand total of $88.95, plus tax, and then counts out the change without a whimper.

Christine wonders if it's time to press her luck.

Dustin Garcia is not a crime reporter as such, and he is not familiar with any of the cops downtown at the Public Safety Building. When he stops at the reception desk in the main lobby, he merely asks for the detective who's handling the Glendenning kidnapping, and waits while the uniformed officer behind the desk plugs into one of the extensions.

"Anyone up there handling a kidnapping?" the officer asks into the phone. He listens, looks across the desk at Garcia. "Who'd you say?" he asks.

"Glendenning. Alice Glendenning."

"I mean *you,*" the officer says. "Who're *you*?"

"Dustin Garcia, Cape October *Trib.*"

"Dustin Garcia," the officer says into the phone. "October *Trib.*" He listens again. "Third floor," he says, "Detective Sloate."

Just as Christine steps off the escalator on the second floor of the mall, she finds an electronics store selling Sony, Hitachi, Samsung, and Philips television sets. She does not know how far she should go here, how much she should risk to test her theory. The salesman is a guy in his sixties, she guesses, another one of the bored retirees down here. He tries at first to sell her a Philips 34-inch digital wide-screen, which, at $2,800, happens to be the most expensive set in the store. She is reluctant to go that high, not because she doesn't have that kind of money—she is still carrying almost five thou in hundreds in her bag—but only because she doesn't want any eyebrows raised.

The salesman figures she's a deadbeat, maybe because she's black, maybe because she's relatively young, who the hell knows or cares? He immediately switches to pitching the cheapest set he has in the store, a Samsung 27-inch that goes for $300.

"If you don't need top-shelf features like a flat screen or picture-in-picture," he says, "this little beauty'll give you good picture quality. And it has an excellent remote control, and V-chip parental control, do you have any children?"

Two, she almost says. Temporarily.

"I had something a bit more upscale in mind," she says.

"Then how about this?" he asks, brightening, and shows her a 32-inch Sony Trinitron Wega that he says is on sale for a mere $1,800.

"This model earned more votes than any other HD-ready model," he tells her. "It can auto-switch to enhanced mode when it detects wide-screen sources, and the pull-down circuitry improves the picture quality of film-based material."

"I'll take it," Christine says.

"It also comes in a thirty-six-inch version, on sale for $2,300," the salesman says.

"No, I'll take the thirty-two-inch," Christine says.

She digs into her handbag.

She guesses he thinks she's searching for a checkbook or a credit card. Instead, she comes up with a wad of hundred-dollar bills, and begins counting out $1,900.

"Will that be enough to cover the tax?" she asks.

"Florida sales tax is six percent," he says. "That comes to a hundred and eight dollars. I'd need another eight dollars from you."

She fishes a five and three singles from her wallet.

"I'll write this up and be back in a minute," he says, and walks to a door on the far wall, and enters what she assumes is someone's office, possibly a manager's. She waits with her heart in her throat. Are they checking the bills on a machine similar to the one the bank had? Will they discover the bills are counterfeit? Are they on the phone to the police this very moment?

She waits.

At last, the door opens, and the salesman comes out smiling.

"Here's your receipt," he says. "Someone's bringing a fresh set down now. Will you need help carrying it out to your car?"

• • •

"What can I do for you, Mr. Garcia?" Sloate asks.

They are in his third-floor office.

A red baseball cap sits on his desktop.

"Are you the man handling the kidnapping?" Garcia asks.

"What kidnapping is that?" Sloate asks.

Garcia knows at once that he is lying. Anglos lie to him a lot. That's because he looks like a Cuban. He has a dark complexion and straight black hair and the rednecks down here think of him as a Cuban-American even though he was born in this country, in this state, in fact. Which in his view makes him an American, right? An American who votes here, by the way, but not for Mr. Bush, thank you, and fuck little Elian Gonzalez, too. It's Garcia's *parents* who are so-called Cuban-Americans, which means they immigrated here from Cuba and became American citizens who also voted, but their votes for Bush outnumbered his vote for Gore by two to one, and besides the Supreme Court had the final say.

Sloate is lying to him, he knows that.

"The Glendenning children," he says. "The little boy and girl who were snatched from school on Wednesday."

"I'm sorry, I'm not familiar with that case," Sloate says.

"Then why'd you tell downstairs to send me up?"

"Courtesy to the press," Sloate says, and shrugs.

"Why are you stonewalling this?" Garcia asks.

"Mr. Garcia, I don't know what you're talking about. I haven't heard of any kidnapping here on the Cape for the past three years. If you think you have information . . ."

"The Glendenning kids have been out of school for the past two days."

"Maybe they're home sick."

"No, I went there, they're not home sick. The mother refused to let me in. If they were there, she'd've let me talk to them. They've been kidnapped, Detective Sloate. You know damn well they've been kidnapped."

"Sorry," Sloate says.

"Here's what the *Trib*'s gonna do," Garcia says. "We're gonna run a big picture of Mrs. Rose Garrity on our front page tomorrow morning. She's the woman who called in to say the Glendenning kids are missing and nobody's doing anything about it. We're gonna run her picture big as life, and we're gonna tell her story. And when we turn inside to page three, we're gonna see a big picture of the school guard who witnessed those two kids getting into a blue Impala driven by a blonde woman who definitely *ain't* Mrs. Edward Glendenning, who isn't blonde and who doesn't drive a blue Impala. We're gonna tell his story, too, his name is Luke Farraday, and we're gonna tell the people that the police in this town aren't doing a damn thing to get those two kids back! How does that sound to you, Detective Sloate?"

"You want to help us?" Sloate asks. "Or you want those kids killed?"

Garcia blinks.

"Tell me," Sloate says. "Which?"

The voice on the phone is a new one to her.

Gravelly and thick, the voice of a habitual unregenerate smoker, it says merely, "Mrs. Glendenning?"

"Yes," she says, and then at once, "Who's this, please?"

"My name is Rudy Angelet, I'm an old friend of your late husband."

Across the room, wearing the earphones, Charlie looks at her, puzzled. Alice returns a puzzled little shrug.

"Yes?" she says.

"I'd like to offer my condolences," Angelet says.

"Thank you," she says, and waits.

It has been almost eight months now since anyone has called to offer condolences. That first week, those first two weeks actually, the phone never stopped ringing. Then news of the drowning became ancient history, and even their closest friends stopped calling to say how sorry they were. She has never heard of Rudy Angelet, though, and she wonders why the call at this late date. So she waits. Warily.

She is wary of any voice on the phone, any knock on the door, fearful that anything she says or does might endanger the children.

"Ah, Mrs. Glendenning," he says, "I'm sorry to bother you about this, I know you've been through a lot . . ."

"Yes, what is it?" she asks.

". . . but we've waited what we consider a respectable amount of time before contacting you . . ."

Waited for what? she wonders.

". . . and we feel it's time we now met to discuss this matter of Eddie's debt."

"Eddie's *what*?" she says.

"His debt. The money he owes us. Mrs. Glendenning, I don't think we should discuss this further on the—"

"I don't know anything about—"

"—telephone. Perhaps we can meet someplace for a cup of coffee . . ."

"I don't even know you," she says.

"My name is Rudy Angelet," he says. "And your husband owes us two hundred thousand dollars. Do you know the—?"

"He *what*?"

"He owes us two hundred thousand dollars, Mrs. Glendenning. Do you know the diner on 41 and Randall? It's right on the corner there. The southwest corner . . ."

"Look, who is this?" she says.

"Last time, Mrs. Glendenning," he says, and the smoke-seared voice is suddenly loaded with menace. "My name is Rudy Angelet, and your husband owes us two hundred thousand dollars. We'll be at the Okeh Diner on 41 and Randall at eleven o'clock this morning. I suggest you be there, too. We'll have breakfast together."

"I've already had breakfast," she says.

"You'll have it again."

"Look, mister—"

"Unless you'd like something to happen to your kids," he says, and hangs up.

"Who was that?" Carol asks.

"Someone who says Eddie owed him two hundred thousand dollars."

"They always come out of the woodwork," Charlie says knowingly.

"He threatened the kids."

"Then call the police," Carol says.

Alice looks at her.

"Do you see the police here?" she says. "Are the police *doing* anything?" she says. "The police in this fucking hick town are sitting on their fat *asses* while my kids—"

"Hey," Carol says, "hey, come on, sis," and takes her into her arms.

It is like when they were children together, growing up in Peekskill, and the kids at school taunted her by calling her "Fat Alice" because she was a little overweight. Well, a lot overweight. But maybe she ate a lot because their father beat her with his goddamn razor strop all the time, the son of a bitch. Carol could never understand why he picked on Alice and exempted Carol herself from punishment. Nothing Alice did ever seemed to please him. Carol could only figure that he resented her being born at all. Or maybe . . .

Well, she didn't believe in pushcart psychology. She knew only that the moment Alice got out of that house, the moment she went off to New York and college, she shed the pounds as if they were water rolling off a tin roof. By the time she met Eddie, she was as slender as a model. Also wore her hair longer, down to the shoulders, though Eddie was wearing his in a crew cut at the time. Dirty blond and raven brunette, they made a striking pair on the streets of a city not renowned for being easily impressed.

But now Eddie is dead and a stranger on the phone has just told Alice her husband owed him two hundred thousand dollars.

"I'll go with you," Carol says.

"No, I'll go," Charlie says.

"I'll go alone," Alice tells them.

9

She sometimes wishes she were six feet two inches tall and weighed two hundred pounds. She wishes she could bellow like a gorilla, pound her chest, smash everything on the road ahead of her. Is that what this kidnapping is all about? she wonders. Is that what this gets down to? Her husband owing money to a man who sounds like a grizzly bear, is that it? Is *that* why they took her children? If so, you *deserved* to die, Eddie, you . . .

I don't mean that, she thinks at once.

God forgive me, she thinks.

I'm sorry, Eddie, please forgive me.

Her knuckles on the wheel are white.

She takes a deep breath.

The man on the phone—Rudy Angelet, he said his name was—threatened the children. Does this mean he actually *has* them? Is he somehow connected with the black girl in the Shell station, oh so fucking confident, looked Alice straight in the eye, never mind worrying about later identification, *Do anything foolish, and they die.* Are they accomplices? Or is Alice merely wasting time here, meeting Mr. Angelet and whoever he's having breakfast with, when she should be home waiting for a phone call? She knows there's more than just him; he said, "Your husband owes *us,*" he said, "*We'll* be at the diner," so there's more than just Mr. Rudy Angelet and his veiled threat. Are there now four of them? More than four? Is this a *gang* she's dealing with, dear God don't let it be a gang! Let it be just the black woman and her blonde girlfriend, and now Mr. Rudy Angelet and maybe one other person waiting for her at the Okeh Diner.

It is unusual to find heavy traffic on The Trail at ten forty-five on a sweltering morning in May. As Eddie once put it, only an iguana would find the Cape habitable during the summer months. And despite what the calendar says, summer starts at the beginning of May and often lingers through October, though many of the full-timers insist that those two bracketing months are the nicest ones of the year. Native residents of the Cape tend to forget that May and October are lovely anywhere in the United States. They also conveniently forget that in May down here, you can have your brain parboiled if you don't wear a hat.

Driving toward the Okeh Diner on Randall and the Trail, Alice suddenly realizes how much she hates this place.

Hates it even more now that Eddie is dead.

Wonders why on earth they ever moved down here from New York.

Wonders what in the world *kept* them here all these years.

God, she thinks, I really do *hate* this fucking place.

She hadn't planned on getting married so soon.

Her plan was to finish film school and then take a job as a third or fourth or fifth assistant director (a gopher, really) with one of the many companies advertising for recent film school graduates to go on location in Timbuktu or Guatemala or wherever they were shooting the latest documentary or low-budget (or even no-budget) independent film. These were learning jobs for single men or women. So marriage definitely was not in her plans.

But along came Eddie, so what was a girl to do?

His own plan was to earn his master's in business that June (which he did) and then get a job with a Wall Street brokerage firm (which he also did that August, to start in September) and then sit back and watch the big bucks roll in (which he never did manage to do, but he was still young, and that was the plan). He didn't reveal the rest of his plan to her until Halloween night of that magical autumn thirteen years ago.

She was dressed as Cinderella.

Eddie was dressed as Dracula.

An odd couple, to be sure, but the pairing was granted some measure of legitimacy by the fact the Eddie was carrying one midnight blue satin slipper in the pocket of the frock coat under his long black cape, and Alice was limping along on one shod foot, the other clad in a skimpy Ped.

"The limp adds vulnerability to your undeniable beauty," Eddie told her.

She was, in fact, feeling quite beautiful that night, all dolled up in a sapphire blue gown she'd rented for a mere pittance at a costume shop on Greenwich Avenue, masses of pitch black hair piled on top of her head, faux diamond earrings (they came with the gown) dangling from her ears, a faux diamond necklace (also courtesy of Village Costumes, Inc.) around her neck, a lacey low-cut bodice to surpass that of the heroine on the cover of any Silhouette romance—but hey, she was *Cinderella,* the romance heroine of all time!

And Eddie was as sinister a vampire count as anyone might have conjured in his wildest nightmares. Alice had never seen a Dracula with a mustache and a pointed little beard, but Eddie was wearing those tonight, together with greenish makeup around his startling blue eyes, creating a sort of hungry look—hell, a *famished* look—that promised an imminent bite on the neck from those prosthetic fangs he was also wearing.

"Are you supposed to be Lucy?" their host asked them. "Or was that her name?"

"Beats me," Alice said. "I'm Cinderella."

"What's Cinderella doing with Dracula?"

"We're in love," Eddie said.

"Ah," their host said.

"See? I have her slipper," he explained.

"Ah," their host said again.

His name was Don Something-or-Other, and he was an NYU student taking classes in Method acting at the Lee Strasberg Theater Institute on East Fifteenth Street. Don himself lived on Horatio Street near Eighth Avenue, in a loft that was probably costing his parents a bundle, and which tonight was filled with a variety of Trekkies, monsters, clowns, superheroes, hookers, ghosts, witches and warlocks, pirates both male (with mustaches and eye patches) and female (in ragged shorts and soft boots), angels, devils and demons, and one girl dressed as a dominatrix (but this was, after all, Greenwich Village). Since this was thirteen years ago, and the first President Bush had recently sent ground forces to Saudi Arabia in preparation for the first of the Bush Dynasty's Persian Gulf Wars, there were also two men wearing Bush masks.

The dominatrix, who said her name was Mistress Veronique, made a pass at Eddie, and Alice whispered in his ear, "I'll break your head!" which seemed to dampen any interest he might have had in whips or leather face masks. He asked Alice what she wanted to drink, and then he made his way to the bar, where a girl who identified herself as a Barbie doll made yet another pass at him. (Apparently there were many would-be vampire victims on the loose tonight, longing for the count to draw first blood.) Eddie made his way back to Alice, cradling a pair of dark-looking drinks in his hands. He made a toast to "All Hallows Eve and beyond" (significant pause), and then led her through the crowd to a pair of French doors opening onto a small balcony overlooking a postage-stamp garden below.

The night was mild for the end of October.

Back in Peekskill, she'd be shivering. But here in New York, on a balcony well-suited to a scullery maid soon to become a princess, or at least already a princess until the horses turned back to mice at midnight, Alice stood looking out over this dazzling city, her one unshod foot somewhat chilled, but otherwise toasty warm in the cape Count Dracula wrapped around her, the better to bite you on the jugular, m'proud beauty!

Eddie took the midnight blue slipper from the pocket of his frock coat.

He knelt before her.

"May I?" he asked.

And tried the slipper on her shoeless right foot.

And, of course, it fit.

"Will you marry me?" he whispered.

The words took her quite by surprise.

They'd been living together since September, when Eddie started work at Lowell, Hastings, Finch and Ulrich. This was, after all, thirteen years ago, and the entire civilized world east of the Mississippi had already been sexually liberated. But marriage had never come up as a viable option. Not before now, anyway. How could a married woman go trotting off to Brazil lugging cameras and running out for coffee while some would-be eminent director filmed piranhas in the Amazon?

She was speechless.

Eddie was still kneeling.

His hand was still resting on her now-slippered foot.

His wonderful blue eyes were asking, "Well?"

"I'll have to think about it," she said.

They were married shortly before Christmas.

She didn't want to get pregnant, either.

That wasn't part of her revised plan.

She had already begun implementing this modified plan by getting a part-time job editing film for an indie who was making a movie titled *The Changing Face of the Lower East Side.* Her idea was to find a series of similar temporary jobs in various aspects of film-related work until she could find full-time employment as a production assistant in a New York–based company.

What she wanted to do, you see, was produce films. She wasn't interested in cinematography or screenwriting or directing or, God forbid, acting. What she wanted to do was create, for all these other people, an environment in which they might make good movies. Movies that won all the prizes. She felt this was an ambition compatible with a good marriage. Eddie was beginning to find his way downtown on Wall Street; she was beginning to find her way in the film industry. Pregnancy was not part of the scheme.

Encouraged by her sister, Carol, who'd been married for two years already and had been successful in avoiding any unwanted pregnancies, Alice consulted her gynecologist about acquiring the same sort of diaphragm Carol had been using so effectively. She was told by Dr. Havram—a woman whose first name was Shirley—that the diaphragm was a flexible rubber cap that a woman filled with a spermicide prior to intercourse and before inserting it.

This, Alice already knew, duh.

She learned, however, that there were some slight, ahem, disadvantages.

To begin with, using it increased the chances of bladder infections. Whee, just what Alice needed, a bladder infection! Next, the cream or jelly spermicide might have an unpleasant taste, not very appealing to Count Dracula, eh, kiddo? Moreover, it might "interrupt the effortless flow of foreplay," as Dr. Havram put it, and added, "Although you can teach your husband to insert it as part of the foreplay."

Not to mention the fact that it was less effective than the condom either as a birth-control device or as protection against STDs. Although Alice knew what an STD was, Dr. Havram informed her anyway that the letters were an acronym for "sexually transmitted diseases" such as gonorrhea, syphilis, chlamydial infection, or herpes, none of which Alice had ever had or ever wished to have.

"Also," Dr. Havram said, "as a contraceptive, the failure rate of the diaphragm is about eighteen percent annually. In fact, it's most effective with older married women who experience intercourse less than three times a week."

("That's nonsense," Carol later told her on the phone. "Whenever Rafe's home, we go at it hot and heavy almost every night of the week, and you don't see any little creatures running around here yet, do you?")

So Alice had herself fitted for a diaphragm.

Dr. Havram confirmed that there was no pelvic infection. Alice emptied her bowel and bladder prior to the fitting. Dr. Havram checked to see that the anterior rim of the diaphragm was just under the symphysis pubis, the posterior rim lying at the vaginal formix, the diaphragm touching both lateral walls and covering the cervix and the upper vagina. She made sure that she could feel the cervix through the diaphragm. She asked Alice if she was aware of anything inside the vagina, and was pleased when Alice answered in the negative.

The diaphragm worked in spite of the Glendennings' heavy sexual activity, which seemed to negate Dr. Havram's dire statistical warnings.

But then one night in April . . .

Eighteen months after she'd inserted for the first time the rubber cap filled with spermicidal jelly . . .

In fact the very night *Braveheart* took the Academy Award for best picture . . .

In the privacy of her own midnight bathroom . . .

Alice tore open the sealed Instastrip Onestep HCG Pregnancy Test kit and removed from it the test strip. With the arrow end pointing downward into a cup of her urine, and being careful not to dip the strip past the MAX line, she left it immersed for the required three seconds, and then removed it from the urine and placed it flat on the countertop. Scarcely daring to breathe, she watched the strip as avidly as she'd watched Mira Sorvino making her poised and articulate acceptance speech for best supporting actress. If only one band appeared in the control region, and no apparent band appeared in the test region of the strip, then no pregnancy would have been detected.

Tick-tock, tick-tock.

In less than a minute, colored bands began to appear in the test region. This meant that a developing placenta was secreting the glycoprotein hormone known as human chorionic gonadotropin, or HCG. Which meant that Alice was pregnant.

She could not believe it.

She had religiously inserted the diaphragm two to twelve hours prior to intercourse each and every time. She had made certain it remained in place for at least six hours after sex. She had never left it in place for longer than twenty-four hours. She had washed it carefully with warm soapy water and stored it in a clean dry place. And now this?

Pregnant?

She absolutely could not believe it.

Ashley was born nine months later.

The Okeh Diner is in a row of stores in a strip mall on the west side of the Trail. The mall itself attempts to emulate Old Florida, and almost succeeds in doing that. Turreted and balconied, shuttered and terraced, the pink-stuccoed and orange-tiled shops partially re-create an aura of graciousness, reminiscent of what Cape October must have been like in the 1920s. Flanking the diner's entrance, a potted umbrella tree stands opposite a dragon tree and a corn plant, all arranged around a sidewalk flower cart massed with purple, white, and pink gloxinias, mums in yellow and lavender, spinning wheels with bright yellow centers and white petals. There are two cars parked in front of the diner. One of them is a white Caddy. Alice wonders why she thinks it belongs to Rudy Angelet.

He is sitting in a booth at the rear of the place, facing the entrance door. He rises the moment he sees her come in. She considers this an ominous sign: he knows what she looks like. Which means he's been watching her. She walks toward the booth.

"Mrs. Glendenning?" he asks.

The same nicotine-ravaged voice she heard on the telephone.

"Mr. Angelet?" she says.

"Please," he says, and opens his hand, using the palm to invite her into the booth beside him. Another man is sitting on the other side of the booth. He is a black man with a sceloid scar running the length of his jawline on the left side of his face.

"My partner," Angelet says. "David Holmes."

"No relation to Sherlock," Holmes says, and shows white teeth and pink gums in a wide grin. "Sit down, Mrs. Glendenning." It is more a command than an invitation. She sits alongside Angelet and opposite Holmes.

"What happened to your foot?" Angelet asks.

"I hurt myself."

"How?"

"I got run over."

"Yeah?"

"Yes."

"Is it broken?"

"Yes."

"That's a shame," he says. "Cup of coffee? Something to eat?"

"Just coffee," she says. "Thanks."

Angelet signals to a waitress wearing a pink uniform.

"Another cup of coffee, honey," he tells her.

The waitress smiles and goes off again. She is back with Alice's coffee not three minutes later. She smiles again at Angelet. It occurs to Alice that she is flirting with him. He is not a bad-looking man. In his late thirties, early forties, Alice supposes, with dark brown eyes and a pale complexion for a Floridian—if indeed he's from Florida. His voice on the phone sounded more like Brooklyn than Cape October. Alice suddenly wonders if he knew Eddie while they were still living in New York. On the phone, he said, "I'm an old friend of your late husband." *How* old? she now wonders.

"I'm glad you could make it," Angelet says.

"This is a serious matter here," Holmes says. "Your husband owed us two hundred thousand dollars when he met with his unfortunate accident. He *still* owes us that money."

"Which is a lot of money," Angelet says.

"A whole fucking *lot* of money," Holmes says.

"I can't imagine my husband owing—"

"Imagine it, lady," Holmes says.

"How . . . how could he possibly . . . ?"

"The puppies, lady," Holmes says.

"The *what*?"

"The hounds."

"I don't know what—"

"The *dog* races. Your husband liked to bet."

"He liked to bet big."

"Too big."

"Losers shouldn't bet so big."

"He was into us for two hundred large when he drowned," Holmes says.

"Drowned too *soon,*" Angelet says.

"Too *fucking* soon," Holmes says, and both men laugh.

Alice gets up to leave.

"Sit!" Holmes says, as if he is talking to a disobedient dog. "And don't get up again."

Alice sits. She looks across the table at him.

"I don't believe a word you're saying," she says. "I don't believe you knew my husband, I don't believe he owes you money, I don't believe—"

"Want to see his markers?" Holmes asks.

"Markers?"

"Show her the markers, Rudy."

"What . . . ?"

"His betting slips," Holmes says.

Angelet reaches into the inside pocket of his sports coat. When his hand emerges again, it is holding a sheaf of three-by-four white papers, some two inches thick.

"They're all dated," he says. "They go back a year and a half. That's when he started betting with us. We were carrying him a long, long time."

"We since found out he stiffed half a dozen other bankers in town."

"We shoulda been more careful," Angelet says.

"You'll probably be getting a few more calls," Holmes says.

"Once word gets around there was insurance."

"What do you mean? How do you know . . . ?"

"A check went out from Garland last week. Seems your lawyer threatened them with a lawsuit . . ."

"How do you know that?"

"It's true, ain't it?"

"How do you—?"

"I'll tell you how we know," Angelet says. "One of the people who bets with us happens to work for Garland, and he also happens to owe us a little money. So when we mentioned to him one day that this fucking deadbeat Eddie Glen—"

"Don't you *dare*—!"

"Stay put, lady, I warned you!" Holmes says, and pulls her down into the booth again.

"When we mentioned to this man, whose name is Joseph Ontano, if you'd care to check, that your husband owed us two hundred large, but he was already dead and we weren't about to let some little pissant like Mr. Ontano stiff us for a mere five, he said the name rang a bell, and he looked up the file when he got back to the office, and sure enough a check went out."

"No, it didn't."

"Lady . . ."

"I haven't received any check."

"You will."

"I hope so. I can use it just now."

"So can we. When that check arrives, we want two hundred of it."

"Before the *other* sharks start circling."

"We'll call you tomorrow," Angelet says. "And we'll keep calling you every day until that insurance check is in your hands. Then we—"

"I don't know *when* a check is coming. I don't even—"

"*Whenever* it—"

"I don't even know *if* one is coming. I haven't heard they're paying. Your Mr. Ontano must be mistaken. When did he say this check went out?"

"Lady," Holmes says, "*whenever* that fucking check gets to you, we want our piece of it. Or we'll break your *other* foot, you know whut I'm saying?"

"You don't frighten me," she says.

"How about your kids? Do *they* frighten you?" Angelet asks.

"Are you in this with the others?" she asks.

Their faces go blank.

"What others?" Holmes asks.

"To each his own," Angelet says, thinking he understands.

"Let them collect their *own* fuckin markers," Holmes says, picking up on it.

They have no idea what she's talking about. With an enormous sense of relief, she realizes they have nothing whatever to do with the kidnapping, Eddie's gambling was not responsible for—

"We'll call you this afternoon," Angelet says. "After the mail comes."

"Keep an eye on the mailbox," Holmes says.

Both men rise in the same moment, as if by prearranged signal. Alice sits alone in the booth, watching them as they go. The waitress in the pink uniform walks over.

"Who's getting this check?" she asks.

Outside, Alice hears an automobile starting. She looks through the blinds on the diner window. The white Caddy is moving out of the parking lot.

Too late, she thinks of writing down the license plate number.

The car is gone.

She calls her lawyer at home from the cell phone in her car.

"Andy," she says, "hi. It's Alice Glendenning, can you hear me?"

"Hello, Alice, how are you?" he asks.

"I'm fine. If we get cut off, I'll call you back. I'm in the car."

"What's up?"

"Have you heard anything more from Garland?"

"No, I haven't."

"Because some people seem to think a check to me has already been cut."

"Really?"

"So they say."

"What people?"

"Some people who knew Eddie."

"I haven't heard anything to that effect. You'd be the first to know, Alice."

"I know that. But they seemed so positive . . ."

"I can call Garland again, if you like."

"Could you, Andy? It'd be nice to know if a check is really on the way."

"I'll do that right now. Are you on the way home?"

"Yes, I am."

"I'll call you there. Say half an hour or so?"

"Thanks, Andy."

When she hangs up, she realizes she's forgotten to give him Joseph Ontano's name.

She tries to call him back, but she can't get a signal.

I'm in a dead zone, she thinks.

Again, she thinks.

Ashley was five months old when the call came from Alice's best friend in film school. Denise Schwartz had set up a low-budget production deal with an independent producer named Backyard Films, who were ready to finance a script Denise herself had written and planned to direct—*and* would Alice care to come in as her partner?

What?

What!

Her heart stopped.

Denise elaborated. The budget was only $850,000, which meant they would both have to wear many hats. Denise would be director and executive producer. Alice would work the camera and serve as line producer . . .

"You were so good with the camera, Alice, please say yes."

"Well, I . . ."

She could barely speak.

"Where will you be shooting?" she asked.

"Toronto," Denise said. "For New York."

"How long is the shooting schedule?"

"I haven't worked it out yet, but I'm assuming six, seven weeks—seven weeks tops. Neither of us will be drawing salaries, Alice, but we'll share in the profits, if there are any. And if we bring this one in on budget, and win a few prizes . . ."

"Oh sure, prizes."

Her heart was racing.

"Why not?" Denise said. "What I'm saying is it's a start, there'll be other ones in the future. Alice. Please."

"I'll have to talk to Eddie," she said. "I'll get back to you."

Eddie didn't think it was such a good idea.

Things weren't going too well at Lowell, Hastings, Finch and Ulrich; he wasn't becoming a millionaire quickly enough. In fact, he wasn't making anywhere near the kind of commissions he thought he should be making by this time.

"So how can we afford your being away for two, three months, whatever it is . . . ?"

"Seven weeks tops," Alice said.

"Seven weeks, okay, even so. We'd have to get a nanny for Ashley, where are we supposed to get the money for a nanny? Line producer and cinematographer are very nice titles, Alice, but you said yourself there wouldn't be any salary while you're . . ."

"If the film shows a profit . . ."

"Oh sure, how many of these indie films make any money?"

"It's what I trained for, Eddie!"

"I know. I'm not saying don't put your training and your expertise to use, Alice, I'm only saying don't do it right this *minute.* Do it sometime in the *future.* This just isn't the appropriate time for you to be running off to Canada."

"But the opportunity is here *now,* Eddie. Not sometime in the future. And why *isn't* this an appropriate . . . ?"

"Because I'm thinking of leaving the firm."

"What? Why would you want to do *that*?"

"Because the bonanza boat at Lowell-Hastings has already sailed, Alice. Which doesn't mean I can't make it somewhere else in the world of high finance. I was thinking . . ."

"Somewhere else? Where, Eddie, New York is our . . ."

"Why can't we move to a small town on the West Coast? Or maybe somewhere in the Southwest? Or even the South? Maybe Beaufort, South Caro . . ."

"Beau . . ."

". . . which I hear is a lovely place to live. Plenty of opportunities elsewhere, Alice. Maybe Florida. Why not Florida? Nice and warm in Florida. But I don't think you should go to Canada just now, honey. Not at this juncture of my career."

Your career? Alice thought.

What about *my* career?

What about the juncture of *my* career that was put on hold when Ashley was born five months ago, what about *that* little career, Count Dracula?

That night, she called Denise and told her she was really sorry, but she couldn't go in with her at this time.

"Thanks, Denise," she said. "I wish I could, but I can't."

"That's okay," Denise said. "Another time. "I love you, hon."

"I love you, too. Good luck with it."

"I'm gonna need it," Denise said.

The pill Alice's new gynecologist prescribed was "*The* Pill," a combination of the synthetic female hormones progestin and estrogen, as differentiated from "The *Mini*-Pill," which contained only the one hormone, progestin. Dr. Abigail Franks recommended the combination pill because it was supposed to be 99 percent effective as opposed to the 97 percent effectiveness of the progestin-only pill. This meant that if a hundred women took the so-called combination-pill every day of the year, only one of them would become pregnant.

Alice took the pill every day at the same time, right after she brushed her teeth and just before she went to bed, because it was easier to remember taking it that way. She gained a little weight at first, and she experienced some spotting, but these side effects went away after her first three or four menstrual cycles, and after that the daily routine became as fixed as bathing Ashley in the morning or kissing Eddie goodbye before he went off to work.

And then one day, she missed her period again.

She didn't think this was possible. She hadn't skipped a day of taking the pill, so how was this possible? Besides, ever since she'd started taking the pill her periods were always very light, sometimes nothing more than a brown smudge on a tampon or in her panties. So she knew that if she hadn't missed any pills—which she was certain she hadn't—then even these light periods counted as menstruation. That was because the hormone doses in the pills were so very low that not much uterus lining built up, and very little blood needed to come out each month.

But this particular month, there was no blood at all.

Nada, zero, zilch.

So Alice went to the nearest CVS pharmacy and bought herself a trusty old reliable Instastrip Onestep HCG Pregnancy Test. And guess what? All the colors of the goddamn rainbow showed up after she dipped the test strip in a little cup of her pee.

Just her luck, Alice turned out to be the one woman in a hundred who got pregnant taking the pill that year!

Jamie was born in the month of October, a year and five months after his sister came into the world. That same month, Denise's film

Summer of Joy won the $100,000 Leone dell'Anno Prize at the Venice Film Festival. When she called Alice to ask if she would join her on her new venture, Alice regretfully had to decline again, she was so very sorry.

"That's okay," Denise said. "Another time. I love you, hon."

Just before Thanksgiving that year, the family moved to Cape October, where Eddie began his new job with the investment firm of Baxter and Meuhl.

At the time of his drowning last year, Eddie still hadn't made his first million dollars. In fact, they were still paying off a $150,000 mortgage on the house, and making monthly payments on the *Jamash,* and the two cars, and what suddenly seemed like far too many other things.

Long before then, Alice had given up her girlish dream of making movies that would win all the prizes.

When she gets back to the house, a faded maroon Buick is parked in the driveway behind her sister's black Explorer. The police, she thinks. A maroon Buick. Gee, fellas, what took you so long?

"I had to let them in," her sister explains. "They have badges."

"Sorry to bother you again," Sloate says.

He is here with Marcia Di Luca, who has already made herself at home behind the monitoring equipment, sipping a cup of coffee Alice assumes her sister prepared.

"Long time no see," Alice says.

She cannot quite hide the enmity she feels for these people.

"Let me fill you in," he says. "To begin with—"

"To begin with," Alice says, "they know you followed them."

"How do you—?"

"The woman called me," Alice says. "They know a maroon Buick followed them. Is that the car outside?"

Sloate makes a sort of helpless gesture.

"Even so," he says, "the bills are marked. We feel certain someone will spot the serial numbers and call us."

He now explains that genuine hundred-dollar bills are printed in so-called families, with serial numbers starting with different letters of the alphabet, but that the super-bills supplied for the ransom drop are all A-series bills, and they all bear the identical serial number, which happens to be A-358127756.

"Once the perps try to cash any of those bills," he says, "someone will spot that number."

"How is anyone going to . . . ?"

"We sent out a list to every merchant and bank in the state," Sloate explains, almost apologetically.

"Nobody looks at serial numbers."

"We're hoping they will."

Alice shakes her head. She is at the mercy of nitwits. She is in the hands of total incompetents.

"What else did she say?" Sloate asks. "When she called?"

"What difference does it make?"

"Please, Mrs. Glendenning."

"She said they had to check the money."

"And?"

"She said the kids were okay. She said they just needed a little time."

"Anything else?"

"Nothing."

"Didn't inadvertently say anything about where they might be holding the children, did she?"

"Nothing," Alice says again.

"Well," Sloate says, and sighs heavily, which Alice finds somewhat less than reassuring. "Let's get ready for her next call."

This time, a so-called plan is in place.

This time, Alice knows exactly what she is to say to the black woman when she calls. *If* she calls. Alice is not at all sure she *will* call. How long does it take to "check" $250,000 in hundred-dollar bills? Whatever that's supposed to mean, "check" them. Count them?

Well, you can count twenty-five hundred bills, that's what they came to, in ten, fifteen minutes, can't you? Half an hour? An hour tops? So what's taking them so long? Have they discovered the bills are fake? Will they kill the children because the bills are fake? If anything happens to the children . . .

"Nothing will happen to them," Sloate assures her. "Please, Mrs. Glendenning, don't worry."

But Alice can't stop worrying. She still believes these people are more interested in *catching* whoever's holding Jamie and . . .

Well, that isn't quite true.

Certainly, they want to get the kids back safe and sound. But in addition to a rescue operation—and she has to think of it as that—they also want to capture the "perps," as Sloate keeps calling them, and this is the farthest wish from Alice's mind. She does not give a damn *who* has the children, does not give a damn if they're *ever* caught. She wants her kids back. Period.

Apparently, they have located the blue Impala.

"Our techs are going over the car right this minute," Sloate tells her. "If we get some good latents, we're halfway home." He hesitates and then says, "There was a red cap on the backseat of the car."

He shows her the cap now. It is in a sealed plastic bag with an evidence tag on it. It is indisputably the cap Jamie left at home Wednesday morning, the one she took to him later. His lucky hat. Which means he was in that blue Impala sometime during the past three days.

"What we can't understand," Sloate says, "is why the kids would've got in a car with a strange woman."

Alice is thinking there are a lot of things Sloate can't understand. She looks at the clock. It is now a quarter to one, and still no call. If they abandoned the car, have they abandoned the children as well? Are Jamie and Ashley now sitting alone in some apartment or some house waiting for . . . ?

Or . . .

God forbid . . .

No!

She won't even think that.

The telephone rings.

Her heart leaps into her throat.

"Pick it up," Sloate says. "Remember what we said."

Marcia Di Luca is putting on her earphones.

Alice lifts the receiver.

"Hello?" she says.

"Alice?"

"Yes."

"It's Rafe. How's it going there?"

"Where are you?"

"On the road. Just thought I'd—"

"Carol's here, did you know that?"

"Yes. That's why I'm calling."

"Hold on. Carol?" she says. "It's Rafe."

"Rafe?" Carol says, surprised, and takes the receiver from her sister. "Hi, honey," she says into the phone. "Is everything all right?"

"Yes, fine. I'm just calling to see how you are. I called home last night, found out you were heading down."

"I figured Alice could use a hand."

"Bet she can," Rafe says. "Fact, I was thinking of stopping by there again myself. You think that's a good idea?"

Carol covers the mouthpiece.

"He wants to come by," she tells Alice.

"Where is he?"

"Where are you, hon?"

"Just over the state line. In Alabama."

"Alabama," Carol tells her sister.

"Who's that?" Sloate asks.

"My husband."

"Tell him to save it for another time," Sloate says. "We're busy here."

"Rafe, it's not a good time just now," Carol says.

"Whatever you say. Give her a hug for me, okay? Tell her I hope this all works out." He hesitates a moment. "Has she heard anything more from them?"

"No, not yet. Rafe, I have to get off the phone. We're hoping—"

"Wish you'da told me you were coming down to Florida."

"Wish I'da known where to *reach* you," Carol says.

"What's that supposed to mean?"

"Nothing."

"No, Carol, what's it supposed to mean?"

"Rafe, I have to go now," she says.

"We'll talk about this when we get home."

"Yes, good-bye, Rafe," she says, and hangs up.

"Everything all right?" Alice asks.

"Yes, fine," Carol says.

But Alice knows it isn't.

The clock bongs one o'clock.

And they still haven't called.

She doesn't want to hear her sister's troubles.

She wants the phone to ring, that's all.

But they are in the kitchen now, brewing a fresh pot of coffee, and Carol takes this opportunity to unburden herself. The door is closed; all those law enforcement geniuses out there can't hear what they're saying.

"I think Rafe's running around on me," Carol says, flat out.

Alice remembers Rafe's comment about Jennifer Redding after she drove off in her red convertible. She says nothing.

"I've had the feeling for a long time now."

Alice still says nothing.

"He's gone so much of the time, you know," Carol says.

"Well, that doesn't means he's—"

"Oh, I know, I know. It's his job, after all . . ."

"It is, Carol."

"But he never calls when he's on the road."

"That doesn't mean anything, either."

"This is unusual, his calling now."

"Well, if you think . . . why don't you just ask him about it?"

"No, I . . ."

"Ask him flat out. 'Rafe, are you cheating on me?'"

"I don't think I could do that."

"Why not?"

"I just don't think I could."

Alice looks at her sister.

Carol turns away.

"What is it?" Alice says.

"There are the kids," Carol says, and suddenly she's weeping. She puts her head on Alice's shoulder. Alice holds her close. The kitchen is silent except for Carol's soft sobbing. In the other room, Alice can hear the law enforcement people talking among themselves. This is a nightmare, she thinks. At last, her sister nods, moves away from her. Drying her eyes on a tissue, she says, "I'm all right, it's okay."

"Leave him," Alice says. "Kids or not."

"Would you? If Eddie was still alive, and you found out he was . . . ?"

"In a minute," Alice says.

"Did he ever?"

"Never."

And the telephone rings.

She snatches the receiver from the phone on the wall. She doesn't give a damn if anybody out there in the living room is trying to trace the call or not. They haven't succeeded so far, and she has no reason to believe they ever will.

"Hello?" she says.

"Alice, it's Andy Briggs."

"Hi, Andy. What'd you find out?"

"Well, Garland is closed today, but I spoke to a man named Farris, at home, asked him if he knew anything further about a settlement on Eddie's policy. I told him word had it that a check had already been sent out. He said as far as he knew the matter was still pending."

Alice nods silently.

"Alice?"

"Yes, Andy."

"I still think we should wait till the beginning of June. If nothing happens before then, we'll start an action."

"It's just that these people . . ."

"Yes, what's *that* all about, Alice? I mentioned to Farris that some people seemed to have inside information, but he said he didn't know how such information could have come from Garland since 'the matter is still pending,' his favorite expression. Who *are* these people? And where'd they get their information?"

"Well, they may be wrong," Alice says.

"Apparently so. Be patient, okay? We'll resolve this, I know we will."

"Yes, I'm sure," she says. "Thanks, Andy."

"Any time," he says, and hangs up.

She puts the receiver back on the wall. Outside, she hears the sound of a car pulling up. She looks out through the kitchen window. It is the mail truck.

The mailman greets her as she comes out the back door and walks up the path to the mailbox. He comments on the hot weather they've been having, and she agrees it's been awful, and then he gets back into his truck. Next door, Mrs. Callahan waves to her as she comes out to her own mailbox.

"Morning, Mrs. Glendenning!"

"Morning," Alice says.

Everything as normal.

Except that her children are gone.

She leafs through the envelopes. Nothing from Garland. Inside the house again, she goes through the mail more thoroughly. A bill from Florida Power and Light . . .

"Anything from the perps?" Sloate asks.

The perps.

. . . another from Verizon. A third from Burdines. Two pieces of junk mail, both soliciting subscriptions to magazines she's never heard of. But nothing from Garland. And nothing from the perps, either, no.

"Nothing," she tells Sloate, and the phone rings again. Sloate grabs for the earphones.

Alice glances at the grandfather clock.

One twenty-five.

She picks up the receiver.

"Mrs. Glendenning?" he says.

She recognizes the voice at once.

"Yes?"

"Has the mail come yet?"

"Yes, it has."

"Is the check there?"

"No. I'm sorry."

"I'm sure it's on the way," he says. "I'll call again Monday."

"Mr. Angelet . . ."

"I'll call again Monday," he repeats, and hangs up.

"Who was that?" Sloate asks.

"A friend of Eddie's."

"What check was he asking about?" Sloate wants to know.

"A check he says he mailed."

"A check for what?"

"He owed my husband some money."

Sloate looks at her.

She senses that he knows she's lying.

But she doesn't care.

10

Christine is almost afraid to break the news to him.

There is something very frightening about this man.

He's never hit her or anything like that, he's not a violent man, although you never can tell with the ones who look as delicate as he does. Once, back when she was still living in North Carolina, she used to date this Latino who looked like a stork, he was that slender and dainty. Actually, he was dealing dope, but that was another matter. The point is, the minute she started living with him, he began batting her around. "What're you gonna do?" Vicente used to ask her, that was his name, Vicente. "Call the cops?" No, she didn't call no cops. She just left. Fuck you, Vicente.

The situation is very different here. Christine knows she could never end this relationship, even if he ever did hit her, which he better not try, but she's not afraid of that, really. He's never hit her yet, and they've been together—what? It must be almost three years since they met, and a year since he cooked up this scheme of his, she can still remember the day he told her about it, she thought he was crazy. That intense look in his eyes, that's the word for him, she guesses, intense. Everything about him is so fucking *intense,* man. You can almost feel him vibrating sometimes.

She thinks maybe the reason she's afraid to tell him what she's discovered is that this whole idea was his to begin with, and now he may think she's trying to muscle in on it, come up with an idea of her *own,* you know? That was one of the things used to get Vicente in a rage all the time, her coming up with ideas of her own. It's like these delicate guys have to prove they're not as feminine as they look, so they put you down whenever you try to express yourself. And if dissing you doesn't work, there's always the fists, right? They can always give you a black eye or a bloody lip. That hasn't been the case here yet, but she's a little gun-shy, she has to admit, of somebody who so perfectly fits the Vicente profile of profound passion in a slight body.

He hasn't yet asked her why she's back so late.

All she was supposed to do this morning was ditch the Impala and rent a new car, which she did without any trouble. But going to the bank to break down the hundreds into smaller bills was her idea, not because she suspected any of the bills were counterfeit but only because cashing a big bill in a shitty little town like Cape October could become a hassle.

He's watching television when she comes in.

The kids are locked in the forward stateroom of the boat. She doesn't ask him how the kids are. Truth be known, she doesn't give a shit about the kids. Now that they've got the money, all she wants to do is turn the kids loose and get the hell out of here. A quarter of a million dollars can take them anywhere. Stop playing hide-and-seek with the locals here. Go to Hawaii or Europe or the Far East, wherever. Go someplace where a black woman and a white man with blond hair won't attract the kind of attention they do here in Crackerland.

But she still has to tell him about those three queer bills, and her idea about the rest of the money.

"Where've you been?" he asks.

"Here and there," she says, and goes to him and kisses him on the cheek.

"Did you get the car?"

"A red Taurus."

"Can't wait to see it," he says, and gets up to give her a hug, flicking his long blond hair as he rises. His hair was short when they met three years ago, made him look more butch. She doesn't dare tell him he looks a bit faggoty with the longer hair, which he didn't start growing till after all this started, even though they moved out of town where nobody could possibly recognize him.

"I missed you," he says. "What took you so long?"

"I bought some things," she says.

"Uh-oh," he says, but he's smiling.

"Want to see them?"

She puts the Victoria's Secret shopping bag on the kitchen table. He's already recognized it, his eyes are already dancing. He may look like a pansy, but man, the opposite is true when it comes to reaction and performance, you know what I'm saying? She removes the boxes from the bag one by one, stacks them on the table. She shows him the push-up bras in the black hydrangea and the cheetah print. She shows him the leopard-print low-rise thongs. He rubs the fabric between his forefinger and thumb, as if he's testing one of the hundred-dollar bills. She shows him the red sequin-lace baby-doll nightgown. He especially likes the black lace garter belt.

"I'll wear it for you tonight," she says.

"How about now?" he asks.

"We have to talk," she says.

"What about?"

"I also bought a television set. It's in the car."

"A television set? What for?"

"Cost me nineteen hundred bucks."

"What? Why'd you spend . . . ?"

"To test the bills."

He looks at her.

"Three of the bills were counterfeit," she tells him.

"How do you know?"

"I tried to cash them at a bank. They've got a machine. The bills are what they call super-bills . . ."

"Hold it, hold it . . ."

"Honey, please listen to me."

There is that familiar intense look in his eyes. He is afraid she's going to tell him that all their careful planning was for nothing. She has already told him three of the bills—

"Honey, please," she says. "It's not bad, really. Just listen."

"I'm listening," he says.

"The bank refused to cash them. In fact, they—"

"Why'd you go to a bank?"

"To get some smaller bills. Honey, please, for Christ's sake, *listen*!"

She sees him tense the way Vicente used to, sees the muscles in his jaw tightening, is fearful that in the next minute he is going to punch her or slap her or shove her . . .

"I'm listening," he says again.

"They call them super-bills. They make them on some kind of presses the U.S. sold to Iran when the shah was still in power. They use German paper to print the bills. You can't tell them from the real thing, honey, except with these machines the Fed has, and now all the Southwest Federal branches. Which is how they flagged the bills, they ran them through their machine. But a diner where I had breakfast accepted one of the—"

"Slow down," he says.

"A diner cashed one of the hundreds. So did Victoria's Secret. Which is why I bought the television set. I paid for it with nineteen hundred in cash, and nobody batted an eyelash. Do you know what I'm saying?"

"You're saying the rest of the money is real. You're saying we don't have to worry . . ."

"No, honey. I'm saying it don't *matter* if they're real or fake or *whatever.* We cash them where there are no machines, and we're home free."

He looks at her.

He is nodding now.

And now he is smiling.

"Let's go celebrate tonight," he says.

• • •

The features editor of the Cape October *Tribune* is a man named Lionel Maxwell, who has been in the newspaper business for forty years now, and who doesn't need a twerp like Dustin Garcia telling him about placement. Garcia is saying he wants his weekly column to run on the first page of tomorrow's Sunday section.

"That is patently absurd," Maxwell says.

This is a small newspaper, circulation only 75,000 in a town of 143,000, which tells you something, doesn't it? In addition to being a star reporter in his own mind, Garcia writes this column he calls "Dustin's Dustbin," and it usually runs on page five of the Sunday section. But now Garcia is insisting it should run on the first page instead.

"Give me one good reason," Maxwell says.

He knows the good reason. Garcia wants greater exposure. His picture runs at the top of the column—"Dustin's Dustbin," for Christ's sake!—but that isn't good enough for him. He wants his picture and his precious words to run on the section's first page, where anyone too lazy to turn to page five will see it at once.

"I think it's an exceptionally good column this week," Garcia says.

He can't tell Maxwell that running it on the first page of the section is Detective Wilbur Sloate's idea. Detective Sloate is looking for higher visibility. He wants to make sure that the people who have those kids will see the piece without having to go digging through the paper for it. But Garcia can't explain that to his boss.

Nor can he tell him that the story he's written is a complete fabrication. He's afraid that Maxwell won't run it at all if he knows not a word of it is true. Well, the kids being picked up at school is true, but the rest is all a crock. Garcia feels he's performing a public service here, helping to get those kids back. He doesn't want to run into bureaucratic red tape from an old-timer like Maxwell who doesn't know what new-wave journalism is all about. He doesn't want to hear him sounding off about libel suits, the way he did that time Garcia wrote a column about municipal garbage pickups regularly and routinely being ignored in the predominately Cuban Twin Oaks area, which actually did happen one Friday, the garbage not being picked up, and which even Garcia had to admit was not exactly an epidemic of neglect, but the city hadn't sued anyway, so what was all the fuss?

"Also," Maxwell says, "I'm not sure I like all these Shakespearean references."

"That's what makes the column special," Garcia says.

"Half the rednecks down here never even heard of Shakespeare."

"Come on, Lionel, everybody knows Shakespeare."

"Wanna bet?"

But he is softening.

Garcia is thinking if his column helps crack a kidnapping case, he'll get the Pulitzer.

"Please, Lionel?" he says. "Give me a break, okay? Front page of the section, upper right hand corner. Please?"

"I must be out of my mind," Maxwell says.

They pick up I-75 ten miles east of the Cape, and then drive the Taurus north toward Sarasota. He tells Christine he's afraid they might be spotted if they try any of the local restaurants, most of which aren't any good, anyway. In Sarasota, there's a wider selection.

They both must realize that Alice is sitting by the phone, waiting for a call from them, but they aren't talking about her, or the kids locked in the forward stateroom of the boat. As long as they catch the last ferry back at ten-thirty, the kids will be okay. Instead, they talk about where they should go now that they have all this money.

The Unicorn is a restaurant all the way out on Siesta Key, secluded and quiet in the off-season. A month ago, it would have been thronged with Midwesterners. Tonight, they are virtually alone in the place. He orders a bottle of Veuve Clicquot. They toast to their success, and then order from the truly magnificent menu.

He sips at his champagne, gives the glass an admiring glance, eyebrows raised. He is dressed casually, tan slacks and a brown cotton sweater that perfectly complement the long blond hair. Christine is wearing an off-the-shoulder yellow dress, strappy yellow sandals, dangling yellow earrings. In Florida, especially during the off-season, no one dresses up for dining out.

She wants to talk about where they should go, now that they have all this money. She wants to talk about leaving Cape October forever, now that everything's worked out the way they hoped it would, now that they're finally rid of his wife.

"She's not a bad person," he says.

"I thought—"

"It's not her fault that we happened to meet."

"You and her, you mean?"

"No, you and me. It's not her fault that I met you and fell in love with you."

"Nice save," Christine says, and hesitates a moment, and then asks, "Are you glad you met me?"

"Of course," he says.

"And fell in love with me?"

"I am *very* glad I fell in love with you."

She remembers the way they met.

Thinking back on it now, it seems to her they fell in love that very first instant. This will always be a source of amazement to her. That they met at all. People tend to forget that Florida is the South. In fact, it is the *Deep* South. And he is white and she is black. But they met. And fell in love.

He looked almost like a teenager. Three years ago, he was wearing his blond hair in a crew cut well suited to the summers on Cape October. Down here—and she was only just learning this because she'd recently moved down from Asheville—the summer months were horrendous. In Asheville, she'd worked serving burgers at a Mickey D's. Down here (big improvement!) she was scooping ice cream at a place called The Dairy Boat. That's where they met. At the Boat.

"Which are the no-fat flavors?" he asked.

Crew-cut blond hair. T-shirt and shorts, Reeboks. This was a Saturday, he'd probably been out running, high sheen of sweat on his face and his bare arms.

"Up there on the chart," she said.

"I can't read," he said, and grinned.

That grin. Jesus!

"Chocolate-vanilla swirl," she said. "Strawberry. Coffee crunch."

"What's the coffee crunch?" he asked.

"It's got like these little chunks of chocolate in it."

"Is it good?"

"I like it."

"What else do you like?"

Little bit of double intender there?

She looked at him.

"Lots of things," she said.

"You like walking hatless in spring rain?"

She looked at him again.

"You flirting with me?" she asked.

"Yep," he said.

"You too young to be flirting with a grown woman," she said.

"Thirty-three last month," he said.

"You look younger."

"How old are you?"

"Twenty-seven."

"Nice age difference," he said.

"You think?"

"Don't you?"

"How about that *other* little difference?" she asked.

"The Great Racial Divide, you mean?"

"No, I mean the gold band I spy on your left hand."

"Oh," he said. "That."

"Yeah, that."

"Yep," he said.

"So whut's a married man like you doing flirting with a nice colored girl like me?"

"Gee, I really don't know," he said. "What time do you get out of here?"

"Six o'clock."

"Want to come for a ride with me?"

"A ride where?"

"To the moon," he said.

That was the start of it.

"You still love me?" she asks now.

"Adore you," he says.

"Even after what we had to do?"

"Well," he says, "desperate people do desperate things."

"Desperate, huh?"

"Is what we were," he says. "We *had* to do what we did. There was no other way."

"Here's to all that money," she says, and raises her glass in a toast. They clink glasses. Her eyes flash with sudden awareness.

"Why's that waiter staring at you?" she whispers.

He turns to look.

"The bald guy over near the serving station."

"He's not staring at me."

"He was a minute ago."

They drink.

"Good," he says.

"Yummy," she says. But she is still looking toward the serving station.

"I wonder why they gave us fake money," he says.

"*If* it's all fake. We don't really know."

Still looking across the room.

"It must be, don't you think?"

"Doesn't matter," she says. "Good as gold either way."

He pours more champagne for both of them. They sip silently for several moments.

"So where do you think we should go?" she asks. "After we turn the kids loose?"

"Where would you like to go?"

"Bali."

"Okay."

"You serious?"

"Sure. Why not Bali?"

"Oh, wow, I'd *love* that."

"Fake money, fake passports, why not?"

"Can we get them? The passports?"

"Oh, sure."

"Do you know somebody?"

"Same guy who made the other stuff."

"Then let's do it."

"We will."

"Let's get out of Florida tonight," she says, really excited now. "Let's give her a call . . ."

"Well, not yet."

". . . tell her the kids are all right . . ."

"Well . . ."

". . . drop them off someplace, and get the hell out of here."

"Well," he says, and takes another sip of champagne. "The kids may be—"

"Excuse me, sir," a voice says.

He turns.

The man standing at his elbow is the waiter who Christine says was staring at him a few minutes ago. Fifty years old or thereabouts, tall and lean, with a balding pate and clear blue eyes, an apologetic smile on his face now.

"I don't want to interrupt your meal," the man says. "Just wanted to say it's nice seeing you here again."

"I . . . uh . . . I'm sorry, but this is the first time I've been here."

"Ah? From some other restaurant then? I used to work at Serafina's out on Longboat . . ."

"Never been there."

"Or The Flying Dutchman downtown?"

"Don't know either of them. Sorry."

"No, *I'm* sorry to've bothered you. I thought sure . . . well, excuse me, I'm sorry."

He nods, smiles, backs away from the table.

"Do you know him?" Christine whispers.

"Never saw him in my life," Eddie says.

Faking his death was the easy part.

It had to look like a sudden whim.

Take the sloop out for a moonlight sail when it's too late to get a sitter on such short notice. *Gee, Alice, I'd like to take the* Jamash *out tonight, would you mind?* Sudden inspiration, you know? But in preparation for this seemingly impetuous idea, he's been watching the daily forecasts, waiting for a night when the seas will be high and the wind will be blowing out of the east.

They keep the boat at a ramshackle landing pier called Marina Jackson. It doesn't have any hoists or storage racks, which they don't need anyway because they never take her out of the water except to have the bottom scraped periodically, and they have that done at a true marina out on Willard. The guy running Marina Jackson is named Matt Jackson, and he's surprised to see Eddie driving in at eight o'clock that night, fixing to take the boat out when the Coast Guard has issued small craft warnings. Eddie tells him he'll be staying on the Intercoastal, which isn't his plan at all, but Jackson frowns at him, anyway, and tells him to be careful out there tonight.

The sloop is a thirty-foot seaworthy Pearson that can sleep four, perfect for the Glendenning family, with a V-berth that can accommodate two up forward, and a port settee in the main salon that converts to a double berth. Eddie does indeed start out under motor on the Intercoastal, but the minute he rounds the tip of the key, he hoists sail and grabs the first wind that takes him westward, into the pass and out into the Gulf.

Man, it is not fun out here.

Expert sailor though he is, he knows this is goddamn dangerous, knows he can *really* drown out here tonight, if he doesn't get off this boat fast, before it gets too far from shore. He inflates the rubber dinghy, carries it back to the stern platform and lowers it into the water. Clinging to the line that holds it to the *Jamash,* he climbs down into the dinghy, and starts its fifteen-horsepower Yamaha engine. He lets the line fall free of the sloop's cleat. Still under sail, the *Jamash* seems to fly away westward into the night, disappearing from sight almost at once.

He is still fearful that he might really drown.

Waves crash in over the sides of the rubber dinghy, drenching him, threatening to capsize the small boat. He keeps its furiously bobbing nose pointed consistently eastward, constantly checking a handheld compass, squinting into the squall, his heart beating wildly in his chest.

At last he sees the light marking the entrance to the pass and the Intercoastal. He shifts course slightly, adjusting for the wind that threatens to blow him and the dinghy farther out into the Gulf. When he comes to within a hundred yards or so from the white sand beach that marks the tip of Willard Key, he removes a bait-cutting knife from its sheath and rips two gaping slashes in the dinghy's orange rubber hide. He is over the side and swimming for shore as the deflating dinghy, weighed down by the engine, sinks out of sight.

He lies on his back on the sand, breathing harshly.

The night rages everywhere around him.

But Eddie Glendenning is dead.

Isn't he?

Christine is silent all the way back to the ferry landing. She is still wondering about that waiter in The Unicorn. They park the car, lock it, and board the ferry at ten-thirty. Ten minutes later, they are approaching the marina.

Years ago, when Ashley first saw the place, she began applauding. Jamie, who was then four, began clapping his hands, too, in imitation, and not knowing what he was cheering. Both children kept clapping as Eddie brought the *Jamash* in. The only approach to Marina Blue was by water. You either came on your own boat, or you took the rickety ferry over from the end of Lewiston Point Road.

Then, as now, the docks were painted the palest tint of azure, streaking the wood like a thin wash of watercolor. Before the site was turned into an eccentric boating hideaway, the grounds had served as an artists' retreat called The Cloister. Here, in the dim distant past, as many as a dozen writers, painters, and composers at a time could be housed and fed for periods as long as two months, while they worked on projects proposed to and accepted by The Cloister's board of directors.

Isolated on this secluded stretch of land a thousand yards off the northern tip of Lewiston Point, a wide assortment of creative men and women lived and worked in wooden residences affording views of tranquil Crescent Inlet to the east, and the sometimes turbulent Gulf of Mexico to the west. The largest of the dwellings served as a community meeting place, where the transient citizens of the retreat gathered nightly to discuss and sometimes vociferously evaluate each other's work in progress.

It was rumored that back in 1949, when Marina Blue was still The Cloister, John D. MacDonald wrote his first novel, *The Brass Cupcake,* while living on a houseboat here. It was further rumored that this earlier experience afloat served as inspiration for Travis McGee's *Busted Flush.* Adding credence to the hearsay was the large framed photo of the writer now hanging in the marina dining room, which had once been the community meeting hall. None of the other wooden buildings remained, although there were now tennis courts and a swimming pool on the grounds as well, luxuries not thought essential to the creative process back then in the bad old days.

The long weekend the Glendennings spent at Marina Blue provided the fondest of memories for the entire family. Eddie guessed he was still in love with Alice at the time. He had not yet begun gambling heavily. He had not yet met Christine. He later supposed he started gambling only when he realized he could not make his fortune as a stockbroker. In his view, betting on the dogs was a lot like buying and selling stocks, bonds, and commodities. It never occurred to him that one was a job and the other was an addiction.

He later also supposed that he'd started up with Christine only because he was no longer in love with Alice. It never occurred to him that he might have fallen out of love with Alice only because he'd already started up with Christine.

The way Eddie looks at it now, he chose Marina Blue as a hideaway only because he thought it would be a safe, familiar, and therefore comforting place to hold the kids until all this was over and done with.

It never occurs to him that he might have been trying to re-create for himself one of the happiest times of his life—before it got too late.

It never once occurs to him that it might already be too late.

Eddie doesn't think of himself as a criminal. He met criminals while he was working at Lowell, Hastings, Finch and Ulrich, thanks, men who engaged in insider trading and were later caught and sent to prison. He was never one of those. Which was perhaps why he'd never made a killing in the market, he was never a goddamn criminal. And he is not a criminal now.

There are men all over these United States, perhaps all over this *world,* righteous men who take their children away from negligent or promiscuous mothers, men who *rescue* their children, in effect, from households that are hopeless—though he can't claim to have done that, no. That would be lying to himself. And Eddie has never in his life lied to himself.

He knows that in the eyes of the law, he has kidnapped his children, which is a crime, but he is not a criminal. In the eyes of the law, he has taken his own children away from their mother, a woman perceived to be a widow. Which, by the way, and for all intents and purposes, is patently true. Since he is legally dead, or at least *presumed* to be dead, who is to say that someone declared dead isn't actually dead?

Who is to say that Alice is not truly a widow if, in her own perception, she is in fact a widow? Who indeed?

And who is to say that Edward Fulton Glendenning did not cease to exist on that night of September 21 last year, which was when Edward Fulton Glendenning disappeared? And is it a crime to vanish from the face of the earth? Does this make him a criminal?

He was certainly not a criminal when he first began seeing Christine on the sly, began cheating on Alice, so to speak, his wife of so many good years; that did not make him a criminal. Florida is supposed to have state laws going all the way back to 1868, and these laws govern adultery, unmarried people living together, and oral sex—but they are never enforced. When he first started seeing Christine on a regular if clandestine basis, Eddie got curious about these laws so he went into the legal department of Baxter and Meuhl, where he was then working, and checked out the Florida statutes in their brown leather covers embossed in red and gold, but he couldn't find any of those laws anywhere in any of the books. So if they weren't in the statutes, were they even laws at all, or just myths? So he convinced himself that he was not doing anything criminal by seeing a sexy little black girl once, and then twice, and then three or four times each and every week, he was certainly not a criminal.

But Chapter 61.052 of those same Florida statutes informed him that if he and Alice ever got divorced because the marriage was "irretrievably broken," then according to Chapter 61.08, titled "Alimony," the court could consider "the adultery of a spouse . . ."

Uh-oh.

". . . and the circumstances thereof in determining whether alimony would be awarded."

Which was not such good news.

By the time he met Christine, Eddie was into Angelet and Holmes for thirty grand. When he finally decided he had to do something to get out of this desperate situation, he owed them two hundred thou. With this huge debt hanging over his head, getting a divorce and paying alimony besides was entirely out of the question.

In Eddie's mind, the two "problems" (he called them) became

inextricably linked. If he could not get rid of Alice, he could not be with Christine full-time, and he would have to keep sneaking around corners and taking her to cheap roadside motels for quick afternoon fucks, which was not fair to either one of them. And if he could not get rid of his debt to Angelet and Holmes, then he could not get a divorce with its attendant alimony "penalties" (he called them).

So what to do?

Well, he could always kill Alice.

This was not a joke. Although he was not a criminal, killing Alice seemed to him a perfectly viable solution to at least one of the problems. Kill Alice, and he wouldn't have to divorce her. He would be free to marry Christine and be with her night and day, you are the one.

Unfortunately, this still left the other little problem, which was a debt of two hundred thousand dollars, payable on demand or he would either be killed or hurt very badly, these people did not fool around.

What to do, oh what to do?

Well, desperate people do desperate things.

When he first told Christine about the insurance policy on his life, she thought this was very interesting but did not see how it applied to their current situation.

"If I die in an accident, the death benefit is doubled," he told her.

"So?"

"Two hundred and fifty thousand."

"So?"

"So if I die in an accident, Alice gets two hundred and fifty thousand dollars. And we get to start a new life together."

"One," Christine said, "how do we start a new life together if you're dead?"

"I'm not dead. I'm presumed dead."

"And two, if *Alice* is the one who gets this insurance money, how do *we* get to start this new life together?"

"We kidnap my kids and hold them for ransom," Eddie said.

• • •

After he faked the drowning, they moved out of the state entirely. It might have been safe to settle on the East Coast of Florida someplace, but from Fort Myers to Palm Beach was just a short hop across the state on U.S. 80, and farther south you could jump onto Alligator Alley at Naples and be in Fort Lauderdale in what, two, three hours? They couldn't take that chance. Eddie Glendenning was dead. They didn't want any travelers from Cape October to run into his ghost in a bar someplace.

They chose New Orleans.

Easier to get lost in a big city.

Fun town besides. The Big Easy, they called it. And nobody looked cockeyed at a black-white relationship there. Plenty of those there already; Eddie and Christine didn't even merit a raised eyebrow.

He knew you could buy a fake ID on the Internet, but he was reluctant to do that because he felt it would leave some kind of paper trail that might come back to bite him on the ass later on. He was also leery of contacting anyone . . . well, *criminal* . . . who might be able to help him establish a new identity. By faking his own death, Eddie had already committed insurance fraud, and he was about to commit the crime of kidnapping, but he still did not think of himself as a criminal. He had not given up gambling—just because a person is dead doesn't mean he has to stop gambling—but gambling wasn't a crime. Gambling was an addiction, even though Eddie wasn't quite ready to admit he was an addict, either.

However, some addictions are related, and so there were gamblers in New Orleans who also used narcotics, and the sale or possession of controlled substances was a crime in Louisiana, the same as it was in any other state of the union. And these gamblers who were also using drugs knew the people who were *selling* these drugs, of course, and these people *were* criminals, even Eddie had to admit that. And these drug-dealer criminals knew people who were involved in yet other types of criminal activity, and one of those activities happened to be the manufacture and creation of false documents like passports, birth certificates, driver's licenses, credit cards, and even diplomas from Harvard University.

So by asking around—cautiously, to be sure—Eddie finally got a line on a man named Charles Franklin ("No relation to Ben," he told Eddie with a grin) who was able to provide a false driver's license issued to one Edward Graham residing at 336 East 120th Street in the city of New York, State of New York, with Eddie's new signature on it and everything.

And he was able to provide first a false American Express card under the cloned name of Michael Anderson, which he said would take Eddie through the month of October when the company would bill the real Michael Anderson, who would begin squawking about charges he'd never made. Franklin then created a cloned Visa card (true owner a man named Nelson Waterbury) that would take Eddie through November, and then a cloned Master Card for December and a cloned Discover card for January. By then, Eddie had found a job selling computer equipment and established a bank account of his own. When he applied for a bona fide credit card under his new name—Edward Graham, no middle initial—it was granted at once. He had no trouble passing a Louisiana driving test, either, and acquiring a legitimate driver's license as well.

By then, he had also married Christine Welles, who became Christine Graham, thereby adding the crime of bigamy to Eddie's already growing list of denied crimes.

Then again, it wasn't Eddie Glendenning who married her.

Eddie Glendenning was hardly a memory by then.

Always mindful of leaving a trail that can somehow be picked up, Mr. and Mrs. Edward Graham fly not to Fort Myers—the closest airport to Cape October—but instead to Tampa, where they rent a car and drive to a marina he knows in St. Pete. Using his new name and his new legitimate credit card and driver's license, Eddie rents a forty-foot Sundancer, a Sea Ray power cruiser that, with its pair of twin Volvo 430-horsepower engines, is capable of high performance in open water—although he plans only to take her down the Intercoastal to Cape October. In effect, he needs the boat more as a floating hotel than as a means of transportation.

Once on the inland waterway, he motors leisurely southward past the towering Sunshine Skyway to Anna Maria and Longboat, into Sarasota Bay, and past Venice and Englewood, and finally rounding Cape Haze and coming past Boca Grande. On the first day of April, he exits the Intercoastal at October Bay, where he finds the marina he and the family stayed at aboard the *Jamash* several years ago. Here on the northern end of Crescent Island, a thousand yards from where Lewiston Point Road dead-ends into Crescent Inlet, the azure docks of Marina Blue beckon in brilliant sunlight as he parks the Sundancer and cuts the engines.

He reminds Christine that this is April Fool's Day.

An appropriate time to be setting their plan in motion.

Eddie Glendenning drowned in the Gulf of Mexico on the night of September 21 last year. Surely the insurance company has paid the death benefit by now. Even so, they do not plan to take the children till the middle of May, after they've gone over the ground a hundred times, walked it through again and again to make sure there will be no mistakes.

Two hundred and fifty thousand dollars is riding on this little venture.

Their entire future together is riding on this little venture.

He does not dare wander very far from the boat, for fear someone will spot him, and recognize him, and blow the whole scheme.

It is Christine who purchases the hinged hasp that Eddie himself fastens to the door and jamb of the forward stateroom. In the same hardware store on the Trail, she buys a padlock that fits into the hasp, to keep the children secure until it is time to release them.

It is Christine as well who takes the ferry over to Lewiston Point, and phones for a taxi to carry her to the Fort Myers airport.

They dare not choose any of the rental car companies that line U.S. 41. It is their reasoning that if she rents at a smaller site, she might be recognized later on. There is a lot of traffic at an airport the size of the one in Fort Myers. No one will remember her. Or so is their reasoning.

The flat rate for the ride from the Lewiston Point ferry landing to the airport is seventy-five dollars. She goes directly to the Avis counter and presents her Clara Washington credit card and her Clara Washington driver's license with her Clara Washington photograph and signature on it, and within fifteen minutes she is driving a blue Chevrolet Impala out of the airport.

She picks up Route 78 West, and drives directly to the Cape.

At the Shell station on Lewiston Point Road, she crosses U.S. 41 and drives out over the bridge to Tall Grass. At the end of the road, she parks the car and again boards the ferry to Crescent Island.

It has taken her exactly thirty-two minutes from the gas station to Marina Blue.

She is still worried about that guy in the restaurant.

It is now almost midnight, and they are lying in each other's arms on the converted double berth in the middle stateroom, several feet from where the children are asleep in the locked master stateroom. It is Christine's expectation that tomorrow they will turn the children loose and leave Cape October behind forever—but she can't stop wondering why that guy in the restaurant thought he knew Eddie.

"Are you sure you never saw him before?" she whispers.

"Positive," he says.

She nods. The boat bobs gently on the water. Her eyes are wide open in the dappled dark.

"Suppose he recognized you?" she asks. "Suppose he knew you were Eddie Glendenning sitting there in that restaurant?"

"I don't think that's likely."

"But suppose."

"Who cares? We'll be out of here tomorrow night. Bali, remember? And we'll never come back. So who cares what some old fart in a restaurant—?"

"Why don't we leave tonight?"

"No," he says. "There are still some things I have to figure out."

"What things?"

"Well . . . the kids, for one."

"What's there to figure out? We drop them off someplace, and we're on our way."

"I'm not sure we can do that, Christine."

"Do what?"

"Just drop them off like that."

"I don't know what you mean, Eddie. Why can't we . . . ?"

"It's not as *simple* as that, Christine! I have to figure it *out*!"

His voice is a sharp cutting whisper.

She catches her breath.

Then, very slowly, she asks again, "What is there to figure out, Eddie?"

"We kidnapped them," he says. "We held them for ransom," he says. "That's what there is to figure out."

They are both silent for several moments.

"Why don't you take this off?" he whispers, and lifts the hem of the baby-doll nightgown she bought at Victoria's Secret.

On the other side of the locked master stateroom door, the children are wide awake, listening to every whispered word.

Sunday

May 16

11

Garcia's column is indeed in the coveted upper-right-hand position of the Sunday section's first page. His photograph runs in a box at the top of the column. It shows him smiling at the camera.

The story that leads off "Dustin's Dustbin" is titled:

ALL'S WELL THAT ENDS WELL

The subhead reads:

MUCH ADO ABOUT NOTHING

The story reads:

A simple failure to communicate caused a dollop of confusion and measure for measure of consternation these past few frantic days. It all began when a blonde in a blue Impala drove into the parking lot of Pratt Elementary School at the end of the school day Wednesday and picked up James Glendenning, 8, and his sister Ashley, 10. When the children did not show up for school the next morning, and when the school's calls to the home of Alice Glendenning, the children's mother and a recent widow, went unanswered, school officials became alarmed.

"It was all a comedy of errors," Mrs. Glendenning told the

Dustbin last night. "It was my sister who picked up the children. She was down here from Atlanta, visiting with her own children, and we decided to take the kids to Disney World, which is where we've been for the past two days. I should have called Pratt, I guess, but it was a spur of the moment decision, and we didn't think missing a few days of school would cause such a tempest."

Carol Matthews, Mrs. Glendenning's sister, is now back in Atlanta.

And the Glendenning children will return to school on Monday.

Which is as you'd like it.

There are some people out there who know that Garcia's little story is a pack of goddamn lies.

Well, not Phoebe Mears.

She accepts unconditionally that Alice Glendenning took little Jamie and Ashley to Disney World and forgot to tell the school about it. But if she sent her own sister to pick up the kids after school Wednesday, then what was that phone call from her asking about did they miss the bus and all? Had she also forgotten her sister was picking up the kids?

Phoebe knows that Mrs. Glendenning has been through a lot lately, her husband drowning and all. In which case, she can be forgiven a lapse of memory every now and then. So she agrees that all's well that ends well, and that everything was probably just much ado about nothing, after all. Which is just as she likes it, yes.

Luke Farraday can't figure out why that newspaper reporter would give him fifty bucks to tell him about the blue Impala and the blonde driving it if he knew all along that it was Mrs. Glendenning's sister picking up the kids. And also, what was that business about wanting to put an announcement about a party in the social calendar, when instead it turns out the kids went to Disney World with their mother? Or is the party next week sometime? Is it a birthday party? Is that why Mrs. Glendenning took the kids to Orlando? Was it a birthday present? Is it one of their birthdays coming up?

Sometimes, Luke gets confused.

Then again, it said in the paper that "A simple failure to communicate caused a dollop of confusion and measure for measure of consternation these past few frantic days," so maybe *everybody's* confused and consterned about whatever arrangement the sisters made between them.

One thing good about it, though.

He now knows why those kids would've got in the car with a stranger. It was their aunt all along.

Anyway, the hell with it.

He's still fifty bucks ahead.

Jennifer and Rafe are in bed when they read the story in the *Tribune.* In fact, except for the five minutes it took Jennifer to put on a robe and go out to the mailbox for the paper, they have not budged from that bed since they climbed into it late Friday night. Rafe even called his wife from Jennifer's bed yesterday afternoon.

Rafe knows an old joke that goes like this:

"Do you always tell your wife you love her after you have sex?"

"Oh yes. Wherever I am, I make a point of calling her."

Rafe told Jennifer this joke after he'd spoken to Carol yesterday. It did not seem to trouble him that he had his head on Jennifer's left breast while he spoke to his wife. It did not seem to trouble Jennifer, either. She laughed when he told her the joke.

They are not laughing now.

They have just finished reading Dustin Garcia's little story.

"Total bullshit," Rafe says.

"What makes you think so?" Jennifer asks.

"Think so?" Rafe says. "*Think?* I know for a fact that there is not a word of truth in this article. To begin with, my wife is not a blonde. She has black hair. So does her sister. So it wasn't my wife *or* her sister who picked up those kids after school. That's the first thing. The second thing is my wife didn't get down here to Florida till yesterday morning, so she couldn't have been going to Disney World with her sister and the kids on Thursday, whenever the article says it was, that's the second thing. And the third thing, I was *in* my sister-in-law's house, the fucking place was crawling with cops, they *know* the kids've been kidnapped, so this whole story about Disney World is pure and total bullshit. Either it's something Alice herself gave to the paper to protect herself because the paper was pestering her, or else the cops themselves planted it for some reason or other."

"That's what I think it is," Jennifer says.

"The cops planted it?"

"Yes."

"Which means they were working with this Cuban fuck, whoever he is," Rafe says. "Where'd he get that name Dustin, anyway?"

"His mother probably was a fan."

"Of Dustin Hoffman's, you mean?"

"Yes, of *course* Dustin Hoffman," Jennifer says. "Who else is named Dustin besides Dustin Hoffman?"

"Well, *this* guy, for example," Rafe says, and taps the byline on the column. "In fact, maybe it's the other way around," he suggests. "Maybe Dustin Hoffman was named after Dustin Garcia."

Jennifer gives him a look.

"So you think that's it, huh?" she says. "They figured this out between them. Garcia and the cops?"

"Don't you think?"

"But why?" she says. "I don't see what they hope to accomplish."

"Here's his picture right here," Rafe says, and grins like a barracuda. "Why don't we just go ask him?"

Tully Stone, the special agent in charge of the FBI's regional office seventy-two miles north of Cape October, has copies of all the southwest Florida newspapers on his desk that Sunday morning, but the one that interests him most is the Cape October *Tribune.* There on the first page of the Sunday section, someone named Dustin Garcia has written a droll little story about Alice Glendenning—the woman Stone's agents have been busting their asses over—taking her kids to Disney World for a couple of days and thinking it's comical that everyone's in an uproar about them being missing.

"It's a plant," Sally Ballew tells him.

"No question," Felix Forbes says.

The two agents read the story early this morning, and then drove all the way up here to Stone's office at regional HQ, an hour's drive in very light traffic. Stone was perturbed on the telephone, and he is visibly upset now, to say the least.

"It's nothing to worry about," Sally tells him. "Just another example of the way the Mickey Mouse department down there is handling the case."

"Do you think there's any truth to it?" Stone asks.

"Not a word," Forbes says.

"Pure misinformation," Sally amends.

"Did they advise you of this?"

"That they were planning to do it? No."

"Then how do you know it was them?"

"Who else could it've been?" Forbes asks.

"Maybe the woman herself."

"Why?" Sally asks.

"Let the perps think she's being a good little girl. Let them think she hasn't called the cops."

"Well, I guess that's a remote possibility," Sally says dubiously, "but my guess is a plant."

"Shall I call them?" Stone asks.

"Why not?"

"See what's on their alleged minds." He pulls the phone toward him, begins looking through his directory.

"He's probably at the Glendenning house," Forbes suggests.

"Have you got that number?"

"Sure," Sally says, and writes it down for him.

"What's his name down there?"

"Sloate. Wilbur Sloate."

"That's a name, all right," Stone says, and begins dialing. Sally is thinking "Tully Stone" ain't such a winner, either.

"Hello?" a woman's voice says.

"Mrs. Glendenning?"

"Yes."

"Is Detective Sloate there?"

"Who's this, please?"

"FBI. Special Agent in Charge Tully Stone."

"Just a minute, please."

Stone waits.

"Sloate," a voice says.

"Detective Sloate, this is Special Agent in Charge Tully Stone, calling from FBI Regional?"

"Yes, sir," Sloate says.

"It was our understanding till now that a kidnapping has taken place down there, which of course if true would naturally attract our attention . . ."

"Yes, sir, it already has. Agents Ballew and Forbes were down here visiting with us already."

Visiting, Stone thinks.

"I am aware of that," he says. "But, Detective, I have here on my desk a copy of this morning's Cape October *Tribune,* and on the first page of the Sunday section there's a story written by a man named Dustin Garcia . . ."

"Yes, sir, I'm familiar with the story."

"Then you know it says the Glendenning children weren't kidnapped at all, they merely went on a little outing to Disney World."

"Yes, sir, that's what the story says."

"Tell me, Detective, did you folks plant that story?"

"Yes, sir, we did."

"Would've been nice if you'd told us what you were up to."

"Would've been nice if you'd told us you had a make on the woman who rented that blue Impala at the airport."

Stone says nothing.

"Or that the name she gave Avis is a phony. Would've been nice to know all that without us having to go digging all the way to New York on it."

"If we've been remiss—"

"You have indeed, sir."

"—then I'm sorry, Detective. But the lines are somewhat blurred here . . ."

"They wouldn't be if we could share information and work this together."

"What do you think that story's going to accomplish?" Stone asks, changing the subject.

"We're hoping they'll turn the kids loose and go on a spending spree."

"Have they given any indication that they're about to do that?"

"No, sir. But we're with the Glendenning woman now, awaiting further word from them. We're hoping—"

"Does she know you planted that story?"

"Yes, sir, she has been informed of that."

"What was her reaction?"

"She did not seem terribly pleased, sir."

"Neither are we," Stone says flatly. "It's my understanding that a ransom was already delivered. Is that the case?"

"Yes, sir. The drop was made on Friday morning at ten o'clock."

"And no word from them yet?"

"Well, she called . . ."

"She?"

"The black woman. One of the perps. She called Mrs. Glendenning to tell her the kids were okay, and they were checking the money."

"What does that mean, checking the money?"

"I don't know, sir. Those were her exact words."

"And that was when?"

"Friday afternoon, sir."

"This is Sunday. What makes you think they aren't in Hawaii by now?"

"They could be, that's true."

"Well, has the mother heard from them since then?"

"No, sir. What we're hoping is the black woman and her blonde accomplice—"

"What blonde? Is this a new development?"

"No, sir, we've known all along it was a blonde woman who picked up the children after school on Wednesday. I believe your people know that, too, that's one of the things we shared. What I'm saying is the ransom notes are marked, and we're hoping—"

"How are they marked?"

"The serial numbers. The bills are supers, difficult to detect without special equipment. But they're all A-series bills, and the serial number is identical on each and every bill. We've circulated that number to every—"

"Who the hell's gonna check serial numbers?" Stone asks.

"Someone might."

"Or someone might meanwhile *kill* those kids," Stone says.

The line goes silent.

"Here's what I'm gonna do, Sloate."

No more "Detective," Sally notices. The gloves are off.

"I'm sending Forbes and Ballew to the Glendenning house. They should be down on the Cape by . . ."

He looks up at the wall clock.

". . . eleven, eleven-thirty. Let's say twelve noon to be safe. They'll be running the case from now on, and I expect your full cooperation in bringing it to a swift and—"

"With all due respect, sir, it's *your* department that hasn't been—"

"You don't understand me, Sloate, do you? This just went *federal* on you. The case is *ours.* Ballew and Forbes are running it from this minute on."

Sloate says nothing.

"Think you've got that?" Stone asks.

"Yes, I've got it," Sloate says.

"Good," Stone says, and hangs up.

He looks across his desk at Sally.

"You heard," he says.

"We heard," Sally says.

Ashley is complaining that it's Sunday, and they want to have waffles.

"We always have waffles on Sunday," she says.

Christine explains that there isn't a waffle iron here on the boat, but she can make pancakes if they'd like. Would they like her to make pancakes?

"Why'd we have to come here, anyway?" Ashley asks. "And why can't I talk to Mommy again?"

"Yes or no, honey?" Christine says. "Pancakes or cereal, which?"

"Daddy always makes waffles on Sunday," Ashley says. "Where is he, anyway?"

"Up at the front desk. Getting the newspapers."

"I'm gonna tell him you wouldn't make waffles for us."

"Fine, tell him," Christine says. "Pancakes or cereal?"

"Pancakes," Ashley says grudgingly.

Eddie comes back with the newspapers some ten minutes later.

"She wouldn't make waffles for us," Ashley tells him.

"That's okay," he says. "Pancakes are good, too."

"Not as good as waffles."

"But I see you ate them all, didn't you?"

"When are we going home, Daddy?"

"Soon," he says. "Why don't you go watch television awhile? Lot of good shows on Sunday morning."

"Jamie?" she says. "You want to watch TV?"

Jamie nods and gets up from the table.

"You got a kiss for Daddy?" Eddie asks.

Jamie offers his cheek, but doesn't say a word. It breaks Eddie's heart that his son doesn't talk anymore. He wonders if that has anything to do with the drowning, some kind of reaction to the supposed drowning. He'd hate that to be the case. But he hates a lot of things about this entire undertaking. He only knows that a man has to do what he has to do. Intently, he watches his children as they go into the forward stateroom. He hears cartoons starting on the television set. He sighs heavily.

Taking Christine topside, he shows her the Sunday section.

"What do you make of it?" she asks.

"Well, we know it isn't true," he says. "It's just some story she invented for this reporter."

"But *why*?"

"To let us think she didn't call the police."

"We *know* she called the police!" Christine says. "They followed us. And she knows that, too. I *told* her we were followed. So why this story in the paper?"

"She's trying to convince us she knows nothing about that maroon Buick. She's telling us the cops *don't* know anything at all about this, we've got the money now, so just let the kids go."

"I think you're right," Christine says. "That's what it means, honey. She's promising safe passage, is what this story is. Let the kids go, and we're home free."

"If only it was as simple as that," he says.

"What do you mean?" she says.

"Nothing," he says.

"No, tell me, hon. What's the matter?"

"Nothing," he says again.

Wearing a pale blue sports jacket with darker blue slacks, a blue straw hat with a snap brim, and blue loafers with a fancy Gucci buckle, Dustin Garcia feels he looks quite dapper on this sticky hot morning. He comes walking out of the *Trib* building jauntily, a man secure in the knowledge that he is a big-time celebrity in this little town that is Cape October.

As he is about to enter his car in the parking lot behind the building, the pair of them suddenly appear. Big burly man, tall beautiful blonde woman.

"Mr. Garcia?" the man says.

"Yes?"

Fans, Garcia thinks. He is not surprised. His photo is at the top of his column and he has even been approached for an autograph once or twice, which can become annoying when a man is having dinner in a restaurant.

"Few questions we'd like to ask you," the man says. "Want to come with us, please?"

"Who . . . ?"

The man grabs Garcia's right arm, just above the biceps. He squeezes hard. *Not* fans then. In which case . . . ?

"The red car," the man says. "Right over there."

Garcia says nothing as they lead him to the car and open the front door on the passenger side. The man urges him inside with a polite little shove. The blonde takes a seat beside him, behind the wheel. Car doors slam. The blonde twists the ignition key, starting the car and the air conditioner.

"You know, of course—" Garcia begins.

"We just want to ask some questions," the man says.

"It doesn't look that way."

"It *is* that way," the blonde says.

"All right, I'll accept that. What are your questions?"

"Why'd you and the cops concoct that story in your column this morning?"

"I have no idea what you mean."

"About the Glendenning kidnapping. Why'd you make up a fake story?"

"What kidnapping? I don't know anything about a kidnapping."

"Your Disney World story," the blonde says.

"You know those kids didn't go to Disney World," the man says.

"You know those kids are missing," the blonde says. "So why the phony story?"

"Those are the facts as I collected them," Garcia says.

"From who?"

"From Mrs. Glendenning herself."

"That's a lie and you know it."

"Look," Garcia says, "who the fuck *are* you people?"

"Language, language," the man warns.

The car has cooled off rapidly. Outside in the parking lot, the black asphalt reflects shimmering waves of heat, but it is cool here in the car now, and yet Garcia is sweating. He wonders who these people are. Is it possible they're part of a gang that took the Glendenning kids? Is there in fact a gang instead of just the black woman and her blonde accomplice, as Sloate and his people seem to think? If so, and if these two *are* part of a gang, if there *is* a gang and not just the two women, and if this ape of a man is part of the gang, then Garcia is in danger here. So tell them what they want to know, he thinks.

Instead, he asks, "How do you know about any kidnapping? If, in fact, there's *been* a kidnapping?"

"You know there's been a kidnapping," the man says.

"The Glendenning kids," the blonde says.

"You know a quarter of a million dollars in phony bills has already been paid."

As a matter of fact, Garcia does not know this. Neither Sloate nor anyone on his team ever once mentioned that the ransom money was counterfeit. They told him the bills were marked, yes, but they did not say they were fake. So this, now, is a new development. He is once again sniffing Pulitzer prize in the air.

"Let's say the children *were*—"

"Look," the man says, leaning closer to him and talking directly into his ear, "let's cut the shit, okay? The kids were snatched, and you know it. All we want to know is what the *cops* know about whoever done it."

"Did *you* do it?" Garcia asks.

"Don't be a fucking moron," the man says.

Garcia's mind is reeling. If these two are not, after all, part of any gang that kidnapped the Glendenning kids, then who or what *are* they? And what do they want?

"The cops only know it's a blonde and a black girl," he says, and looks the blonde directly in the eye, hoping she will blink. She does not.

"Locals?" she asks.

"Probably not. It was a rental car."

"The Impala?"

"Yes."

"Who rented it?"

"The black girl."

"What's her name?"

Garcia doesn't know her name. Sloate didn't tell him her name. All he said was that a black girl rented the Impala at the Fort Myers airport, and that this led them to believe the perps had flown in.

"What's she look like, this black girl?"

"Hot. Jungle meat."

"And the blonde?"

"Delicate features, hair to her shoulders." He pauses. "Like you," he says.

The blonde still doesn't blink.

"What else?" she asks.

"That's all they've got."

"Why the phony story?" the man asks.

"I don't know."

"You *wrote* the fucking thing . . ."

"They *told* me what to write!"

"But not why, huh?"

"Only broad strokes."

"Let's hear the broad strokes."

"Sloate wants . . . he's the local cop on the case," Garcia explains.

The man nods. He already knows this. But if they have nothing to do with the kidnapping, how . . . ?

"He wants the black girl and her blonde accomplice to believe that Alice Glendenning followed their instructions and did not go to the police. The black girl warned her not to go to the police, you see. Told her if she wasn't alone when she dropped off the ransom money, they'd kill the children. Told her if she wasn't back where she was supposed to be in half an hour, they'd kill the children. So my story was all about protecting those two kids. If the kids went to Disney World, there was no kidnapping, you see? In which case, it's safe to return them, drop them off on a street corner someplace, anyplace, just get rid of them. Sloate wants those kids back safe and sound. That's what he hopes the story will accomplish."

"It just might," the blonde agrees.

"Do the cops have any idea where these people are holding the kids?" the man asks.

"If they knew that—"

"Do they even have a fucking *clue*?"

"Not that I know of."

There's one thing Garcia hasn't given them. He hasn't told them that once the two dames let the kids loose, Sloate hopes they'll go on a spending spree. Run out to spend all those marked hundred-dollar bills. Buy themselves some fur coats and diamond rings. Leave a trail a mile wide. That was one of the purposes of the story. But he hasn't told them this.

"Okay to go now?" he asks.

"No, now we're gonna shoot you," the blonde says.

For an instant, Garcia's heart stops.

But the blonde is laughing.

Garcia is still sweating when he steps out of the red Thunderbird into blistering heat.

As the pair drive off, he hears more laughter from inside the convertible.

His name is Joseph Ontano, and that is the name he goes by at work. But Angelet and Holmes know him as Joey Onions because in addition to being an insurance adjuster, Joey is also a gambler, and they are the men with whom he places his frequent bets. At the moment, and by their virtually infallible count, Joey Onions is into them for some fifty thousand bucks, give or take. Which is why he is always so happy to provide them with sometimes valuable information about the inside workings of Garland Insurance. The numbers racket, as Angelet and Holmes both know, is premised on the insurance business, which is why it is also sometimes known as the "policy game"—but that's another story, and that's not why they're looking for Joey today.

Angelet and Holmes know exactly where to find him because that is their business, even on a Sunday. At ten minutes past noon, on this particularly sweaty hot Sunday in May, when the dogs aren't running, they look for Joey at a cockfight in the black section of Cape October. Florida's HB 1593 makes it a felony to breed, sell, or possess dogs or birds for the purpose of fighting. But hey, man, this is Colleytown.

Colleytown was, in fact, once a real town named Colley before it got incorporated as part of greater Cab'Octubre after the Civil War. Minuscule in comparison to some of the sprawling black ghettoes elsewhere in the South—there are maybe, what, two, three thousand people here?—Colleytown can hold its own with the worst of them. Because Cape October is a resort destination with sandy beaches and palm trees and fishing piers and little hidden lagoons, one tends to forget that it's a part of the South, or that the entire state of Florida, in fact, is really the *deepest* part of the South. In the South, there are ghettos. And in ghettos, there are drugs and prostitution and gambling, and the gambling often includes illegal sports events like cockfights. Then again, that holds true for almost every city in the United States. So who gives a shit about what happens in the rest of the world? Holmes thinks. Then again, Holmes is black. And he considers himself lucky that he's here in Florida living off the fat of the land instead of getting shot at in some foreign hood like all his dumb fuckin brothers in Bush's stupid fuckin crusade.

The cockfighting season in Cape October roughly coincides with the tourist season, though not too many tourists are attracted to what its devotees call "a blood sport." The end of May will mark the official end of this season's fights, but even now, in the middle of the month, there are fewer fights than there were last month or the month before then. Actually, the fights began tapering off shortly after Easter, which is when the tourist season unofficially ends. There have been only two or three fights a week since then, at different times and in different venues, depending on how much advance knowledge the police have managed to gather. This Sunday's fights were supposed to take place last night at a venue in Bradenton. Instead, the local fuzz were alerted, and so the venue was changed to Colleytown, and the time was changed to Sunday afternoon, when most good people are home reading the comics.

This Sunday afternoon, there are plenty of good people about to watch the first of the fights, which is between a rooster named Ebony because he is as black as midnight, and a rooster named King Kock because he has been crossbred with a very large pheasant and is positively enormous. Nurtured on steroids to increase their muscle tissue, dosed with angel dust to numb any pain, both birds are equipped with fighting spurs before they enter the carpeted ring. In India, where the "sport" enjoys wide popularity, the birds fight bare-heeled using only their God-given claws to shred and destroy. In Puerto Rico, a long plastic apparatus that resembles a darning needle is attached to each of the bird's heels. Here in this part of Florida, the chosen artificial device is called a slasher. It is a piece of steel honed to razor-sharp precision. These spurs are fastened to both claws. One of these birds will die a horrible death in the next few minutes.

King Kock is the favorite to win, the odds on him being five-to-six. This means that if Joey bets two grand on the bird's nose—or his beak, to be more accurate—he will take home twenty-four hundred dollars, which is not a fortune but which is better than a kick in the face. He has been on a losing streak this past month, which is why he's into Angelet and Holmes for such a large sum, and so he takes the favored bet, King Kock to win at five-to-six.

Ebony turns out to be a vicious little bastard.

The crowd roars, "*Kill him, kill him!*"—this is such a genteel sport—as he tears King Kock apart, limb by limb, feather by feather.

Joey Onions has just lost a lot of money on this stupid fuckin King Kock, and he's not happy. He is even less happy to see—entering the barn enclosing the ring—the two men to whom he still owes fifty large. Sometimes these people come around to collect at the most inopportune times. Like now, when he has just dropped two thousand dollars on a bird that couldn't peck shit out of his own grandmother. If they are here for even part of the fifty, they haven't got a prayer. But if they decide to get ugly about this, he may very well go home with a broken kneecap.

This is not what Joey Onions enjoys about gambling. He does not enjoy losing, but even less does he enjoy crossing the path of an irate bookie. Or bookies, as is the case here and now, pushing their way through the crowd toward him, one of them Hispanic and the other black, and both of them bigger than the big bald guy at the door, who Joey now wishes hadn't let him into the ring in the first place, where he's just lost two grand he could now be handing over to these two thugs if that's why they're here, which he certainly hopes isn't the case.

"Hey, guys," he says jovially. "What gives?"

"No check in the mail, bro," Holmes says.

Joey doesn't like it when a nigger calls him "bro," but he's willing to take any kind of insult so long as this isn't about the money he owes these guys. Or is that what Holmes means by "No check in the mail, bro?" Is that his cute nigger way of saying "You still owe us fifty large, bro, and here you are throwing away money on the birds"?

"Which check might that be, Dave?"

"We spoke to the lady yesterday," Angelet says. "No check in the mail."

"And which lady might that be, Rudy?"

"That lady might be Alice Glendenning, who you said a check went out to from Garland last week."

"Oh," Joey says.

So that's what this is about.

What occurred, actually, was the last time these two came around asking about money matters and such, they happened to mention that they were still in the hole for two hundred K from a guy named Glendenning who drowned out on the Gulf seven, eight months ago, it must've been, and whereas they might be getting stiffed by *him* because he was dead and all, this didn't mean they were going to let themselves get snookered by a small-time little *shit* like Joey who was still alive, was actually what they'd called him. Which was when Joey happened to mention that he recalled the name Glendenning from some correspondence back and forth between Garland and a lawyer, and he would look into the matter for them if they so desired.

So he went back to the office and checked the files, and sure enough there was indeed a claim filed by a woman named Alice Glendenning as beneficiary of a $250,000 double indemnity policy on the life of her husband, Edward Fulton Glendenning. According to the records, this claim had not yet been satisfied, though it looked as if it might soon be.

Now Joey is not a very big reader, but he is fond of the sequence in George Orwell's book *Nineteen Eighty-four* where the hero is being tortured with caged rats about to eat his face, and he yells, "Do it to Julia!" who is his girlfriend, telling them to put the rats on her face instead of his, thereby betraying her to save his own skin.

So Joey stretches the truth a tiny little bit and goes back to Angelet and Holmes with news that a check has already gone out to the Glendenning woman, and they should look to her for payment of her husband's gambling debt, instead of coming around breaking his balls all the time for a lousy fifty G's.

"Yeah, that check went out," he tells them again now.

Which is another lie.

"You sure about that?" Holmes asks.

"Positive," Joey says.

And then—figuring it can't do any harm, can it?—he embroiders the lie just a tiny little bit more.

"In fact, it was already cashed," he says. "I saw the cancelled check last week sometime."

"Then the fuckin bitch is lying to us," Holmes says.

"I'll bet," Joey says.

What the hell, he thinks.

Let *her* mother worry.

The FBI arrives at twenty minutes past noon.

Brusquely and bustily informing Sloate and Di Luca that the Feds have now taken over the case, Sally Ballew immediately begins detailing the way things will be handled from this moment on.

"First," she says, ticking the point off on her index finger, "Mrs. Glendenning will never again talk directly to the kidnappers. Is that clear? Detectives? Mrs. Glendenning?"

"What if they ask for me?" Alice says.

"Hand the phone to me."

"That can be dangerous," Sloate says. "They told her not to call—"

"They already know we're in it," Sally says. "From what I understand, you blew surveillance."

"A garbage truck intervened," Sloate says.

Sloate offers the excuse like a kid explaining that the dog just ate his homework. Sally merely gives him a look.

"Second," she says, using her middle finger to tick off another point, "no one outside of law enforcement enters this house again." She turns to Carol as if just discovering her and asks, "Who are you, miss?"

"I'm Alice's sister," Carol says.

"She stays," Alice says.

"Fine, just keep out of the way," Sally says, dismissing her.

"How do you plan to get my children back?" Alice asks.

"Exactly the way we've done it before," Sally says.

"And how exactly is that?"

"First," Sally says, using her fingers again, "we let them think they're running the show."

They *have* been running the show, Alice thinks. And they're *still* running it. They've got the money, and they've got my kids. What does that add up to, if not running the show?

"They *are* running the show," she says.

Sloate says nothing. He is enjoying seeing someone else in the hot seat for a change. Marcia is enjoying this, too. She hasn't liked Sally from minute one, and her opinion of her hasn't changed an iota. The two local dicks can barely suppress smiles.

"Next," Sally says, ticking it off on her ring finger, "we find out where they are . . ."

"And how do we do that?" Alice asks.

"We are still currently checking hotels, motels, bed and—"

"Suppose they rented a private house?" Alice asks. "Or a condo? There are hundreds of—"

"We're checking real estate agents as well. We have the woman's false name, we're hoping she may have used that. Once we learn *where* they are, we contain them there with the children, and we move in."

"Move in?" Alice says. "What about my kids?"

"Don't worry, they'll be completely safe."

"How can you promise that?"

"Trust us," Sally says.

The telephone rings.

Marcia is about to put on earphones. The phone rings again. Sally grabs the earphones from her and puts them on her own head. The phone rings a third time. "Take it," she tells Alice. "If it's them, put me on. I'll do the talking." Alice picks up on the fourth ring.

"Hello?"

"Mrs. Glendenning?"

"Yes?"

"This is Rudy Angelet. You're lying to us. We'll be there to pick up the money in half an hour."

The line goes dead.

"Who the hell was *that*?" Sally asks.

12

At the Shell station on Lewiston Point Road and U.S. 41, they buy a road map and two containers of coffee, and then go out to Jennifer's T-Bird to study the map.

The top is up and the air conditioner is blowing full blast; Rafe is afraid his wife might be out buying a container of milk or something, and he doesn't want her to spot him in an open red convertible with a gorgeous blonde. For all Carol knows, he's on the road to Atlanta, which reminds him that he ought to call the kids when he gets a chance, make sure they're okay. He hasn't yet mentioned this to Jennifer, because he knows how women feel about another woman's kids. Rafe thinks he knows a lot about women.

Poring over the map, sipping at their coffees, he and Jennifer could easily be two tourists trying to figure out the best way to get to Sea World or someplace. Instead, they are trying to figure out the best way to get to the black woman and the blonde who have Alice's children and incidentally $250,000 in so-called super-bills.

"Half hour's drive from here," Jennifer says.

"Is what the man said."

Told her if she wasn't back where she was supposed to be in half an hour, they'd kill the children.

Was what Garcia said, exactly.

Half an hour from the gas station here on 41 and Lewiston.

"Means what?" Rafe says. "Thirty or forty miles in any direction?"

"Depending on traffic, right."

"Is there a scale on this thing?"

They turn the map this way and that until they find a scale of miles in the lower left-hand corner. They don't have a ruler in the car, but it looks like an inch equals thirty miles, more or less. An inch is about the length of the top joint of Rafe's thumb. So if the two chicks are holding the kids someplace a half hour away from the Shell station here, then using the station as the center of a circle, and using Rafe's thumb joint as the radius . . .

Thirty miles to the east of Cape October would put them in the middle of the General George C. Ryan Wildlife Refuge. Is it possible they're keeping the kids in a tent out there?

"I don't want to go anyplace where there are any snakes," Jennifer says. "Fuck the two-fifty."

"Me, neither," Rafe says.

But he wouldn't mind facing a few snakes if it meant getting his hands on all that cash. Hell, people on *Survivor* did that for a lot less money.

Just southeast of the refuge, on route 884, is the town of Compton Acres, which Rafe has never heard of. About a half hour *north* of the Cape, on U.S. 41, there's Port Lawrence. About a half hour *south* is Calusa Springs. To the west of the Cape are the offshore keys and the great big Gulf of Mexico.

"Let's call some real estate agents," Jennifer suggests.

On her way home from twelve o'clock Mass, Rosie Garrity picks up the Cape October *Tribune.* She does not begin reading it until she is in her own kitchen sipping a cup of hot tea. She knows at once that Dustin Garcia's story is a complete lie.

First, she was right there in the Glendenning house when that black woman called and told Mrs. Glendenning she had the kids.

Next, she has met Mrs. Glendenning's sister—Carol Matthews is her name—and she knows damn well that woman ain't no blonde. Her hair is as brown as Mrs. Glendenning's, the two of them could pass for twins, in fact, there ain't no way the blonde in the blue Impala could be Carol Matthews, no way at all.

So what is this all about?

Is this some kind of cop trick?

Are they working in cahoots with the newspaper?

In which case, the police have taken some action, after all. In which case, her efforts have not been in vain. There is still hope for those two innocent little kiddies.

But what are they trying to accomplish with their lies about Mrs. Glendenning's sister and a trip to Disney World? Rosie knows Mrs. Glendenning and her sister didn't take their kids to no Disney World. Little Jamie and Ashley, poor dears, were picked up by a blonde in a blue Impala, all right, but that wasn't no Carol Matthews, and there wasn't no trip to Orlando in the offing. That was somebody working in cahoots with a black woman who called to say she had the kids and would kill them if the police were informed.

She feels like calling Mrs. Glendenning right this minute, tell her that instead of screaming at her on the phone the way she did Friday night, she should get down on her hands and knees and thank God for people like herself, Rosie Garrity, who *did* in fact inform the police, and who is damn glad she did!

Something's in the wind now, she feels certain of that, all those lies in the paper.

"So what's new today?" her husband asks.

"Bunch of lies, is what," Rosie says.

"Who's lying now?" he asks.

He is still in his pajamas. She hates it when he comes to the breakfast table without even throwing on a robe. Almost one-thirty, he's still in his pajamas.

"Mrs. Glendenning," Rosie says. "What time did you get in last night, George?"

"Little before midnight," George says, and pours and drinks a glass of orange juice. "What's she lying about?" he asks, and pops a pair of frozen waffles into the toaster.

"Her kids getting kidnapped."

"Oh?"

"I told you, remember? She's now saying they weren't kidnapped at all."

"Why would she do that?"

"'Liar, liar, pants on fire,' is why."

"Uh-huh," George says, totally uninterested, and pours himself a cup of coffee from the pot on the stove. He butters the waffles, pours maple syrup on them, and then sits down at the table to eat. He is silent for several moments. Then, suddenly, he snaps his fingers.

"*That's* who he looked like!" he says.

"I don't know what you're talking about, George."

"Her husband who drowned."

"What about him?"

"I thought I saw him last night."

"Well, *that'd* be some kinda miracle," Rosie says, "seein' as how he's been dead these past eight months."

"Well, of course," George says. "I know it *wasn't* him. I'm just saying it *looked* like him. Even though the blond hair was long, like a hippie. Besides, he was with some black girl, so of course it wasn't him. Especially since he's dead."

Long blond hair, Rosie thinks.

Black girl, she thinks.

"Holy Mary, Mother of God!" she says aloud.

If the FBI or the local cops knew that Edward Fulton Glendenning was still alive, their check of real estate agents on the Cape and in neighboring vicinities would most likely include a search for an Edward Fulton as well as any recent renter with the initials EG. As taught in Identity Change 101, they know that a person deliberately getting lost will often use his own initials in choosing a new name, or simply use his existing middle name as his new surname. Rarely will he change his given name. He is too used to being called Frank or Charlie or Jimmy.

But the law enforcement people making phone calls in Alice's living room do not know that Edward Glendenning is still alive, or that he is now an entirely new individual who calls himself Edward Graham. So their calls to various real estate agents and condo rental offices ask only for a possible renter named Clara Washington, the only name they have, who they know is a black woman in the company of a blonde.

Listening to them making their fruitless phone calls, Alice realizes they are merely clutching at straws. She stopped believing in God on the morning they informed her that her husband had drowned in the Gulf of Mexico. If God truly existed, He would not have allowed such a thing to happen. But now she begins praying, desperately and silently, that Clara Washington and her blond girlfriend will call again soon to tell her they've now "checked the money," whatever that means, and are letting the children go. *Please, dear God,* she prays, *let the phone ring.*

It does not ring.

Instead, the doorbell does.

The first thing Holmes sees when the door to the Glendenning house opens is a chesty black woman holding what looks like a nine-millimeter Glock in her fist.

He backs off at once, almost knocking Angelet off the front steps.

"Hey, sistuh," he says, holding up both hands, palms toward her, "ain' no need for the cannon."

"You're no brother of mine," Sally says.

Angelet is already turning to run.

"Hold it right there!" she snaps.

He freezes in his tracks.

"Both of you step inside here," she says.

Holmes goes in first, sidling past her, looking around as he enters. Angelet comes in behind him. Sally closes the door. Neither of the men knows what the hell is going on here. Is this a holdup they've stepped into? Everybody seems to be strapped, except for the Glendenning woman and another woman who looks just like her. There are four women and two men altogether. The big busty sister who answered the door with a gun in her hand—and it is a Glock, Holmes now confirms—another woman wearing a shoulder holster and sitting behind what looks like some kind of electronic equipment, plus the Glendenning woman and her look-alike. The two men are also wearing shoulder holsters and packing big weapons. It suddenly occurs to Holmes that perhaps Alice Glendenning has informed the law on him and his good buddy Rudy here. Which, if true, was not a very nice thing to do.

"Look," he says, "I don't know what's going on here, but nobody's done nothin to—"

"What's going *on* here," Sally says, "is you're trying to extort money from Mrs. Glen*denning* here . . ."

"Extort? Hey, no . . ."

"Hey, no, no," Angelet says, holding up his hands in denial. "All we're doing—"

"All you're doing is threatening to harm her if she doesn't make good on her—"

"No, no, hey—"

"—deceased husband's *debt*!"

"*Threaten* her? *Who* threatened her? Lady, did we threaten you?" Holmes asks Alice, and takes a step toward her, which must appear menacing to the lady with the Glock because she raises it again and points it at his head.

"Hey," he says, "watch it with that gun, okay? Who the hell are you, anyway? What's it to you, this woman's—?"

"Special Agent—"

"—husband owes us—"

"Sally Ballew, Federal Bureau of—"

That's enough for Holmes. He knows the rest of the sentence, doesn't have to hear the rest of it. The titty sister here is an FBI agent. Eddie Glendenning's widow done called the fuckin FBI on them!

"Okay, we're out of here," he says. "Lady, forget what your husband owes—"

"Just one damn *second*!" Sally shouts.

Alice blinks.

The pistol is steady in Sally Ballew's hand. It is undeniably pointed straight at David Holmes's head. It is aimed directly between his eyes, as a matter of fact.

"Put it in writing," Sally says.

"Whut?"

"Put it in writing. Felix, get the man a pen and some paper."

"Yes, Sally," Forbes says, and reaches into his inside jacket pocket to remove from it a genuine bona-fide fountain pen, which Holmes didn't know people actually wrote with anymore. Forbes tears a page from a little leather-bound notebook, and hands both pen and paper to Holmes, who looks at Sally and shrugs expectantly.

"Write what I tell you," Sally says.

"Yes, ma'am."

"Satisfaction of IOU," she says. "Write it."

"How do you spell 'satisfaction'?" Holmes asks.

Angelet spells it for him. He is very eager to get out of here. He will sign a satisfaction agreement or whatever the hell this document is supposed to be—which he doubts is legal, by the way, and talk about extortion—he will even sign his own mother's death warrant if he can get out of here before the black FBI agent puts any holes in him. Holmes is already writing. He's not too enthusiastic about hanging around here, either.

"Satisfaction of IOU," he repeats aloud, writing.

"Underline it," Sally says.

He underlines the words.

"Now write the name Edward Glendenning . . ."

"Edward Glendenning."

"And under that . . . how much was it, Mrs. Glendenning?"

"Two hundred thousand dollars."

"Two hundred thousand dollars," Sally says.

"Two hundred thousand dollars," Holmes repeats, writing.

"Two hundred thousand dollars," Angelet agrees, and gives a little encouraging nod to Holmes, urging him to write faster so they can get the hell out of here.

"Now write 'Paid In Full . . .'"

"Paid In Full," Holmes repeats, writing.

"And both of you sign it."

Holmes signs it. Angelet takes the pen from him at once. He signs his name with a flourish, and then puts the cap back on the pen and hands it to Forbes.

"Now fold it and give it to Mrs. Glendenning," Sally says.

Holmes folds the page. He hands it to Alice.

"Thank you," she says.

"My pleasure, ma'am," Holmes says.

"The debt is satisfied, is that correct?" Sally asks.

"Yes, ma'am, the debt is satisfied," Holmes says.

"It's satisfied," Angelet agrees, nodding.

"Which means you have no further reason to bother this woman, is that also correct?"

"That is correct, yes, ma'am," Angelet says.

Until now, he always thought it might be pleasant to go to bed with a black woman. He has now changed his mind about that.

"And just for your information," Sally says, "in case you ever decide to come near Mrs. Glendenning again, in the state of Florida extortion is a second-degree felony punishable by up to fifteen years in prison and a ten-thousand-dollar fine. Not to mention the civil suit that might ensue if you breach the document you just signed. My advice?"

Both men look at her like kids who've been rowdy in class and are now in the principal's office.

"Crawl back in your holes and don't come out again," Sally says.

"Good advice, ma'am," Angelet agrees. "Can we go now?"

"Go," Sally says, and points the Glock toward the front door.

They are gone in a flash. Alice goes to the drapes, parts the Venetian blinds. She sees the white Caddy burning rubber out of her driveway, hears it scratching off. Behind her, Sloate tells Sally, "That paper they signed is total bullshit."

"I know," Sally says.

Alice is wishing that she herself could behave the way Sally Ballew just did. She is thinking that from the minute she met Edward Fulton Glendenning, she was dependent on him for her every move. And the minute Ashley was born, and later Jamie, she became even more and more reliant on her husband, until finally she lost sight of herself entirely, became merely an extension of Eddie, a mere "Mrs. Glendenning" who was essentially unable to function without him.

She remembers an argument she and Eddie had several weeks before the accident. The fight was about money. That was the only thing they ever fought about, money. There never seemed to be enough money. Even though he was always at the office working late, studying his damn computer, trying to figure out his next market move, they never had enough. The argument that night . . .

"I'm investing in stocks for us," he tells her.

"Well, when do these stocks begin paying off, Eddie? I look at our savings account, it just keeps going *down* every month."

"Well, shit," he says, "*I* wish I had a crystal ball, too, Alice, but I don't. I'm just a poor working stiff trying to earn enough money to support—"

"Oh, please, Eddie, where are the violins?"

"You're worried so much about money, why don't you go get a job at Mickey D's?"

"I *have* a job, Eddie! I'm raising two kids."

"I mean a *real* job."

"That *is* a real job, Eddie."

"Yes, I know, you've told me at least—"

"And I'd *have* what you call a real job if—"

"Yes, here we go again."

"Yes, if I'd gone in with Denise when she—"

"Right, you'd be a big movie producer now."

"I'd be *somebody,* Eddie. Instead of a person whose husband thinks raising two kids isn't a real—"

"Oh, fuck the kids!" he shouts.

"Don't you *dare . . .*"

"You keep using the kids as an excuse for—"

She rushes him with her fists clenched and raised, her eyes blazing, ready to strike him for what he just said.

"No, Mommy!"

Jamie's voice.

She turns. He is standing in the doorway to his bedroom, tears in his eyes.

"Don't hurt Daddy," he says.

She takes him in her arms.

She hugs him close.

"I'm sorry, honey," she says. "I'm so sorry."

Three weeks later, Eddie drowned at sea.

And she wonders now if Jamie stopped talking only because he overheard their bitter argument and somehow blamed Alice for what happened out there in the Gulf of Mexico.

Ashley is talking in whispers because she doesn't want her father or Christine to hear what she's saying. She knows they are going to get under way as soon as it's dark. She has heard them discussing this. She is afraid of what might happen *after* they get under way.

"What Daddy said is that he *kidnapped* us, do you know what that means, 'kidnapped'?"

Jamie nods and pulls a face.

"And he asked for a ransom, do you know what 'ransom' is?"

Jamie rolls his eyes heavenward.

"So what he told Christine is that he can't just let us go, he's got to figure out what to do with us."

Jamie looks puzzled.

"I think he's afraid we'll tell on him," Ashley says.

Jamie is listening intently now.

"I think he's going to drown us, Jamie."

They get their first real clue on a call they make to Calusa Springs. The woman at Barker Real Estate there says, "What's all this sudden interest?"

"What do you mean, sudden interest?" Sally asks.

"Second call we've had today about a black woman and a blonde," the woman says.

"Oh?" Sally says. "What do you mean?"

Alert now. Alice senses this in her posture, her entire attitude. Doesn't know exactly what Sally's hearing on that telephone, but realizes it may be important.

"Policeman called here an hour or so ago," the woman tells Sally. "Said he was trying to locate two women traveling together, a blonde and a black woman, who may have rented recently here in Calusa Springs. I told him I hadn't rented any property to any people answering that description."

"Nor anybody named Clara Washington, is that right?" Sally asks at once.

"Now how do you know *that* name?" the woman asks.

"How do *you* know that name?" Sally asks.

"She called me, had to be two months ago, said she'd seen on the Internet I had some cottages for rent, wondered how much they were renting for and whether I had one available for April and May."

"Called from where?"

"New Orleans."

"This was when did you say?"

"Had to be the middle of March."

"Said her name was Clara Washington?"

"Yes, she did."

"Did she give you an address where you could reach her?"

"No, but she gave me a phone number. Is she wanted for something?"

"May I have that number, ma'am?"

"Well, I don't have it anymore, I'm sorry. I told her I'd need a hundred-dollar deposit if she wanted me to hold the rental and I also told her I could only hold the reservation for ten days. When I didn't hear from her again, I tossed the number."

"But it was a number in New Orleans, is that correct?"

"It was a 5-0-4 area code. That's New Orleans, isn't it?"

"That sure is New Orleans, ma'am. Tell me about this policeman who called you. Did *he* give you a name?"

"Yes, he did."

"Would you happen to remember it?"

"Well, it was only an hour or so ago, I guess I can remember it."

"Can you tell me what it was?"

"Ralph Masters," the woman says.

Sally merely nods.

Alice knows she's onto something. Maybe there's a God, after all.

"Thank you very much," Sally says, and hangs up, and turns to where Carol is sitting alongside her sister on the living room sofa.

"Mrs. Matthews?" she says.

"Yes?" Carol says.

"Your husband's name is Rafe, isn't it? Rafe Matthews?"

"Yes?"

"He ever use the name Ralph Masters?"

"No. Ralph Masters? No. Why would he?"

"Just curious," Sally says. "His own initials being RM and all. Maybe he's sticking his nose where it doesn't belong." She turns immediately to Alice. "We're going to have to leave you for a while," she says.

"What is it?" Alice asks.

"Clara Washington called Florida from New Orleans. If the phone company can give us the information we need—"

"What's my husband got to do with this woman?" Carol asks.

"He called Calusa Springs to ask about her maybe renting there."

"That's not likely," Carol says, shaking her head. "Rafe's on the road to Atlanta. In fact, he's probably home by now."

"Maybe so," Sally says, and turns to Sloate. She is all efficiency now, not a wasted motion, not a wasted word. "You and Marcia might want to go back to *your* office, too, Wilbur."

"What for?" Sloate asks.

"Help us find that number Clara Washington called from in the middle of March. From someplace in New Orleans to Barker Realty in Calusa Springs. Knowing how *cooperative* . . ."

She lands heavily on the word, almost sneering, almost spitting it out.

". . . the *phone* company can be . . ."

Stressing that word, too.

". . . maybe we should *all* try our luck."

"What's happening?" Alice asks. "Can you please tell me?"

"Will you be okay here alone?" Sally asks.

"She won't be alone," Carol says pointedly.

"Here's where you can reach me if you need me," Sally says, and hands Alice a card with the FBI seal on it. Not two minutes later, she is out the door.

"I need a road map," Carol says, and goes out to the Explorer.

"Where's Calusa Springs?" she asks Alice.

The map is open on the kitchen table.

"About a half hour south of here," Alice says. "On U.S. 41."

"Why would Rafe be phoning a town *south* of here, if he was heading *north* to Atlanta?"

"I don't know," Alice says.

She is wondering what Sally Ballew plans to do with a New Orleans phone number, if ever the phone company gives her one. She is wondering how a New Orleans phone number will help them locate Clara Washington—if that's her name—and the blonde woman who together have stolen her children.

"Why would he call a real estate agent at *all*?" Carol wonders out loud. "And what did she mean about him using the name Ralph Masters?"

"I don't know," Alice says, and suddenly remembers what Clara Washington said to her on the phone Thursday night.

If you don't come to that gas station alone, your children will die. If you don't have the money with you, your children will die. If anyone tries to detain me, your children will die. If I'm not back where I'm supposed to be in half an hour, your children will die.

"I don't like that woman, do you?" Carol says.

"I think she knows her job," Alice says.

If anyone tries to detain me, your children will die.

"She's very bossy, I think," Carol says.

If I'm not back where I'm supposed to be in half an hour, your children will die.

Half an hour, Alice thinks.

They're half an hour from the Shell station on Lewiston and 41!

"Let me see that map," she says, and grabs it from her sister, and locates the scale of miles, and then roughly measures thirty miles north, east, south, and west from the gas station.

Port Lawrence to the north.

The wildlife refuge to the east.

Compton Acres to the southeast on route 884.

Calusa Springs due south.

"What are you doing?" Carol asks. "What is it?"

And to the west, the keys and the Gulf of—

"They're on a *boat*!" Alice says.

She finds the card Sally Ballew left, goes to the phone at once, and dials the number.

"FBI," a male voice says.

"Sally Ballew, please."

"Moment, please."

She waits. She can hear ringing on the other end.

"Special Agent Warren Davis," another man says.

"Sally Ballew, please."

"Sorry, she's not here just now," he says. "Anything I can help you with?"

"Yes, can you please give her a message when she comes in? Tell her Alice Glendenning called . . ."

"Yes, ma'am."

". . . with something I don't think she's considered yet."

"Yes, ma'am, and what's that?"

"I think my children may be on a boat. We've been checking land accommodations, but they may be on a boat someplace. Miss Ballew may want to alert the Coast Guard, or—"

"Yes, ma'am, I'll tell her."

"Thank you," Alice says.

There is a click on the line. She has the feeling she's just been brushed off. She replaces the receiver on its cradle, and is staring at the phone in anger and disbelief when suddenly it rings.

She picks up the receiver at once.

"Hello?" she says.

"Mrs. Glendenning?"

"Yes?"

"This is Rosie Garrity. Please don't hang up, ma'am."

"What is it, Rosie?"

"My husband, you know? George?"

"Yes."

"He's a waiter out on Siesta Key? In Sarasota? A restaurant called The Unicorn?"

"Yes, Rosie, what about him?"

"He was working last night when this man came in for dinner. A white man with a black woman."

"Yes?"

"George thought he recognized him, so he went over to the table and introduced himself—"

"Rosie, what is it you're—?"

"Do you remember that Saturday my car broke down and George

had to drive me to work? And he met Mr. Glendenning going out to the mailbox for the newspaper?"

Alice is suddenly listening very hard.

"Well, George thought this man last night was your husband. Was Mr. Glendenning."

"Why . . . why would he think that, Rosie?"

"Well, this man was the same height and build, and he had blue eyes, and blond hair."

"Even so, Rosie . . ."

"Though now he's wearing it much longer. To his shoulders, actually."

"What are you saying, Rosie?"

The line goes silent.

"Rosie? You said he's wearing it much longer. What are you trying to tell me? *Who's* wearing it much longer?"

"God forgive me, your *husband*!" Rosie says. "Mr. Glendenning."

"Rosie, that's imposs—"

"I know, I know. Your husband drowned last year, how can I believe it was him sitting there in that restaurant?"

Mom, I can't believe it!

The words her daughter shrieked into the phone.

"But this man paid the bill with a credit card, and the last name on the card was Graham, but his first name was Edward . . ."

Oh Jesus, Alice thinks.

". . . so I can't help believing . . ."

"Oh *Jesus*!" she says aloud.

"Mrs. Glendenning?" Rosie says. "Please don't fire me. I just had to tell you what I was thinking."

"You're not fired, Rosie. Thank you. I have to go now."

"Mrs. Glendenning? Do you think it really was—?"

Alice puts the receiver down on the cradle.

Her heart is pounding.

"What?" her sister asks.

"Eddie's alive," she says.

"What!"

"He's alive. He was out last night with that black woman, he's *alive*!"

"That can't be."

"It is."

She goes into the bedroom and takes the .32-caliber pistol from her top dresser drawer.

"Come on," she tells her sister.

13

"He's the one who has the kids," Alice says. "Him and this black woman . . . whoever she is."

They are driving out to Lewiston Point. Alice is thinking that she doesn't know who the woman is, and she doesn't know who Edward Graham is, either. Edward Fulton Glendenning no longer exists. These people are both strangers to her.

"He knows boats," she says. "He'd be comfortable on a boat. And they'd be less obvious on a boat than in a hotel or a motel. Besides, we took the kids there four years ago. They loved it. They'd feel safe and protected there."

"Where, Alice? Where are we going?"

"Marina Blue. That's what Ashley was trying to tell me on the phone. Not Maria, not Marie, but Marina Blue. Out on Crescent Island. Half an hour from the Shell station."

The women are silent for several moments.

The Mercedes truck bounces along Lewiston Point Road, which in the past few minutes has gone from potholed asphalt to rutted dirt. Either side of the road is lined with thick mangroves. Beyond, they can hear the gentle lap of water. The sun is beginning to set. Nightfall comes quickly here on the Cape, especially near the water, where the sky turns from red to violet, to blue, and then black with a suddenness that can stop the heart.

"That's why the kids got in that car," Carol says, nodding. "It wasn't a stranger, it was their father."

Was, Alice thinks.

Was their father.

Who knows what he has become now?

Eddie has paid the marina bill, refueled the boat, and brought it back to their dockside mooring. Christine knows that his plan is to get under way as soon as it's dark. She knows nothing beyond that. When she comes topside, he is sitting at the helm, alone and silent, smoking a cigarette. He raises the flip-up bolster, making room for her on the upholstered companion seat. She sits beside him and takes his left hand. It is a warm evening, but his hand is cold to the touch.

"You okay?" she asks.

"Yes, fine. What are the kids doing?"

"Watching television."

He nods.

"When do we call Alice again?" she asks.

"Well, there's no hurry," he says.

"Because we should tell her where we're leaving the kids, you know."

"Yeah," he says, and nods, and takes a long drag on the cigarette.

They are silent for several moments.

Out on the water, a fish jumps.

Then all is still again.

"Are we going to just leave them here on the dock?"

"No, that wasn't my plan," he says.

"Because I thought we were getting under way . . ."

"That's right."

". . . soon as it got dark."

"Right."

"Which is pretty soon, Eddie."

"I know it is."

"So where are we going to leave the kids?"

"You see . . ." he says, and then stops, and shakes his head.

She looks at him.

"They saw me," he says.

He draws on the cigarette.

"They know I'm alive," he says.

She is still looking at him.

"We can't turn them loose," he says.

"We can't take them with us, either, Eddie. The police'll be looking for them everywhere we—"

"I know that."

"We *have* to let them go, Eddie."

"But we can't," he says.

"Then what . . . ?"

He draws on the cigarette again.

"We'll move out in about five minutes," he says, and looks at the luminous dial of his watch. "We'll head straight out to the Gulf."

"I don't understand. What about . . . ?"

He does not answer.

He turns away from her penetrating gaze and tosses the cigarette overboard. Its glow arcs against the sudden blackness of the night and hits the water with a brief dying hiss.

They get to the ferry landing just as the boat is about to leave. Alice pulls the truck into a parking space alongside a red Taurus. Carol jumps out and first begins waving and shouting at the lone dockhand who is already tossing lines aboard, and next at the pilothouse to let the captain know they're here. Alice slams the door shut on the driver's side. They both run for the dock.

"Take it easy, you've got time," the dockhand says.

The ferry carries passengers only, no cars. There are perhaps half a dozen people aboard when the captain gives a final warning toot on his horn and begins backing away from the dock. He makes a wide circle, coming around, and then points the boat's prow toward Crescent Island, some thousand yards across the inlet.

Ten minutes later, the boat is docking on the island side.

The night is balmy and still.

Eddie has already started the engines.

The Sundancer is idling at the dock.

The two women come striding out of the darkness beyond, moving rapidly toward where he is crouched over the forward line. He does not recognize them until the dockside stanchion lights pick them up, and then he sees that it is Alice and her sister, Carol. He shakes his head and smiles because Alice looks so utterly ridiculous and helpless, her left foot in a cast, limping across the dock like a cripple. And then he sees the pistol in her hand, and the smile drops from his face. He loosens the line from its cleat and tosses it aboard. In the next instant, he leaps aboard himself, and reaches into a locker alongside the wheel.

"Where are the kids?" Alice shouts.

He is already behind the wheel.

Alice does not raise the pistol in her own hand until she sees that what he's taken from the locker is a gun.

"Put it down!" he yells.

The thirty-two is shaking violently in her fist.

"Give me the children and leave," Alice says. "You're Edward Graham now, you can forget all this."

"But will *you*?" he says, and smiles thinly. "Will your *sister*? Will the *kids*?"

The gun in his fist is a nine-millimeter Glock. It looks very large and very menacing, and it is pointed at her head.

"You know the penalty for kidnapping in the state of Florida?" he asks.

His tone is almost conversational. He could be giving a little talk on the wisdom of investing in growth stocks.

"You can leave Florida," she says. "Take your girlfriend and—"

"My wife," he corrects.

"Your . . . ?"

"Kidnapping is a life felony, Alice. If they ever catch up with us . . ."

"No one will even *try,* Eddie. Just let the kids *go*!"

"Well, no," he says, "I'm afraid I can't do that."

And throws the engines into reverse.

She hears a click in the dark.

Is there a safety on the gun?

Has he just thrown off a safety?

She hears two simultaneous voices.

"*Don't,* Eddie!"

"No, Daddy!"

The first voice is the voice Alice has heard so many times before on the telephone, the voice of the woman she came face-to-face with outside the Shell station's ladies' room, the woman she now sees again, rushing up from below, holding out her hand beseechingly to Eddie. His wife, Alice thinks. His wife.

The second voice is a voice Alice has not heard since the morning they learned that Eddie drowned out on the Gulf.

The second voice belongs to her dear son, Jamie.

"Don't hurt Mommy!"

His son's voice has no effect on him. He still has the Glock in his right hand, pointed at Alice's head. His left hand is still steady on the stainless steel wheel as he starts to maneuver the Sundancer away from the dock.

This is the man who once matched her foot to a midnight blue slipper.

This is the man she once loved with all her heart.

She squeezes her eyes shut.

Opens them again at once, and fires.

Fires another time.

And yet another.

Blood spurts on his yellow windbreaker. She sees him crumpling over the wheel. The boat swerves back and bangs violently against the dock. She throws down the gun, and leaps onto the boat, and rushes to her son where he stands trembling just outside the slatted wooden doors leading below. The black woman whose name she still does not know says nothing. Her eyes are darting, calculating.

"Mom?"

Ashley comes from below, her eyes wide.

She glances once at her father where he lies slumped and still over the stainless steel wheel smeared now with his blood. Then she, too, rushes into Alice's arms.

The black woman hesitates a moment longer, and then suddenly leaps ashore.

"Gee, no," Carol says, and points the pistol at her head.

They have called all the real estate agents and condo rental offices they could find in the Yellow Pages, and have even visited one personally, but have not come up with any information on a blonde and a black woman having rented any kind of dwelling at any time during the past two months. Or at any time at *all,* for that matter.

So there is nothing to do now but make love again.

Rafe reflects afterward, as they both lie spent and damp on rumpled sheets in Jennifer's bedroom, that there's a certain time of day in Florida when a hush seems to come over the entire land. The traffic seems to come to a halt, the streets are all at once deserted, even the insects and the birds seem to fall suddenly still. Overhead, the ceiling fan rotates lazily, scattering dust motes climbing shafts of silvery moonlight. Lying on his back beside her, Rafe thinks that maybe it's this way everywhere in the world after you've just made love to a beautiful passionate woman, maybe there's just this, well, this sort of serenity that comes over you. A stillness that causes you to believe your heart has stopped, causes you to believe that maybe you're even dead. And causes you to think.

He knows he's going to be leaving here soon.

He knows he's going to get out of this bed, and shower in this lady's bedroom, put on his Jockey shorts and his jeans and his denim shirt, and his socks and loafers, and then either take a taxi or ask her to drive him to the truck stop where he's parked the rig, knows he is going to walk out of this bedroom, and out of this house, and never see this woman again. Because no matter what Eminem has to say about opportunity knocking just once or whatever the words were, seize the moment, seize the music, he knows that maybe such dreams are okay for a talented kid on 8-Mile Road, but they're just not there for people like Rafe who don't know how to rhyme.

Opportunity may have come knocking when he learned about all those phony bills out there someplace, and maybe it kept knocking and knocking when he found this beautiful passionate woman willing to chase the dream with him, but man, there is no way on earth he is going to find those two chicks sitting on that fake bread, no way in the world at all. He has tried to seize the moment and the music, but his hands have closed on nothing but thin air.

So he knows he will now go back.

Knows he will go back to Carol and the kids, knows in his deepest heart that eventually he will go back to jail, too, that's what recidivism is all about. It's all about making the same mistakes over and over again. Going back home again to a woman he no longer loves and kids he never wanted, going back on the shit again, too, and getting caught with it, and going back to jail as a three-time loser who once upon a time heard opportunity knocking, and opened the door to let it in, and found nobody standing there, nobody at all.

It's kind of sad, really.

It's kind of so fucking sad.

She drives him to where he parked the rig.

They stand outside the cab in the harsh bright overhead lights, and they hold hands, both hands, his outstretched to hers, hers clasped in his, and he tells her he's sorry this didn't work out the way he was hoping it would, tells her he can still think of a hundred and six ways the two of them together could have spent all that money.

He tells her he's never met a woman like her in his entire life, tells her that these few days he's spent with her have been the happiest days in his life, he wants her to believe that. He tells her that there are a couple of things he still has to straighten out back home in Atlanta, but that as soon as he's taken care of these few little odds and ends, he'll be coming back down here to Florida, where he hopes she'll be waiting for him.

"Wait for me, Jenny," he tells her, though she's asked him not to call her Jenny, but he's already forgotten this.

Still holding both her hands in his, he draws her close to him, and kisses her on the mouth. She kisses him back. They pull apart from each other at last, still holding hands, and he nods silently and solemnly, and finally drops her hands and climbs into the cab and rolls down the window.

"I'll be back soon," he promises, and starts the engine.

She watches as he backs the truck out of its space. She watches as he drives it over to the exit. Before he pulls out onto U.S. 41 North, he waves back at her from the open window. Then he is gone.

She walks over to where she parked the red convertible. She puts the key into the ignition, and sits there for a long while without starting the car. Then, aloud, she says, "You're all so full of shit," and starts the car, and turns on the radio very loud, and drives out of the lot.

Monday
May 17

14

Sally Ballew calls her boss at eight-thirty in the morning. She sounds jubilant. She tells him that GTE here in Florida was able to provide a New Orleans phone number for the call made to Harper Realty in Calusa Springs.

She tells him that Ma Bell in New Orleans was able to give them the name of the subscriber for that number, and the name wasn't Clara Washington, it was Edward Graham, no middle initial.

She tells him that the FBI's regional office up there in the Big Easy was able to obtain a list of calls made from Edward Graham's number to Florida in general and more specifically to Cape October, and one of the numbers called was for a marina out on Crescent Island.

She tells him that a call to that marina . . .

"Which happens to be called Marina Blue," she says, "which I think is what the little girl was trying to tell her mother on the phone . . ."

"Uh-huh," Stone says.

"A call to the marina," she says, "confirmed that a man named Edward Graham booked docking space there for the months of April and May—"

"Have you been watching television?" Stone asks.

"No. What? Television? No. Why?"

"It's been on television since late last night," Stone says.

"What's been on television?"

"The woman shot him. They got both him and his accomplice. Her husband and his bimbo."

"I don't know what you're talking about," Sally says.

"The Glendenning woman. Her husband never drowned, Sally. In fact, he's *still* alive after she plugged him three times. They got the woman, too. Where've you been, Sally?"

"I've . . ."

Sally looks at the list of phone numbers she's been calling.

"Who gets credit for the bust?" she asks.

"A security guard at the marina," Stone says.

There are television cameras all over Alice's front yard when Charlie gets there at nine-fifteen that morning. Her sister's Explorer is still parked in the driveway. He pushes his way through all the microphones being thrust at him, and almost knocks a young reporter on his ass as he shoves his way to the front door and rings the doorbell.

"Are you a cop?" a woman reporter asks him.

"I'm a painter," he says, and rings the doorbell.

The door opens. The crowd of reporters instantly surges forward, but Charlie has already eased his way in.

"You okay?" he asks Alice.

"Fine, Charlie."

"The kids?"

"Asleep."

"Did they book you?"

"Not yet."

"Will they?"

"I don't think so. They said there'd be an investigation."

"You should've seen her," Carol says proudly.

"I almost killed him, Charlie."

"You should have," Charlie says. "Is there any coffee?"

• • •

The story that runs in Dustin Garcia's column that morning makes it sound as if the Cape October *Tribune,* and more particularly Dustin Garcia himself, played a major role in locating and apprehending the couple who'd kidnapped the Glendenning children.

Were it not for the fabricated story this columnist reported in the "Dustbin" yesterday, the perpetrators would not have ventured to be so bold as to . . .

And so on.

No Pulitzer prize maybe, Garcia thinks, but close enough for a cigar.

At ten past eleven, Reginald Webster appears at Alice's front door. Through the peephole, she sees behind him a phalanx of reporters still waiting patiently for a glimpse of her. It appears that she has achieved fifteen minutes of fame she is not especially eager to claim.

"Want me to get rid of him?" Charlie asks.

"No," she says, and opens the door.

Flashbulbs pop, and cameras begin rolling. The same woman who earlier asked Charlie if he was a cop now shouts, "How'd it feel to shoot your own husband, Mrs. G?"

"Good morning, Alice," Webb says.

"Good morning, Webb," she says.

"Was your little girl molested?" a male reporter shouts.

"I was worried," Webb says. "I saw it on television this morning . . ."

"I'm all right," she says.

"Well, good," he says.

"Were you trying to kill him?" another reporter yells.

"I still want a house down here, you know."

"I'll find one for you."

"Is that a promise?"

"It's a promise."

"I'll hold you to it," he says.

As he starts up the walk to where he's parked his rented Mercury at the curb, the woman reporter shouts, "What are your plans now, Mrs. G?"

Alice merely smiles, and closes the door, and goes to where Charlie is brewing a pot of coffee in the kitchen.

About the Author

In 1998, **Ed McBain** was the first American to receive the Diamond Dagger, the British Crime Writers Association's highest award. He also holds the Mystery Writers of America's prestigious Grand Master Award. His most recent 87th Precinct novel was *Hark!* Under his own name—Evan Hunter—he has enjoyed a writing career that has spanned five decades, from his first novel, *The Blackboard Jungle,* in 1954, to the screenplay for Alfred Hitchcock's *The Birds,* to *Candyland,* written in tandem with his alter ego, Ed McBain, to *The Moment She Was Gone,* published in 2002.